To my darling Eileen & Rob,
Love ♡ Jun

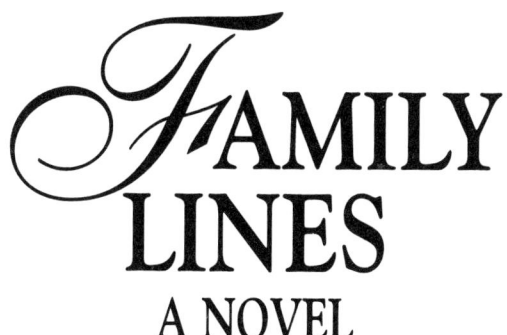

ALSO BY GWENDOLINE FORTUNE
Growing Up Nigger Rich

FAMILY LINES

A NOVEL

Gwendoline Y. Fortune

PELICAN PUBLISHING COMPANY
Gretna 2003

Copyright © 2003
By Gwendoline Y. Fortune
All rights reserved

*The word "Pelican" and the depiction of a pelican are trademarks
of Pelican Publishing Company, Inc., and are registered
in the U.S. Patent and Trademark Office.*

Library of Congress Cataloging-in-Publication Data

Fortune, Gwen Y. (Gwen Young)
  Family lines : a novel / Gwendoline Y. Fortune.
    p. cm.
  ISBN 1-58980-146-6 (alk. paper)
  1. African American women—Fiction. 2. Corporate culture—Fiction. 3. Businesswomen—Fiction. 4. Conspiracies—Fiction.
I. Title.
PS3556.O7534 F36 2003
813'.54—dc22
                                                2003016462

Printed in the United States of America
Published by Pelican Publishing Company, Inc.
1000 Burmaster Street, Gretna, Louisiana 70053

For Georgia Mittie McCain Young, my mother. She was a fey (preternatural) lady who carried the stories of the great-grands with knowing reverence.

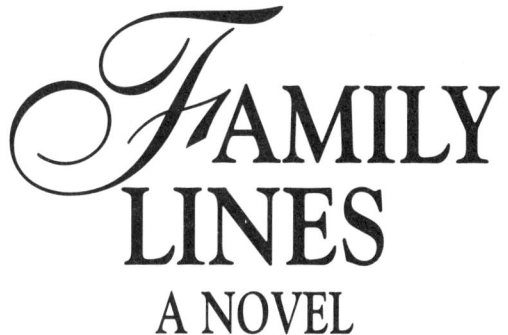

CHAPTER 1

"Good morning, Mrs. Jones-Keyes." Rosamund's secretary greeted her from her neat desk outside Rosamund's office. "Mr. Warner wants to see you as soon as you're settled in."

"Thanks, Lois. And please, call me JK. 'Jones-Keyes' is a mouthful." Rosamund smiled at Lois, who looked to be about her own age: thirty-two.

"Okay, Mrs. JK." Lois smiled at her accidental rhyme. She continued to sort the morning mail.

Inside her office, one of three identical offices that angled behind Lois—each one smaller than a walk-in closet—Rosamund did a little twirl, humming under her breath. "Rosamund, we're on our way girl," she said softly, tapping her fingers over her white desk, then on a matching, laminate bookcase that held three folders. She imagined those shelves filled with computer printouts and folders bulging with reports. "Soon," she said, a little louder than before, "Dectel Global, Atlanta G-A. I like the rhythm," she said.

Rosamund Jones-Keyes had dropped her first name, Sariah, when she married. Her great-great-grandmother's name was a reminder of her African heritage. Rosamund didn't know if it had been a slave name or if it was a remnant of an exotic original. Dr. Taylor, her graduate-school professor, had said that an African-sounding name might prejudice Rosamund's chances in the corporate world. *Not that I'm ashamed of my African roots,* she thought. *How can I be? All anyone has to do is take one look and here I am.* Rosamund was five feet-nine inches tall, the color of copper with a hint of gold. Her earlobe-length, dark brown hair was copper tinged. Her nose was a bit too wide for classic beauty—by some standards—but she was a good-looking woman to most observers.

A knock on her office door was followed by a man's head and torso. "I know you've just gotten in, but I was told to bring this report," he said, in an accent that was clearly Southern.

His voice had an edge that might have suggested disapproval or dislike—or simple uncertainty. Rosamund didn't know and didn't care to find out. She wasn't particularly fond of blond, grey-eyed white men. She'd never considered why—could it have been the creep in fifth grade who'd called her "Sticks"?

"Oh, Mr. Shuggs, are you assigned to me? I haven't been told who my statistician will be." Maybe she pushed *my* just a tiny bit.

"I was assigned when I came in this morning," he said. Shuggs' color heightened. He lingered in the open doorway.

Rosamund felt that maybe the guy has a sour face all the time. "Sure, Mr. Shuggs. Come in, I'll take care of it." She moved her notepad from one corner of her desk, signaling to Shuggs that he could put his folder in the empty spot. The corners of his mouth tightened downward. He placed a blue notebook on her desk as if it were a precious artifact.

Shuggs turned to leave then paused. "I hope you won't get me wrong, Mrs. Keyes—or is it Mrs. Jones? My calculations show that there's something odd in an important section of the report. I think the brass is ignoring a potential problem or holding the cap on a blowup. I flagged my findings, the blue stick-tabs. I don't think the figures were supposed to turn up here, but I take pride in being thorough, even meticulous." He came closer, opened the notebook, and pointed to a chart, "Look, Dectel began buying a new chemical, phiofomel, from ROD, Inc., last year—first, small amounts, then gradually larger batches." Shuggs pointed to several checks; he traced the lines. "Phiofomel is highly toxic and dangerous," he said. "We should not be using it in our manufacturing process."

The tone of his voice caught Rosamund's attention more than his words did. Her practiced eyes scanned the page. Jeffrey Shuggs was definitely past the point of being concerned, more like a major upset. A nudge way down inside Rosamund sent a warning. *Not now*, Rosamund thought. *No dirty business. I've just arrived.* She raised her gaze from the precise entries, "Call me Mrs. JK, Mr. Shuggs."

He nodded, "Yes'm."

She put the notebook in the top drawer of her desk and locked it. Her voice and face offered neither assurance nor rejection. "Excuse me, Mr. Shuggs. Mr. Warner wants to see me."

"Do you understand what I'm saying?" Shuggs dropped his pen, bent to get it. "The amount of money is modest, starts out like nothing for an operation as large as ours; the first order was $25,000, then $85K, and, in the last three months, more than $250K. Somebody in research decided to change the formulation in the transangle system. The long-term effects will be a human and ecological disaster," he said.

Shuggs stood aside, almost stumbling, as Rosamund walked toward the door.

She didn't see the look on Jeffrey Shuggs' face—one of disbelief.

Rosamund left Shuggs near Lois's desk and walked, assuredly, about twenty feet down the hall to where a stylish executive assistant sat. She was ushered into a commodious, cherry-wood-paneled office recessed in its own historical-wallpapered alcove. Approaching the man behind the impressive desk, Rosamund continued to muse on Shuggs' behavior. *I'm not going to take on a crusade,* she thought. *My job is to use my brain as an analyst for Dectel and that's all I'm going to do.* She clenched and opened her eyes. *No civil, environmental, or other "issue" is going to stop me from getting where I want to be.* Her expression, carefully practiced, conveyed nothing.

The man on the other side of the desk stood, extended his hand, and gestured Rosamund to a chair. His blue suit, hint-of-gold shirt, and deeper gold tie were corporate correct. His collar creased into his neck just enough to look uncomfortable.

"Good morning, Mrs. Keyes. I'll get to the point right away. Time, time, always too little time, isn't there? You've been with us only two months and already you've found three inconsistencies in departmental reports. Excellent. In fact, outstanding," Vice-President Edward C. Warner said. "You're going to be a great asset to Dectel."

Rosamund did not request to be addressed as JK, as she had with Lois and Shuggs. *Later,* she thought, *when I'm "inside."*

The VP's high-pitched voice was a contrast to his solid, rotund body. "I want you to know that—well—all eyes are on you. That's a cliché, I know—but it is efficient. You're being noticed, rest assured of that. I expected good things when we brought you in from AMB. Continue as you are, and you'll be rewarded. Your rise in the corporation should be rapid."

"Thank you, Mr. Warner. I always do my best," Rosamund said, warming to the good feeling his words brought. She'd heard the staff called the VP "Mickey" behind his back—he sounded like the Disney character. Warner appeared to be an impatient man who struggled to exude calm control.

"I want you to keep close scrutiny on Jeffrey Shuggs' work. He's an excellent statistician," Warner said, "but sometimes he gets carried away with his interpretations of data—kind of a zealot. Social-consciousness type. Inappropriate in this world."

"I didn't know he was to be my statistician until a few moments ago. I'm ready for all challenges, Mr. Warner."

Rosamund had been introduced to Shuggs, along with everyone in her department, when she arrived at Dectel—almost ten weeks ago. He had not seemed to be particularly outgoing at that time or this morning. She put any unpleasant thoughts about Jeffrey Shuggs out of her mind.

"Don't hesitate to let me know if you want clarification on any Dectel policy—or anything for that matter," Warner said, standing quickly, indicating their meeting was finished.

"I will, Mr. Warner. Thank you," Rosamund held out her hand, closing their good-bye.

Warner's smile disappeared as he watched the back of the company's latest and highest-level "person of color." He pulled a small, red-leather-covered notebook from his jacket pocket and wrote on a fresh page, reading as he did so: "R. J. eager to please, naive." He underlined the final word, saying, "Project closed."

Ed Warner cupped the executive notepad in his hand. The relaxation in his jaw suggested what, for him, passed as a smile. He returned the notebook to his pocket, giving it a final tap. His eyes mirrored the flat, black numerals on the wall clock beside the door Rosamund had exited.

Back in her office, Rosamund asked Lois to come inside. "You've been here longer than I have, Lois. Perhaps, you can give me a bit of insight."

"I don't know if eighteen months is enough to know much, but if I can help, I will." Lois, a petite, pleasant-looking woman with a bittersweet chocolate complexion, black hair, and wide-set dark brown eyes, sat across from Rosamund's desk that was larger than hers, smaller than the executive assistant's, and much smaller than the vice-president's. "The company tries to make us feel comfortable. I like it here," Lois said. "I hear a little gossip, but I keep my mouth closed and listen."

Rosamund shared her secretary with two other Dectel analysts. Lois impressed Rosamund from her first days at work. She was efficient and alert. Rosamund didn't pry. She knew only that Lois Hardy was married to a disabled, former employee, something to do with an industrial accident.

"I don't want you to violate ethics or confidences, but I can be more effective if I know everything I can about the people who will be working with me," Rosamund said. "As an African-American woman overseeing the work of white men, I'd appreciate it if you'd fill me in before issues become problems, if that's okay with you?"

"I understand Mrs. Ke—JK. I appreciate your confidence." Lois sat straighter, pleased with her superior's attention.

"I don't take long to make up my mind," Rosamund said. "You're an intelligent, observant woman. I also know that I won't have even one chance to foul up. Change moves swiftly in this world." Rosamund reached across her desk to shake the other brown hand. "Sisters?" she asked.

"Sisters." Lois returned the grasp.

"Jeffrey Shuggs doesn't seem happy about working for me," Rosamund said. "What do you know about him?"

"Practically nothing," Lois answered, slowly shaking her head in contemplation. "He's a loner—smart, I hear. I think he's from some place north of Atlanta. A 'mountain-man,' I've heard him called behind his back. He looks like he spends a lot of time outdoors. He's polite but not close to anyone, as far as I can see," she said.

The outer phone rang. "Oops, I gotta go," Lois said. "Thanks for taking me into your confidence, Mrs. JK."

"Thank you, Lois. Guess it's time to get on with important stuff." Rosamund did not open the locked desk drawer.

Rosamund stopped at the after-school center. Cars and SUVs were crowding the curb. Children with backpacks were hurrying. Caryl, her nine-year-old daughter, a smaller replica of herself, threw her book bag in the back seat, dropped beside her mother, and slammed the door. "Hi, Mums," Caryl said, buckling in.

"What's the trouble?" Rosamund could sense the disappointment in her daughter.

"This was one long day. I didn't get any of my homework finished. The aides try to keep everybody quiet. No way, Mums. I need my own space." Caryl bounced against the seat back.

"We've talked about the after-school center before." Rosamund's stomach knotted. "I can't get away from the office until 4:30. Understood, right? I don't want you to be a latchkey kid." After the exhilaration of leaving work, she felt self-control slipping away. Struggling to keep dejection out of her voice, Rosamund said, "We're lucky to be in Atlanta, where there are good after-school centers, Caryl." She let out a tiny yoga exhale. "I'll see if I can work something out."

"I know, Mums. I don't mean to be a whiny. If we can't do it better, I'll hang in. We go through everything together, don't we?" Caryl said.

"Right—and stop sounding like me." Rosamund stroked the cheek of her sober-faced nine-year-old. "I'll call Mom and Dad. Maybe they'll have an idea for us."

Rosamund's car turned into the parking garage of the apartment building that was home since they had moved from Ohio. "I'll help you with the rest of your homework, then one video and to bed. I want to catch Mom and Dad before they're asleep."

Rosamund sat on the side of her bed beside the telephone she'd just hung up. She blew off the memory of Shuggs, mouth agape, behind her as she had walked out of her office. *Mom and Dad don't need to know that my perfect new job may not be perfect. A disaster, the man said. Wonderful.*

Next morning, Caryl slipped onto the stool at the breakfast counter. Rosamund set a bowl of cereal beside the glass of juice. She poured herself a third cup of coffee. "We're in luck. Mom and Dad suggested that I call Aunt Pet—Dad's cousin who lives in Shreveport, Louisiana. I asked Aunt Pet if she would be willing to come and live with us for a while. She's by herself now, and she might be willing."

Caryl slammed her glass on the counter, spilling her juice. "I don't want a fussy old woman around. She'll bore me."

"Who says she's old or fussy?" Rosamund ignored the spill. "When I was a kid and I visited Aunt Pet, she was as much fun as any kid. She told great stories, and she played games with your

Uncle Bob and me—fun stories and magic things, too," Rosamund said. "I don't know why I didn't think of her myself."

"But we're a team, Mums. She may not have been old when you were little, she's got to be ancient now." Caryl felt an intrusion in her partnership with her mother, and she wasn't ready to give up.

"I told Aunt Pet that you and I will discuss it. I can't come up with a better idea. Have you? Aunt Pet's mother died a year ago, and her husband's been dead for years, so she is free to help us if we all agree." Rosamund glanced at the clock on the microwave. "Omigosh, we've got to run."

The morning drive—to Caryl's school then to the expressway toward the outskirts of Atlanta—was never easy. "The way this city is growing, you'd think people would learn how to drive—they drive like it's julep-on-the-verandah time," Rosamund fumed, maneuvering skillfully to her exit. She pushed through a fleeting fear: what if she lost her job and couldn't pay Aunt Pet? *I will not let that happen,* her internal voice spoke. Suddenly, she laughed aloud. "I've never seen a julep or a verandah, except in the movies," she said to the empty car.

"I'd rather be on a battlefield," she told the guard when she pulled into Dectel's parking lot. She flashed her badge and found a spot halfway down the lot. He stared at another corporate weirdo. She joined coworkers who were rushing into the cathedral-sized building. Everyone looked, reflexively, at their watches, heads bobbing like pigeons pecking at food thrown in front of them.

Heels clicked on terrazzo then muted on plush, green carpet that ushered everyone into the thirty-foot-high foyer. Rosamund reached her outer office. "Lois, please make an appointment with Mr. Shuggs to go over his report, will you?"

"He's been here already, Mrs. JK. Seemed out of sorts that you weren't ready for him." Lois reached for her phone.

"What does he think I am, a machine? His report is complex. I won't be rushed and end up making mistakes." Rosamund thought: *Southern men! Or is this his way of getting my blood pressure up? He doesn't know me. The more intensity there is, the more I like it. I'll bet he doesn't know the brass is on his tail.*

"I don't think it's you, Mrs. JK. Mr. Shuggs took longer on those last stats than Mr. Warner wanted," Lois said.

"Thank you for that, Lois. It's good to know when the pressure rises." Rosamund laid a copy of her comments on Shuggs' file. "Tell him I'm ready for him—five minutes only."

"Yes'm," Lois said.

Shuggs' tie hung loosely—not Dectel protocol. "I assumed you wanted to see me to sign off on the report." Under his healthy outdoorsy complexion, redness moved into his face. "Will you please tell me the problem? Is my presentation difficult to follow?" he asked.

"On the contrary, Mr. Shuggs, you are a fine mathematician. I haven't enjoyed working with an analysis this much since I worked with Gene Taylor." Rosamund ran through his report with a facility that caused Shuggs' heightened color to change from ruddy to pale.

"You studied with Taylor?" Shuggs' voice was respectful.

"His graduate assistant for an entire year." Rosamund hid her pleasure at his chagrin as well as she could. "Did you work with him?"

"No, but my favorite professor was a student of Taylor's. He praised the man to high heaven all the time. I've read everything he's written."

"To 'high heaven'? I've never heard that expression before. Is it Southern?" Rosamund was not ready to capitulate, not yet. She enjoyed seeing him back off one more time. "But I think I know what you mean. Taylor is almost a god in the field. Now, as to your project, I see no serious problem, and I can sign off with a few minor changes." Rosamund handed Shuggs the marked copy—a smattering of question marks with a notation or two in the margins.

Shuggs thumbed through the printout. "I pride myself on being thorough. I'll look at this again." His color changed for the third time during their brief meeting. "You didn't comment on the phiofomel. Do you agree with what I see coming on? Someone is covering up a dangerous situation. Lives will be lost. Dectel can lose it all."

"If I've made any errors, I'll be happy to discuss them," Rosamund told him. "Your work is good, but I think it will have clearer impact with my modifications—they are clarifications, really." She ignored his question.

After Shuggs left, Rosamund thought, *if the mountain man had any doubts as to my ability, I think they're gone. Damn, he is good.* She had a grudging respect for the man. *His problem is not mine,* she thought.

Rosamund finished the day's work, saw that she was ahead of schedule, leaned back in her chair, and glanced at the photograph of Caryl smiling.

"Mrs. JK, are you all right?" Lois broke Rosamund's reverie. "I knocked. I didn't want to annoy you with the phone—" she said.

"Lois, do you have a child?" Rosamund stopped Lois in midsentence.

"Twins—a boy and a girl—Mark and Meryl, ten years old," Lois answered. "I noticed your little girl's picture; she looks real smart."

Dectel did not encourage personal relationships in the workplace. The corporation wasn't hostile to families. Its medical program—including psychiatric, dental, and eye care—was a good one. But the organization conveyed that an employee who did not bring personal issues to work would be more efficient, a better player for Dectel Global. This atmosphere snaked from department to department, person to person.

"Caryl and I came to Atlanta from Cleveland three months ago. Dectel offered a package I could not refuse. My daughter and I are it. I'm a widow," Rosamund said. "She's in a good school and a good after-school program, but she's used to being with my parents and lifelong neighbors. She's not happy with the after-school center. I'm looking for a change."

Lois said, "My husband isn't able to work any longer. We have an agreement, he's with the twins until I get home. What work he can do he does while they're at school. Have you found something better for your daughter?"

"Yes, one that is a hard sell." Rosamund decided she wanted to talk through her quandary. She had not made friends in the short time she'd been in Atlanta. She told Lois about Aunt Pet, how much fun she was when Rosamund and her brother took summer vacations in Louisiana.

"Aunt Pet is healthy as two people. She walks three or four miles a day and is not 'old and fussy' the way Caryl thinks. Her mother lived past ninety, worked at something every day."

"She sounds great. You say you and your daughter have a close relationship, maybe a trial run would appeal to her. That sometimes works with my twins."

"What a good idea. Caryl and I can make a compact or contract—not exactly a thirty-day trial but an agreement that if both

18 FAMILY LINES

Aunt Pet and Caryl don't find the arrangement mutually happy we can end the trial with no hard feelings. We can make it a three-month period." Rosamund beamed, a resolution had come earlier than expected.

"I'm glad you think it's worth a try," Lois said. "It was a passing thought. I'll be interested to know how it works." Lois heard her name called through the closed door. "There's my carpool. See you in the morning."

"Young lady, I am neither an invalid nor a yokel."

Passengers glanced at the white-haired, dark brown woman with the patrician nose, then looked away, pretending they hadn't heard or seen anything, the way intrusion into other people's privacy is avoided.

"No ma'am, I didn't mean to hurt your feelings. I thought you might like help getting your luggage together," the flight attendant smiled wanly.

"Well, now, thank you, but I am quite capable of looking out for myself. Go help some old person." Aunt Pet, Patricia Thompson, gestured across the aisle of the airplane to a man with a cane.

Waiting for the door to swing open at the end of the Jetway, Caryl contemplated her purple, green, and pink fluorescent sneakers. "Mums, I can manage myself." She caught her lower lip between her teeth—calculated to produce a mother-melt—and mumbled—"I don't need any old lady."

Rosamund closed her eyes. "It's a trial run, Caryl. There's more than after school at stake. Dectel will be sending me away on business, sometimes. You know that. Next week it's Houston. Back in Ohio, you had Mom and Dad. I can't leave you alone overnight, and finding a sleep-over sitter would be harder than winning on *Jeopardy*." Gathering her purse and welcoming bouquet, Rosamund held Caryl's hand. Her voice lilted, "I always enjoyed Aunt Pet the times she came to Ohio and when we went to Louisiana."

Caryl pulled her hand away. She walked as slowly as she could. "I've never been to the country. Do I have to show her how to use the electric stove?"

Rosamund laughed, took Caryl's hand again, and squeezed. "Shreveport, Louisiana, is not the country; it's a city, like Cincinnati or Atlanta. You're going to have fun. Let's move it."

Aunt Pet emerged from the Jetway, red hat balanced on snow white hair, red-and-white pantsuit, a crammed-full red carry-on, and a package wrapped in colorful, mostly red gift paper under one arm. In the other hand, she held a burgundy leather suitcase.

Hugging the older woman, Rosamund sang, "When the red, red robin . . ."

Pet picked it up. "comes bob, bob, bobbing along . . ." Pet planted a loud kiss on Rosamund's cheek. Deplaning passengers grinned. "You didn't forget," Aunt Pet said.

"I didn't remember until I saw you in your favorite color." Rosamund replied. "Outrageous, Aunt Pet, like always."

"My good-luck color and my daddy's favorite song I used to sing you to sleep with. A fine howdy-do." Pet took in the questioning gaze on Caryl's face. "Here's my little Caryl, growing up so pretty." She did not try to hug the girl. "I haven't seen you since you were a baby. My Joe and I came to your christening."

"I didn't know I'd ever seen you." Caryl said, surprised. She looked at her mother then at the woman in red.

"I thought I told you." It was Rosamund's time to sputter.

"Sure, I did, and every time I look at the pictures we took and compare them to the ones your grandma sends me—regularly—I see you growing, and I send you a spirit message to protect you."

Caryl Anne Jones-Keyes had to grow up fast. She didn't remember her father. His name was Carl. Her mother told her that he died in a car accident when Caryl was barely a year old. Caryl never worried about not having a father. She had friends whose parents were separated or divorced, and others who didn't know their fathers.

Sneaking a gaze into Aunt Pet's unusual eyes—deep set, slanted, almost yellow—Caryl moved closer, held out her hand to shake the extended one. It felt strong and soft.

On the drive home, Caryl scrutinized Pet from the back seat and listened to the conversation—grown-up, "do you remember when" stuff. She waited for a lull. "Aunt Pet, sometimes I look at Mums' photo album, where she keeps pictures of my dad. Know what? You look like him."

"Aunt Pet is my dad's cousin, sweetheart. She's family to me, not your dad," Rosamund said.

"I reckon the child is right, Rosamund." Pet shifted to catch

Caryl's eyes with her own. "We're all family all the way back. Look close and you'll see. I have this theory, worked it out years ago. I believe people grow up looking in the mirror—brushing their teeth, combing their hair—seeing how they look. Time comes for coupling, they look for what's familiar, fall in love, and marry. People think married couples grow to look like one another. No sir. Starts out that way, I say." Pet gave a throaty gurgle that passed for a laugh.

"Makes sense to me," Caryl agreed.

"I don't know," Rosamund said. "People said your dad and I looked like sister and brother. Maybe you're on to something, Aunt Pet."

The three of them went into the large building, up the elevator to Rosamund and Caryl's apartment. Aunt Pet started to unpack and arrange things. She went to Caryl's bedroom with the package that had been under her arm at the airport.

"Here's something I made for you. Hope you like it." Pet handed Caryl the brightly wrapped box. Inside was a doll made of sturdy, ebony-colored, cotton cloth, its hair braided in an intricate African style. A wide gold and black skirt, with beads and jewels sewn around the border, flared over the lower half of the body.

"Thank you, Aunt Pet. She's beautiful."

"Turn her upside down," Pet said.

The skirt changed to green and yellow, and the lower half of the doll's body and arms was Indian brown, with pigtails on the head and a blouse of tiny, multicolored beads.

Neat!" Caryl exclaimed. "I love both of them—or her, or hers, or whatever—Aunt Pet."

"You're going to find out I talk a lot," Pet told Caryl, who had forgotten she was not going to be pleased with "any old, fussy lady." "I talk about family, the old-time ways and days. Your doll shows two parts of our family: African and Indian. I like to say the name of the nation—when I know it, like Catawba—so the story was passed on to me.

"Don't worry, Aunt Pet. I remember Granddaddy telling me stories, and I like history at school." Caryl had been won over in three hours. She was having fun.

CHAPTER 2

The Dectel cafeteria had disgorged the noon lunch crowd. Mid-level managers, who took lunch more or less at their pleasure, were seated in the sparsely filled, quiet room. Rosamund found a table shielded by a screen and a large plant positioned at the juncture of two walls and settled into her Cobb salad, roll, and tea.

On the other side of the wall, a voice sounded familiar enough to be noted but not firmly identified.

"She's a smart woman. I give her that."

"The times are changing, they are," an unfamiliar voice teased. "I just don't find it easy to take orders from a woman. Boy Scouts and Girl Scouts have their own troops, don't they? At least mine is blond. You have it tough—a black one."

"Hold a minute." The first voice turned steel-like. "Race—color is not a problem for me. I don't play that game. It's just that where I grew up, women didn't push. I'm not used to seeing ladies way up the 'boss' ladder."

Rosamund tried to place the voice that seemed familiar but changed in the high-ceilinged space. Southern cadence and timbre—recent, she thought.

The stranger said, "Don't kid me. You're from these parts. You know *they* only get on and up because of affirmative action."

The almost-recognizable voice said. "My folks raised me to give everybody their chance. Up in the mountains, we didn't have life on a platter, silver or plastic. I grew up watching everybody work hard—black, white, and Indian. It's the woman thing I'm not comfortable with."

Rosamund recognized the voice. Jeffrey Shuggs, the office "mountain man." The out-of-sight conversation turned into an argument.

The stranger said, "You're naive, a fool, lying, or all three, friend. You report to her, that Jones-Keyes. Bet she's plain old Jones, like all of *them*."

Shuggs said, "Sam, you're helping me see my blind spot. I'll tell you one thing: that Jones-Keyes is smart—man or woman. She showed me an angle in my latest stats that was brilliant—and a help to me. You know what? I thank you for opening my eyes."

The man Shuggs called Sam replied, "Stay in this city long enough and you'll wake up. You're still asleep, Mountain Man."

Rosamund pushed her chair from the table, got up, and walked to the other side of the wall. Seeing her, both men blanched.

"Mr. Shuggs, I'm pleased to work with you," she said with a broad smile.

"I-I didn't know . . . you—" Shuggs stammered.

"And I didn't mean to overhear. The cafeteria is quiet this time of the afternoon." She glanced toward the huge plant that shielded the two sections. "Sorry."

The stranger—Rosamund had not seen him before—hung his head. "I didn't mean any harm," he said.

"Oh yes, you did." She stopped him with a glint and tone as steely cold as she felt. "You are, without doubt, the majority opinion in this building—same as outside. Thank high heaven for fair-minded people." She gave Shuggs a look of acknowledgment when she said "high heaven." "We're going to get on, Mr. Shuggs." Rosamund left the men, and the rest of her lunch, feeling fine.

"Say, what are you doing? That's my game." Caryl grabbed the back of the boy's jacket. She turned him around and wrestled a brightly colored plastic box from his hands. "Darren?" she gasped.

"Don't tell the teacher. Please?" The squirming boy begged. "I don't know why I took it. . . . It's 'cause I like you."

"If you like me, ask to play with my stuff. When you like somebody, you take their stuff?" Caryl asked.

Darren, eight and three-quarters, and half a head shorter than Caryl, sniffled. She tugged his shirt, guiding him to the side of the playground.

"Come on, talk," she demanded.

Darren wiped his nose with a tissue Caryl took from her backpack. "I borrowed it for when I'm by myself. Makes me feel better. Like I'm not so much by myself."

"Am I the only one you steal from 'cause you like me'?" Caryl asked.

"I don't steal. I don't have to steal. I got money—five dollars." His eyes clouded. "You won't tell the teacher, will you? He'll call my dad, and Dad'll be mad."

"I won't tell *this* time. But you need counseling, man—the way I see on the *Oprah* show."

"How about you be my counselor? Kids can talk to each other better than they talk to grownups." The boy pleaded. "I'm not bad." Darren had noticed Caryl when she came to Randolph School in September. "You have lots of friends. You're in with the smart kids, and you play soccer really good."

"I see you with the boys. You have friends."

"No matter how it looks, I don't feel too good," he moaned. "I don't like Atlanta."

A loud buzzer went off. "We can't talk anymore. It's time to go back to class. Do you want to make an appointment?" Caryl knew her mother made appointments. She knew how to sound.

"You mean, you'll talk to me regularlike—every day?" Darren jumped from the bench.

"Not every day. Once in a while," Caryl said. "Wait a minute. Can't you talk to your mother? Does she know how you feel about Atlanta and having friends?"

"My mother doesn't live with my dad and me. She's a singer with the Ridge Boys."

"What's that?" Caryl asked.

"They're a band. They tour most of the time, all over the country. Even when they're not on the road, they're recording or rehearsing. Mom has an apartment in Nashville."

Caryl tried her counseling voice. "My mother and I—and Aunt Pet—live together. I get lonesome sometimes, but I don't 'borrow' things from friends."

"I only did it once. And I'll never do it again. You scared me off. I promise." Darren pleaded.

"We'll talk tomorrow," Caryl said. She put her game in her backpack. "How do you spell your last name, Darren? I'll write it in my notebook."

"S-h-u-g-g-s."

The black-haired, brown-skinned girl and the blond-haired, pink-skinned boy went into the school building.

A couple of hours later, the school bus stopped at the apartment complex where Caryl lived. She got off, waved good-bye to her new friends, Misty and Jennifer, and went inside.

"What's that good smell?" Caryl called as soon as she was inside the front door.

"Made-from-scratch gingerbread," Aunt Pet called back. "Wash your hands and come tell me your news."

Caryl climbed onto a stool to a saucer of gingerbread with lemon sauce and a glass of milk. "This is so cool, better than that grungy after-school center," she said, the side of her fork cutting into the warm, dark square.

"I searched high and low in three stores to find the right ingredients. No box bread for me," Pet said.

In the commodious Dectel Global headquarters, Rosamund was clearing up end-of-the-day tags. Lois had left. She heard a light knock at her door.

"Come in," she called.

Jeffrey Shuggs came in, sheepishness and bravado interchanging on his face. "I apologize for today," he said.

"No apology needed. I respect your honesty and admire your courage," she replied.

"Courage?" The corners of his mouth turned down; his eyes widened.

"Yes, courage. I don't imagine it's easy for one man to admit to another that he has changed his mind—especially on hard subjects like gender and race."

"I see. That's darn good of you," Shuggs said.

"You can say, 'damn white' if you want," Rosamund said.

They laughed.

"Would you like to stop for coffee on the way out?" Rosamund asked.

"I would, but I have to go right home."

"Heavy date?" she asked. Shuggs didn't wear a wedding band.

"Something like that." He threw his jacket over his shoulder, grinned, and left.

On her way downstairs, Rosamund heard muffled voices from VP Warner's office. She thought, *the brass is turning over its billions.*

In her bedroom at Rosamund's apartment, Pet Thompson

opened a large cardboard box, one of several delivered from Louisiana. She folded and smoothed an intricately designed quilt and laid it on the foot of her new bed. An aroma of sandalwood caressed her nose. Pet picked up the worn quilt, held it to her face, and took in the aroma. She shook off the shadow of sadness. "Ah, Uncle, I'll hear from you soon. Tonight, maybe?"

Pet cherished and guarded the remnants of heritage to which she was custodian. She lifted a linen-cloth-wrapped wooden box that once held hand-rolled cigars, its corners worn shiny from years of opening and closing. Cushioned in a soft, yellowed cloth were four roughly hewn pieces of flint, each nearly an inch long, and five flat, reddish black, round stones flecked with gold. The nondescript items had been passed to Pet from her mother, Anne, who received them from her mother, Ula, who received them from her mother, Sariah.

Pet wondered if she would be the last of her line, if the family stories and small treasures would cease with her. She had no children. Patricia Sariah Johnson did not worry. The moment she saw Caryl, she knew. The girl would be the one. "I'm to teach her the lessons, right, Uncle? You old tease. You never let on, did you? Never told me what I was left here alone to do." Pet closed the box and put it on top of a tall chest on the north wall of her new home.

CHAPTER 3

"I am not interested in hypothetical conjecture, Mr. Shuggs. The FDA and EPA have the expertise and experience to find out if Dectel is doing anything illegal. You and I are not scientists. I don't understand your insistence." Rosamund leaned back in her chair, placing her fingertips together, as she'd seen thoughtful people do.

"I'm no Ph.D., but my minor was chemistry, and I almost majored in the field, except my math was better than my electron microscope work." Shuggs wanted to convince his analyst, not antagonize her. He was calm, deliberate, and slow. "I've a passion for keeping up with scientific things. I read magazines and books on all kinds of sciences."

"I won't try to explain why the FDA and EPA are not up on this matter," he said, "but I promise you if someone doesn't stop Dectel from doing anything and everything they want to do to make a buck there'll be one gigantic mess-up. It'll be too late to pay up." Jeffrey needed the support of someone closer to top management to get his story heard. Rosamund was that person.

Rosamund pursed her lips and gave him a determined gaze. "I don't have any interest in being a whistle-blower, especially when I haven't proof that you're right. I have a daughter to raise—by myself. I won't compromise her future."

"All right, I'll find someway to convince you, I promise." He shoved one hand in his pocket and pulled on his chin with the other. "From my point of view, what's at stake *is* your daughter's future—and that of a lot of other kids and grownups."

"Let's call this meeting to a halt. I have another appointment. I'm not angry. Just show me, if you can." She handed him his file. "Here's your report, good job—I've told you that." Rosamund tapped her intercom button. "Lois, will you come in, please?"

Jeffrey stood aside in the doorway to let Lois move ahead of him.

"He doesn't look happy," Lois said. "His project has been passed. He should be jumping for joy, I'd think." She shrugged.

Rosamund motioned for Lois to close the door. She disengaged the intercom. "Shuggs thinks that the company is using some sort of dangerous chemical process. He wants me to set a meeting with the brass so he can show them. He sounds all wet to me. I'm not going to go out on a long leash for him."

"May I talk to you, privatelike, Mrs. JK?" Lois asked.

Rosamund heard a catch in Lois's voice. "Of course, is something wrong?"

"My knees sort of went weak at what you said. Now, this is a confidence, too." She went to the outer office door and closed it. Lowering her voice, Lois asked, "Do you know anything about my husband?"

"Nothing, except that he is disabled." Rosamund didn't know if she wanted to hear more. A turning sensation in the bottom of her stomach raised a warning: danger or disaster. "I have fifteen minutes before my next appointment."

"My husband, Liam, worked for Dectel as a technician in the fiber-research lab."

"Liam, interesting name," Rosamund said, checking her desk for her notes.

"My husband's mother is Chinese. She named him for her father. My father-in-law is African American. He was a GI. Met his wife in Taiwan. Liam now has nerve damage, can't walk anymore. The doctors say they don't know what it is, maybe genetic, but Liam thinks something went wrong in the plant one day and that's what paralyzed him. He says the company gave me this job, and a salary better than secretaries with more seniority, in order to keep me quiet."

"Sounds like a TV sitcom." Rosamund did not like the tension surging from her stomach to her forehead. "What do you think?" She leaned over her desk, closer to Lois.

"Sometimes, I think he's gone bitter. He's always been level headed, and he doesn't talk about his trouble most of the time. It's not easy for a young man who loved to run, play ball with his kids, and ride his motorcycle to sit in a wheelchair."

"I'll have to think about what you're saying. Maybe there is a tie-in with what Shuggs says. I need to think on it."

The women heard someone enter the outer office. Lois got up to announce Rosamund's next appointment. "Hope I haven't upset you. It's my problem, and Liam's."

She went to the outer office and returned with the latest sales rep.

At home, Rosamund stopped at the door to Aunt Pet's room. "You're so full of life; the house feels like the roof is about to blow off. Something special happening?"

"Does it show? Guess I'll have to tell you, if it's so obvious."

"Not if you'd rather not, but it's clear to me that you're feeling extraspunky." Rosamund sat in the rocking chair in front of the window.

From the first day of Aunt Pet's arrival, the room had been very different. Pillows, pictures, scarves, and artifacts had changed it from a generic spare room to a comfortable nest. Pet's "family shrine" occupied the top of the six-drawer chest. The shrine was an arrangement of dried flowers, candles of differing heights, a piece of driftwood worn into the shape of a canoe, an old cigar box, and a charcoal drawing of a woman in a high-necked dress.

Aunt Pet began. "I've had to shop all around to find food and ingredients like I like for my cooking. A few days ago, I found this little store, no wider than a truck, run by a woman from near down home—N'Awlins, we say."

Rosamund said, "I'm impressed. In this strange city, you found just what you wanted all the way from New Orleans?"

"I can smell a red, hot pepper four miles away, or it could be second sight. I turned a corner, and Ma Belle's little place sat right there between a boutique and a barbershop."

"You mean, finding down-home food makes you this happy?"

"There's more." Aunt Pet folded the last of the warm clothes from the dryer.

"I'm salivating." Rosamund leaned into the cushioned rocker, playfully licking her lips, enjoying the respite after work on a Friday evening.

"OK." Pet glanced down at her hands, stroking Caryl's favorite shirt. "I was selecting my groceries when I saw a gentleman, about my age, turning and sniffing a piece of fruit—a cassava. I heard myself say—mind you, I didn't intend to say anything, I swear it—but I said, loud enough for a body to hear, 'That's what I like to see, a man who knows how to pick a ripe melon.' Most people thump and shake it to see if it's ready to eat. My mama taught me if it smells ripe, it's ripe."

"Then what?" Rosamund was tickled that Aunt Pet had made contact with, perhaps, a new friend in her new home.

"Next thing I knew, Ma Belle introduced us. I would never 'pick up' a man. His name is P. B. Preston; he's a reverend and he's retired from working at the post office."

"Are Caryl and I going to have the honor of meeting this connoisseur of the orchard? We need to check him out, see if he's good enough for our Aunt Pet." Rosamund was not joking.

"We've only met at Ma Belle's store. He lives a few blocks from the other side of the shopping plaza. We sat and talked in that little park across the way a couple of times. The Reverend Preston is a widower, lost his wife like I lost my Joe.

"I like the way the new Atlanta has grown all through the old city. In some big cities, you can't find little hole-in-the-wall stores—and still in nice parts of town." Pet smiled, knowing that Rosamund would approve of her reasoning.

Rosamund lazily pulled herself from the chair, "Time to get Caryl from dance class. I'm looking forward to tomorrow. Saturday, day of rest."

"Not supposed to be—that's Sunday. Hurry back." Pet lifted the basket of clean clothes.

Rosamund heard the subdued hum of the air-filtering system when she turned off her light after midnight. She was a night person, hated getting up in the early morning. But she'd learned to adjust, do it the normal way; otherwise she'd never get up until noon.

Rosamund had been having strange dreams, strange because usually she either did not dream or didn't remember her dreams. Around the time Aunt Pet came to live with her and Caryl, she started dreaming more. In some of these dreams, two men would stand near her bed, grandfatherly types, watching her. They appeared to be talking to each other, but she couldn't hear anything. She'd never seen anyone who looked like either of them. One of the men was brown; one was white.

In the morning, feeling uncommonly refreshed, Rosamund decided she would let Jeffrey Shuggs in on Liam Hardy's story.

Where did that decision come from? she wondered as she pulled on tights to go for her run. She quietly let herself out of the apartment, so as not to awaken Caryl and Aunt Pet.

Two familiar figures sat on a bench with a third, unfamiliar person about fifty feet ahead. Rosamund jogged closer. "I thought my eyes were playing games with me. How did you get here before me?" Rosamund looked at her watch, then at Aunt Pet, Caryl, and the strange man.

Caryl laughed. "Hi, Mums, we sneaked out so we wouldn't wake you. I peeked in and you were solid sleep."

"We thought we'd catch the early air, and look who's here, my new friend Reverend Preston." Aunt Pet introduced a fit-looking man—fair skinned, hazel eyes, pencil-thin moustache, not very tall, and nattily dressed in a black and green jogging suit.

Hellos exchanged, Rosamund said, "You three seem to be doing great. Glad to meet you, sir. Caryl, Aunt Pet, I'll see you at home, later."

"Aunt Pet, you didn't say he was a white man." Rosamund confronted Aunt Pet the moment she entered the door.

"P. B.'s not white. He's a bright-skinned black man. Don't you know our people are so mixed up lots of times it's hard to tell the difference?" Pet's voice was stern, almost accusatory.

"He looks white to me," Rosamund retorted.

"I could tell right away, by the way he smelled that melon. You haven't had experience like I have. We know our own." Aunt Pet saw a puzzled look on Caryl's face. "I'll explain later, baby. Don't worry your pretty head."

Rosamund was not happy that Caryl had seen her disagreement with Aunt Pet. "Now, don't worry, Caryl. I was surprised, that's all." She tried to smooth over her outburst.

Showering, Rosamund felt, *Yes, it would be better if Aunt Pet unraveled the maze of coloration among "black" people. I'm not sure how the story works myself.*

CHAPTER 4

Jeffrey Shuggs sat on the edge of the chair in Rosamund's office. "This may be exactly the break we need."

"*You,* not *we.* This is your project Shuggs. I'm going along because Lois's husband is willing to talk with you. But I'll only go so far—so far." Rosamund's eyes were unsmiling and guarded.

Lois came in, her face alert with anticipation. "Liam is excited that somebody from Dectel will talk to him. No one has been interested in what he has to say about the accident. I'm glad his mood is up for a change."

On the way to Lois's house, which was located in an older neighborhood of Decatur, the mood in Rosamund's car was a mix of Jeffrey's hopeful expectation and Rosamund's skepticism. Lois pointed to pine-needle-covered roofs and patios. "I don't know why people buy nice houses in good neighborhoods and let the property deteriorate." Lois turned away from a rust-encrusted carport, tree branches dragging the concrete driveway. "It would take one day, just one day, to clean up that place. Neglect pulls the neighborhood down."

"You don't need to feel responsible," Rosamund comforted. "You can't be mother to the whole world."

A little further down the street, Lois asked Rosamund to stop in front of a brick and green-trim trilevel. The yard was planted with neat shrubbery. A white brick border lined the walk to the front door. The door opened, and Liam, looking as if he had recently returned from a workout, smiled from his wheelchair "Come on in," he beckoned and led his guests into a bright living room. "I made iced tea, and Lois did cookies last night. Help yourself."

Drinking Liam's tea and munching cookies, Jeffrey said, "I

filched your file from personnel, Mr. Hardy. I have a friend in the department."

"Call me Liam." Lois's husband was a muscular, pecan brown man with an Asian bone structure and shoulder-length black hair. "I'd sure like to see it. Funny, a man can't see what's written about his own self—it's my body, isn't it?"

"You're right." Jeffrey passed the file to Liam.

Liam slowly turned pages. "That's a lie . . . ain't so," he said several times.

Within the few minutes it took Liam to scan his file, Rosamund watched his face change from bewilderment to anger. "Surely the doctors wouldn't say things about your condition that weren't medically accurate?"

"It's not the treatment, Mrs. JK. That's what Lois calls you—is it all right for me to say the same?" Getting a nod from Rosamund, he continued. "It's what they say about *how* I was hurt—what happened that day in the laboratory. I see why the company got away with simple disability and no responsibility on their part."

"Let's go over the day of your accident step by step," Jeffrey said. He took a notepad from his pocket. "I'm not Dectel, legitimately, you know. I'm trying to figure this on my own. I think there's an iceberg underneath your accident."

Lois went toward the kitchen. "I know the story too well. I'll bring fresh tea. Go on, Liam." She caressed his head as she passed him.

Liam's hands trembled; his eyes turned inward. After a moment, he looked at an empty space between Rosamund and Jeffrey. "I was working with two other techies, moving five-liter vats of solvent from the centrifuge to the lab bench. We had our protective gear: masks, boots, gloves—the works, like always. Dectel doesn't use robots in that lab. I didn't deal with heavy toxics, just experimental stuff. A new chemist, some doctor I never saw before, was with our regular guy. He told us to wait a minute before we transferred the solvent to the big batch. He poured a small bottle of a clear liquid, only about four ounces, into each vat and told us to remove the vats we had brought in. Then, he said for us to take a ten-minute break. The guys and I went to the head, got some pop from the machine outside, and waited.

"Ten minutes later, we were back in the lab, like the big shot had said. The chemists told us to take the vat out. The other techies went to close the doors. I was the one to open the vat cover—it's on levers—it's not hard for one man to do," Liam said.

"So, you're saying the other technicians were not with you when the top came off?" Jeffrey was writing fast, his face more severe with every word Liam spoke.

"Right, Mr. Shuggs. I'd done it—opened a vat alone—a hundred or more times. Never had a problem. That time the odor was different, went up my nose like a fast freight train." Liam pinched his nose. "We always had a little smell—after all, it is a chemical lab—but not like that one. I guess the other men could have smelled it, but they were twenty-five, thirty feet away. The chemists—they had on protective gear, too—they were in the office looking at charts or something."

"You were the only one to get the full effect?" Rosamund asked. "And you think that's when something happened that paralyzed you?"

"Absolutely," Liam answered, his eyes and voice distant and resigned. "I passed out for a second or two, I guess. They took me to Medical. After pumping oxygen into me, they sent me home to rest, said I'd be fine in the morning. But next day, I couldn't move my right leg. It got worse every day until I couldn't stand or walk. But, look here," he pounded on the papers from his file, "Dectel's doctors say that all five of us were in the room, at the same spot, and they didn't get sick. That's a lie. I can tell you one thing, the other techies will testify differently. They've been bought off or scared off," Liam slumped in his wheelchair.

Jeffrey stared at Rosamund, the corners of his mouth pulled down. "I'll check to see if an order of phiofomel was delivered on that date."

Rosamund was quiet on the ride back to Dectel. Jeffrey was positively hyper, a contrast to his usual calm. Back in her office, Rosamund said, "I don't want to throw doubt on your hopes, Jeffrey—I can call you Jeffrey?" He nodded yes. "It seems to me that whenever a worker gets sick, he wants to blame the corporation. I like Lois, and Liam seems sincere, but he could be wrong."

"He may be, but it doesn't look as if Dectel gave him the benefit of an investigation to prove him wrong. It's a vested assumption. Any good analyst would want to exhaust all avenues before drawing a conclusion." Jeffrey noticed the reluctance with which Rosamund spoke. "My father used to sing a song about coal miners—somebody named Tennessee Ernie sang it when Dad was young." Jeffrey Shuggs began to sing in a pleasant voice. "Sixteen tons and another day older . . . I owe my soul to the company store." He stopped, gazing intently at his superior. "If you order me not to spend time on the case—listen to me, sounding like a detective—I'll chase it down on my own time."

"I wouldn't dream of doing that, as long as you finish your projects on time. You're a grown man." Rosamund didn't want to admit that she was affected by Jeffrey's argument, the tingling in her forehead was a sign of excitement, of something important.

Darren followed Caryl, swinging hand over hand across the playground parallel ladder. She dropped to the ground, dusting her hands. He followed.

"This playground stuff is easy. I wish it was harder," Caryl said.

"My dad took me to his Fit 'n Gym. The machines are neat, not babyish like this." Darren did not add that he didn't feel ready to try the high bar.

Caryl dropped to the grass and began breaking pink- and white-clover flowers. She began to thread the stems into a chain. "Aunt Pet showed me how to do this." In a few minutes, she had completed a garland of blossoms as long as a necklace. "This one's for Mums. Do you want me to make one for your dad?"

"Men don't wear necklaces. And flowers—yuck," Darren said.

Caryl found more clover blossoms from the grass beneath the tree where they sat. "Flowers are better than gold chains; they smell good and they're soft. Men wear gold chains. That's a necklace." She worked steadily, slitting one stem and threading another through it.

Completing a second garland, she put it around her neck.

"Darren, do you dream?" she asked, settling on her back into the grass, watching clouds move slowly across the sky.

"I guess so. Mostly I have nightmares when I eat too much."

"I have neat dreams." Caryl's voice was slow, almost as slow as the clouds. "Like the one with the two men in old-style clothes. They talk to me. I don't have to eat too much to dream about them."

"Nobody talks to me in my nightmares," Darren interrupted.

"Maybe animals growl in my stomach. Sometimes I get chased in my sleep, but that's a nightmare, like I said."

Caryl made a monster face, pretending she was afraid of nightmares. Darren knew better, so she stopped. "When I wake up, I remember that the men were talking to me, but I don't remember what they said. Aunt Pet says I will one day. She says I don't have to try hard. I hope so."

A shadow fell across the grass. Aunt Pet stood over them with a shopping bag packed with groceries. "Ready, Caryl? Introduce me to your friend."

Caryl jumped up and hugged Pet. "He's Darren, from school. We're getting to be friends." Caryl gathered her sweater and books. "This is my Aunt Pet. I told you about her. She tells neat stories."

Darren held out his hand to Aunt Pet. Pet set her bag on the grass. "Glad to meet you, Darren. Caryl has to go, now. Maybe you can come over for gingerbread one day."

Caryl handed Darren the second clover garland. "I almost forgot. This is for your dad, from me. I hope he likes it."

"I'll tell him a girl made it."

On the way to the apartment, Caryl held up one side of the shopping bag. "Darren doesn't dream, Aunt Pet. He has nightmares. Doesn't everybody dream?"

"I believe everyone dreams, but some folks don't remember them," Pet said. "Sometimes, when there's been a real bad time in somebody's life, they push down their dreams. There's a fear in them. They don't want to feel the hurting."

Caryl bounced, nearly toppling the groceries. "That's it, Aunt Pet! I bet that's it. Darren doesn't remember his dreams because he's hurting. His mother doesn't live with him and his dad." She gripped the shopping bag more carefully and smiled up to Pet. "You see, I'm Darren's therapist."

"Be careful, child. I know you and the boy are just playing, but you don't want to stir up more than you and he can handle." Pet knew how quick Caryl was, way beyond her years. She didn't know about the boy.

"I don't see how we can do anything wrong, Aunt Pet. Darren wouldn't tell a grownup what he'd tell a kid." Caryl trusted Aunt Pet. She knew she wouldn't tell her anything that wasn't true. "I'll be careful. I might have to ask you for help, OK?"

"That's what I'm here for. Anything on your mind, today, besides your "patient" Darren?" The elevator stopped at their floor. "It's good to be home." Pet let out a long sigh-whistle. She took off her shoes and rubbed her feet across the soft carpet.

The groceries put away, Caryl and Pet sat in the kitchen. Caryl drank milk; Pet sipped tea. "Last night, my two dream men turned into kids," Caryl said. "One of them looked like Darren and one like me. All the time before they've been grownups, with moustaches and beards. But I could tell they were the same two men. Why did they do that?" Caryl was at ease telling Pet her dream. Her mom was busy, and she wasn't old enough to know things like Aunt Pet did.

"It's not for anybody else to tell you what your dreams mean. You have to figure them out yourself, because the meaning is only for you. But, just taking a guess, I could pretend that until last night the men were showing you that you have somebody to look after you, more grown-up men because your daddy's not here to do it for you. You're getting more grown-up, big enough to look out more for yourself," Pet said. "I suppose the people in your dreams are like the ones who have brought me messages all my life. They help me too, like angels, except without wings and long white robes. They're regular people."

Caryl wiped her milk moustache. "One of the men is brown, like me, and one is white, like Darren. But last night when they changed, the one who looked like Darren was my color, and the other way around."

"That's different, I'd say." Pet put her teacup in the dishwasher. "I've seen people change in my dreams, but I don't remember that kind of switch. What do you think it means?" Pet did not talk down to children, certainly not Caryl.

The sound of a key in the door made them stop and glance toward the front entrance. "I don't know," Caryl slid from the stool to meet her mother. "I'll sleep on it, like you say," she flung over her shoulder.

After dinner, Caryl read Rosamund a story, one she was working on for school. Pet was at a table across from them, writing a letter.

"Good job," Rosamund said when Caryl finished. "I've special news. My secretary has twins, a boy and a girl, a little older than you. We're going to make a picnic some Sunday. We'll plan what we'll take as soon as we decide what day. Put that in your computer for a fun time," Rosamund said.

Caryl wanted to ask if she could invite Darren, but something inside told her not now. "Will we take something sweet or something healthy?" she asked.

"Both," Aunt Pet said, never slowing her concentration or the pen that skimmed scented pink paper.

CHAPTER 5

Rosamund stared into the circles that funneled down clockwise then faded to the bottom of her cup. Around and around she stirred, watching the circles slow then become no movement at all. She did not hear Aunt Pet come to the door behind her. Pet watched for nearly a minute, then, coughing and striding into the kitchen as if she had just arrived, she went to the refrigerator and opened the door.

Rosamund mumbled, "Morning, Auntie," without raising her head.

"Uh huh," Pet answered cheerfully. "Good, bad, indifferent. It definitely is morning. How are you?"

"Fine."

"Folks answer automatically. Say, 'Fine,' even if they're dying," Pet said.

"I'm not dying. Stop signifying on me," Rosamund managed a smile. "See, I remember 'signifying' from the talk I heard when I used to visit you in Bayou Country."

"You mean people don't signify in Ohio?" Pet opened her eyes wide and shook her head. "You sure you know what it means?"

"For sure. Our people know much the same things no matter where we live," Rosamund said. "If you wanted to make somebody angry, you told jokes about how they looked or something they said, but the joke couldn't be a direct insult; it had to be an offside."

Pet gave a cackle. "Well, that's your Midwestern way of saying it, but the way we used signifying, you made another kid mad by comparing a member of their family to something bad—an animal, ugly person, movie monster, and so on. If the kid took the insult without fighting, or crying, that meant they were strong.

One thing you never said. If you signified on their mother, you had to fight. Now, that was called 'playing the dozen.' You could get hurt, bad, if you played dirty dozens."

"Did you or did you not signify on me?" Rosamund stopped stirring her cup.

"Maybe a little bit," Pet teased. "I was trying to get your attention. You looked like you were one of those old Supreme Court judges and you had to decide the guilt or innocence of the Pope, the president, and the potentate of Baghdad all at the same time." Pet put the kettle on to reheat for her tea.

Rosamund drained her cup, left her chair, and began to pace. "Why is it that whenever life seems to finally be working well, something comes along to send it careening again?"

"My mama and grandma, all the old men and women, said that this world is like a teeter-totter—up and down, "Pet said. "We've got to stay with the movement to keep our balance. We need to believe that no matter how life shifts around it's going to balance-up right in the end." Pet poured her tea, added honey, stirred it, and put bread in the toaster. "Big problem or middle-sized one bothering you? No one ever admits to a little problem." Pet rubbed Rosamund's shoulders until she felt her begin to relax.

"I've got this great job, and you're here to take care of Caryl for me—she loves you so, I'm getting jealous." Rosamund smiled weakly. "There's something going on at Dectel that I don't want to get into. My gut says it's going to be rough down the road."

"Is it secret or can you talk about it?" Pet asked.

"I can talk. If you hear something that doesn't make sense to you, let me know, will you? I don't get some of it, myself." Not waiting for an answer, but knowing she had one, Rosamund plowed on. "My new statistician—he's the one who works all the numbers, gets them all together, name's Jeffrey Shuggs—thinks he's found out that the company is manufacturing something that can make people sick, maybe kill them. He wants to stop them from using it."

"Making people physically sick is not good, or the spiritual way either. Doesn't the government watch out for that kind of problem?" Pet asked. "They have all those departments with alphabet names."

"That's what I told Shuggs. He sees things differently than you and I do. I can't afford to take a chance with my career. Caryl depends on me, and I have to take care of myself." Rosamund said. "There's no more Carl, no daddy for Caryl, either."

"I don't know how things work in big business. I do know what's right and what's wrong. It's wrong to hurt people, especially if they don't know what's happening to them, like not choosing to get in the ring with gloves on," Pet said. "We come from a line of family that's always had clear vision on doing right. You know about your great-granddaddy Munje. He set the road for us. Long before him, too, I suppose." Pet began to warm to her favorite topics, family, strength, and honor.

"I know the story, Auntie. That old stuff doesn't help in today's corporate culture. It has strict rules on how things have to be done. If I don't follow the rules, I won't be able to work at all."

Pet looked at Rosamund with kind eyes. Her words were calm and firm, "All I know is when my great-uncle Munje had to decide on his life, free or slave, he went for free. Maybe the old-time ways don't work, but seems to me, if people are hurting people, lying, and firing 'em, keeping 'em from earning their daily bread, it's time to do something. Mr. Jeffrey Shuggs sounds like he understands that."

"Shuggs is from the mountains of North Carolina. The folks who used to be called 'hillbillies'. He's smart, I admit, but he's white. At first I didn't like him, but he turned out to be different from what I expected. Why, he stood up against a white coworker for me, another man, too."

"Don't you people eat anything but tea in this house?" Caryl stood in the doorway stretching, her stuffed camel, Lola, in one hand.

Aunt Pet gave her a hug. "Tea is for those who don't want to get fat. You can have whatever you want—as long as it's in the house."

"Right," Rosamund said. "We're not going out today in this rain."

"Rain? I didn't know it was raining. I have an appointment. Guess I can't make it."

"Are you in business for yourself these days?" her mother asked.

"How'd you guess, Mums? It's kind of private, do you mind?" Caryl asked.

"I will not intrude in the free-enterprise system." Rosamund felt a bubble jump in her diaphragm. She might have to eat her words.

"We can talk about your little matter whenever you want—if you want," Pet said to Rosamund as she began preparing breakfast.

Caryl went to the front window to watch the rain.

Two blocks away and around a corner, Darren and Jeffrey were watching the rain whip the cords that tied the awning to the wall, stretching like snakes, only to curl back onto themselves. The push and release was almost hypnotic. "We can't go anywhere today." Jeffrey said. "Looks like a fifty-mile wind. Say, man, take off the long face."

"Oh barf, I have an appointment." Darren grimaced, remembering that he wasn't supposed to tell that he was meeting with his new friend, Caryl. Luckily, the phone rang and his father didn't hear his last words. The strain of keeping secrets was not to Darren's liking. He and his dad shared most things. He'd have to talk to Caryl about secrecy. Still, he felt good. He hadn't taken anything from anyone or anyplace since he and Caryl started talking. Talking with her about his mother and his feelings helped him feel good.

P. B. Preston ate his solitary breakfast, scraping the last bit of pulp and juice from his melon. "Sure is a fine woman," he said aloud. Being alone, P. B. had fallen into the habits of people who have silence for companionship. But this time he looked around his kitchen, feeling guilty. It had been twelve years since his wife, Mattie, died, and his thoughts, somehow, seemed a betrayal of her. P. B. was a moral man. He hadn't been to college to learn to be a preacher. He had read the Bible—too many times to count. Once, he had a little congregation when he and Mattie lived in Waycross. He left for Atlanta when it became clear that they could not expect his congregation to pay him a living wage. Then, too, even though he was born in Waycross, sometimes people looked at him strange when they saw him walking or driving with Mattie.

P. B. hated his white skin, his white daddy, white people. In Atlanta there were so many people he could get lost in the crowds. He felt more at ease. What hurt was that he could find no place for him to preach. The big churches had schooled ministers, and the little ones had their own, too. He didn't know enough people to start his own congregation. No one knew what a sanctified and inspired preacher he was.

Working for the Southern Railroad didn't last long. The railroads died a few years after World War II. Rev. P. B. Preston had been lucky. He passed the civil-service examination and stayed with the post office until he retired.

Spunky Patricia, Pet, was the first woman who had caught his attention since Mattie. P. B. looked at the paper where she had written her telephone number. "Maybe she wouldn't mind if I called her." He cleared away his breakfast dishes and saw that it was after eleven. "She's sure to be up and about by now," he said.

"I don't care if it is raining; Good Lord, I been in rain all my life. I lived right off ol' Father Mississippi." Pet was fastening her raincoat close around her neck.

"I don't see any need to go to the store for something as simple as spice for a pie," Rosamund protested. "If it's that important, I can go for you. Tell me what you want."

"You'll get the wrong thing, and I like to walk in the rain," Pet returned the protest.

"I don't think you know how treacherous the weather in Atlanta can be. We're eight floors up. We don't know how windy it is down in the street," Rosamund insisted. A determined set to the older woman's jaw showed her that she was getting nowhere. The telephone rang as she tried to think of something to deter Aunt Pet.

Caryl called out, "It's for you Aunt Pet. I think it's your boyfriend, Reverend P. B."

"Grownups have gentleman and lady friends, not boyfriends," Pet answered. "It's probably someone wanting to sell me something, insurance or long-distance service." She swatted at Caryl's bottom and was surprised to hear P. B. on the line.

After Pet put down the phone, Rosamund asked if she insisted on going to the store after all. Pet said that the Reverend Preston was going to come over when the rain slowed—he liked rain just as she did—and the two of them were going to a movie.

"Why don't you stay here and watch a video?" Caryl asked. "I can make popcorn."

"Yes, and I can get to know the gentleman," Rosamund said.

"I'll suggest it," Pet said. "But I like to get outside. You know

46   FAMILY LINES

I'm not used to an apartment. Rain is good to walk in. I can hear when it talks to me."

P. B. agreed to a video. Surprisingly, to Rosamund, he and she hit it off. They found similarities between the bureaucracies of the post office and big business. They agreed on the mountains of paperwork. "How come, Miss Rosamund, we're supposed to have less paper with computers and we have more?" he asked.

"I don't know," she said. "Copies have to go to everyone on the network, and we have to make copies—back up—everything. Sometimes we're off-line for a while, and we're all on edge."

Pet said, "Making all the copies sounds, to me, like people having habits; they write down what they want to remember, then store it up, like photo albums, names in Bibles, school notebooks. I have report cards and certificates from ever since I was six years old."

"Patricia, you come up with the smartest ideas I ever heard," P. B. beamed. "I think you're right on. Folks are like pack rats, don't throw anything away. But I like notepads and books better."

And as an aside to Rosamund, "Your kind of backup can't be pulled out and held in your hand like a book or a letter."

Caryl piped in. "You can't smell them either. I like to smell old paper, like the ones Aunt Pet has about my great-great-great-great-grandparents."

"You added some 'greats' I don't know about," Pet said.

"Makes no difference," P. B. said. "Ancestors go back forever, whether we know them or not."

By the time P. B. went home, the rain had stopped. Rosamund went to her bedroom to work, and Aunt Pet invited Caryl to climb on her bed and hear family stories.

"Aunt Pet, you dream a lot, don't you?" Caryl sat in the cozy rocking chair beside Pet's bed.

"Just like you and everyone else—except for Darren. *He* dreams; he just doesn't know it, yet. Do you have good dreams?" Pet asked.

"I think so. Sometimes, I feel like I'm being teased. I almost hear or see something, then it goes away."

"That happens to everybody. Pictures and words come into my mind, and I don't know where they come from." Pet turned the album so that Caryl could see the likeness of a distant cousin.

"Is that dreaming?" Caryl's eyes were large as she moved closer to the lamp to see the faded photograph.

"Not a real dream. That's intuition talking to you. Reverend P. B. is right about ancestors. Our ancestors are parts of us, just like air coming in and out of our lungs. I read that all the people who have ever lived are around us in the air, and every time we breathe, we take in a little bit of them." Pet stopped and stared at the child to see if her words were frightening her. She saw rapt attentiveness.

"Go on, Aunt Pet. I love it." Caryl bounced back into her chair, causing the braids on her doll's head that she nestled in the curve of one arm to sway.

"If you hear or see something, and it feels really good down inside you, then you know you're learning from the source, from the Great Spirit. That's what my granny told me. Away, back in Africa, we had Ifé or Olodumare. Makes no difference about the word, the meaning is what's important.

"There are as many names for what we are, where we come from, as there are languages; God, Goddess, Zeus, or Nut. I hope you remember some of what I say. People will try to confuse you. You have a good head on you; don't you let that happen. Don't let anyone steal your spirit." Pet paused, wondering if she had said too much.

Pet had always spoken her truth whenever it came to her. Whatever tonight meant, she had followed her inner guidance. She hadn't meant to say all those things to Caryl. But they came out.

"Seems I've put enough thoughts in my girl's head, tonight," she said. "I hope you don't have a headache."

"My head is full of exciting things." Caryl was eager. "I feel like dancing. Show me, again, about the breathing. I'm going to try to get the dream men to stay with me tonight until I can hear what they say."

Pet stretched her body to full length in her bed. "You already know how. Watch." She placed her hand on her abdomen, slowly inhaled. Her hand lifted with her breath. She counted—one, two, three—then gently, slowly exhaled, letting her hand follow her body to resting position. "Once you get the rhythm, you don't need your hand. Just count until it is a part of you."

Caryl got up from the chair, holding her two-headed doll that

Pet had brought her from Louisiana. She kissed Pet's soft, sweet-smelling cheek. "G'night," she whispered.

Pet watched the rapidly growing child leave. She settled into her bed. "You're visiting her, too, Uncle. I guess that means you're almost through with me. I'll go out in the morning for my spice. Rosamund ought to know she can't teach this old dame different tricks, particularly when it comes to my cooking."

CHAPTER 6

Lois pushed the wobbly wheeled, overflowing shopping cart to her car. She tried not to notice the wear and tear of the eight-year-old vehicle, its faded paint and two wheel covers less than a full complement. The twins were arguing over who got to play Ninja next.

"Please, you're giving me a headache. Toss a coin, will you? Who wants heads?" Stopping the cart at the trunk, Lois noticed that the car tilted forward.

Mark and Meryl ran to the front of the car. Mark dropped to his knees. "Mom, the tire is flat," he yelled. Meryl was on the other side of the car yelling the same thing.

"Impossible," Lois said. "Two tires don't go flat at the same time." She rushed from one side of the car to the other. "Mark, open the trunk. Oh no, there's only one spare."

The lanky teenager collecting carts stopped. "You've got trouble, lady. You can call somebody to help you in the office. I'll tell the manager."

Leaving the twins to watch the groceries, Lois went to call a tow truck. "Not another unplanned expense," she groaned.

"Do you know anyone who has a grudge against you, Mrs. Hardy?" The tow-truck driver held one tire in the crook of each elbow. "Somebody slashed your tires, same place on each side. Looks like they knew what they were doing."

Lois was mystified. "You've gotta be kidding. Some punk with nothing to do, fooling around, did it. We shop here all the time."

"Maybe," the driver said. He gave her the bill and ran her credit card through his portable frame. "Like I say, I don't know—plain daylight and all. Never saw this done before, except by pros."

The twins were subdued on the ride home. Lois was silent. Nearly home, Mark said, "Mom, did you see that white car cruising our house the last couple of days?"

"You mean Mr. Brown's car?" Lois asked.

"I know his car, Mom. This is a different one," Mark insisted.

"I didn't see any strange car," Meryl said.

"You were too busy with your head in Ninja," he replied.

"Stop it, I beg you." Lois drove into the yard. "Nothing but coincidence . . ." Her voice trailed off.

The twins went upstairs to their rooms. Lois and Liam used the downstairs family room for their bedroom, because of his wheelchair. Liam confided that he had recently answered two strange telephone calls—open wire, glasses clinking in the background, but no voice. He had finally hung up.

"I thought it might be someone casing the house to see if anyone was home, you know, before a burglary. Or it could be a wrong number."

"Did the calls come before Mrs. JK and Mr. Shuggs were here?" Lois asked.

"I'll be damned," Liam exploded. "First one came the day after." He placed both hands over his face, dragged his fingers from forehead to neck—a gesture of confusion. "No, I don't believe it. Just coincidence," he peered solemnly at his wife.

"I think we shouldn't say anything to Mr. Shuggs and Mrs. JK—or anyone—until we see if anything else weird goes on." Lois reached for and grasped his hand. "We haven't done anything wrong. Have we?"

"I don't think so," Liam said. "But I have an idea we'll find out soon enough."

Darren and Caryl were in their favorite spot in the neighborhood park. The rainstorm of the day before had cleared, and although cool, the day was sunny. They could see the street, the school across the way, and the adult supervisor's station at the corner of the fenced playground. Anyone noticing them saw two children in animated conversation.

"You're sure if I breathe the way you say, I'll stop having nightmares?" Darren did not look convinced. But, his faith in Caryl was nearly absolute.

"No, I didn't say that," Caryl told him. "What I said is, 'if you practice breathing like Aunt Pet, you might start dreaming good dreams.' Since Aunt Pet showed me and I've been doing it, I remember more cool dreams. I even dreamed about you."

"What did I do in your dream?" Darren asked. "Were you in the dream with me?"

"You, your dad, Mums, and I were riding a Ferris wheel. You guys were in one seat. Mums and I were in another. Funny thing, every time the wheel went around, we got closer together. Just when we could almost reach out and touch, I woke up."

"Dreams are supposed to mean something, right? What does that mean?" Darren asked.

"Aunt Pet told me that a dream can only be in-ter-pre-ted by the person who dreams it. What my dream means to me is different from what your dream means to you. You have to do your own dreaming and figure it out. Got it?" Caryl felt older than nine years. Words seemed to be pushed up into her head by a different part of her than her everyday self. She wasn't scared. Aunt Pet told her to listen to everything, especially her inside voice.

"Your dream sounds like a happy one to me. How about you?" Darren liked the idea of being able to make up his own story about his dreams. Sometimes adults—not his dad, but teachers and strangers—thought they could make up his mind for him.

"What I think about my dream is—I guess it means that your family and mine go on a trip together, and we're friends." Caryl remembered that she had a job to do. "Okay. Is there anything else on your mind?"

"Mom called last night. About every three or four months, she calls to tell me where she is, what she is doing—and she cries a lot. She tells me she loves me. I wish she wouldn't do that." Darren stared across the street, through the fence. He swung his legs, kicking the air.

"You mean you don't like her calling, or you don't like her crying?" Caryl wondered if she might be getting in too deep, like Aunt Pet had warned her. She took a deep breath, all the way down in her body, the way Aunt Pet showed her. She counted slowly when the breath came out. Her insides felt better, no butterflies. Yep, she was doing all right with Darren.

"At first I liked her calling, hearing her talking, but the crying hurt. Now, I don't think I like her calling very much." Darren wondered if he was being disloyal, telling family secrets.

"You don't need to feel that you can't feel the way you feel,"

Caryl said. "You've got your feelings, like me and everybody. You're not telling a lie, are you?" she asked.

"Did you read my mind right then?" Darren asked. "How did you know what I was thinking?"

Caryl laughed and jumped from the bench. "No, silly. All I did was see how your face looked. Aunt Pet says, 'mind-reading is no big deal; just watch the face, the hands, and the whole body,' she says."

"Your Aunt Pet is a smart lady," Darren said.

Caryl turned a cartwheel on the damp sand. "Yeah, and she says I will be, too, 'cause I'm descended from a ver-r-r-y interesting family. Maybe you come from an interesting family, too. We learn stuff in our dreams. You can try—if you want to." Caryl wouldn't tell Darren that maybe he couldn't because he was white. Her mother could be wrong about some things.

A bell rang. Caryl, Darren, and the other children in the park looked up to see the supervisor waving to them. The children ran to the small shed that served as an office. "We'll have to close the park," the woman said. "More rain is on the way. Guess we had a fluke of good weather for a while. All of y'all get on home, you hear?"

The children and several older people who were sunning on park benches started, unhurriedly, to their houses and apartments.

"See you tomorrow," Darren called.

"Call if you think of anything to say," Caryl teased.

Near the time for Rosamund to come home, Pet found that she didn't have enough sweet potatoes or allspice for the pie she was ready to bake. She had forgotten to write them on the list for Rosamund. It was too late to call the office; she'd be on her way by now. *I can get around the corner to Ma Belle's before anybody knows,* she thought. "Caryl," she called, "I need to go to the store for a couple of things. I'll be gone no more than twenty minutes—ten there and ten back. You stay here. Answer the phone but not the door."

"Aunt Pet, the playground supervisor said that big storm is coming back," Caryl said. "It was really bad yesterday; maybe you should wait." Caryl put down the book she was reading. Aunt Pet had on her green raincoat.

"'Shoulda', 'coulda', 'oughta' I took out of my dictionary long time ago. Dinner won't be right unless I have exactly what I need. I'll be back before you know I'm gone." She started toward the door.

Caryl felt a cold space between her chair and Aunt Pet. "I don't feel you should go," she said.

"Just because you're learning to listen to your feelings doesn't mean you know everything," Pet laughed. She lifted her umbrella from the corner stand in the hall and went out the door.

Miles away, Rosamund was studying her monitor, her face intent. *Something isn't adding up. Last time I looked, all the data from the lab was available. Now everything earlier than a month ago has disappeared.* She tried a variety of commands—each time, nothing. Realizing that she would be late getting home, she murmured, "Better call Aunt Pet and let her know."

"Lois," she called, "something is amiss with this line. Can you get a clear outside line for me?"

Lois replied, "All the lines are dead. We're having freaky weather. At least the electricity is still working."

Sure that everything was all right at home—Pet and Caryl would be in out of the weather—Rosamund settled back to locate the missing file. Half an hour later, Rosamund gave up trying, closed everything down, and left the office. Everyone had left except the custodial people. The giant building was eerily quiet; she missed the hum of a thousand employees. Rosamund took advantage of a lull in the rain.

Caryl went back and forth between the living-room window and her chair. Aunt Pet had been gone for more than an hour. She wasn't frightened of being alone, but the cold she felt when Aunt Pet walked out in her raincoat and umbrella stayed in her body—a chill that wasn't due to the weather. Caryl heard the door open. She ran, "Aunt . . ." She stopped in front of her mother.

"Hi, Puddin'. . ." It was Rosamund's turn to stop in mid-sentence. "You look as if you've never seen me before."

"You should be Aunt Pet," Caryl's words tumbled out. "She went to the store, and she's not back, and it's been longer than an hour." Caryl didn't know if she should tell her mother about the cold feeling. She knew that, right now, she wanted Aunt Pet home more than anything in the world.

"The rain is coming down like a waterfall. She shouldn't be out there," Rosamund went to the hall closet.

Tossing Caryl's raincoat to her, Rosamund headed to the garage for the car, with Caryl following. They retraced the route Pet would have taken to Ma Belle's. At the tiny store, squeezed into an alley-wide space left over from a surveying miscalculation, Rosamund asked Ma Belle if she had seen Aunt Pet.

"Yes, she was here," the tawny Creole woman in black lace and a multicolored blouse said. "I told her she shouldn't be out in this rain—the wind was something fierce, mon Dieu." She crossed herself and made a second obscure movement with her hand. "Pet left time gone by. She should have been home long before now. She says it's only a ten-minute walk. I told her I'd call for her a cab. She said, she'd lived on 'Ol' Miss,' a little Georgia rain wasn't going to stop her."

Rosamund drove up and down every street leading to her apartment, peering through the rain, which began to slack.

"She must have taken shelter in another store or a building along the way." Rosamund watched her solemn daughter, huddled in her corner of the front seat. "We won't panic. Aunt Pet is a strong, resourceful woman. She will be all right," she said. Rosamund hoped her voice was confident. She was not.

"We'll find her," Caryl said. "But, I don't think she's all right."

Rosamund was startled. The voice did not sound like her Caryl, but a mature voice she'd not heard before.

After driving darkening streets several more times, Rosamund decided to return home and call the police. As she and Caryl arrived home, the phone was ringing.

"Miss Rosamund, this is P. B. Preston," a hurried voice said to an anxious Rosamund.

"Reverend Preston, do you know where Aunt Pet is?" If the hour had not been so late, Rosamund would have breathed a sigh of relief that Pet was at his house. No, she would have called long ago. Something was not right.

P. B. said, "Come right over to Emory Hospital—do you know where it is? I won't explain now, just come. Pet's here, and she's being looked after."

"I can find it. I'll be right there."

Caryl stood in the doorway. "I'm coming too, Mums." She was fully dressed and did not look sleepy at all.

The look on Caryl's face made it obvious that this was no time for a motherly decision otherwise.

Rosamund, Caryl, and Reverend Preston sat in the hospital waiting room. A resident—late-night, stubble-showing, fighting-sleep—leaned against a wall. "She has a concussion, a broken leg, and three cracked ribs. I'm not worried about any of that. The problem is that she lay on the wet ground for about two hours before a passing motorist saw her. We're trying to ward off pneumonia—that's the thing that gets older people more than anything else."

"Aunt Pet's not old," Caryl said, aroused at any implication to the contrary.

"The doctor means compared to you or me, Caryl," Rosamund said.

"You're right, little girl. Your aunt is a healthy woman, but she is more than seventy, and we never know. Of course, we'll do everything we can for her." The doctor did not miss the glare that Caryl gave him when he said 'little girl.'

"Can we see her?" Rosamund asked.

"She's still sedated. She won't recognize you. I know what you folks have been through, not knowing where or how she was. I suggest you all go home and get some rest. Come back tomorrow."

"She slipped, or was blown down, and was knocked unconscious." P. B. said to Rosamund and Caryl a second time. Rosamund drove to her apartment. P. B. seemed as upset as she and Caryl were.

He had said, when she and Caryl rushed into the hospital, that Pet didn't take her pocketbook to the store, just a change purse with money and the door key. "At first they didn't know who she was or anything," he said. "Then, a nurse searched Patricia's change purse a second time and found a scrap of paper in the corner with my telephone number on it. The hospital woke me. I called you right away, soon as I saw it was Patricia."

"She left home around five. Why so long?" Rosamund was shaking her head, confused.

"Apparently, it was dark, from the rain and clouds," P. B. went on. When she fell, she rolled near a clump of shrubbery. Seems she must have decided that the weather was worse than she thought, so she started to my apartment. I live closer to Ma Belle's than you do, in the other direction."

"That's why we didn't see her, Mums. We were going the wrong way." Caryl said.

"Right, and I had no idea where you lived, Reverend Preston," Rosamund said.

"P. B., please," he said. "Anyway, what with her green raincoat, if anybody came by, they would have been hard put to see her. About 8 o'clock, a man was pulling into his driveway—the moon peeked out for a little while—and he saw her. He drove her to the hospital. Took about an hour to get her admitted—she didn't have identification, remember? The man who found her said he argued with the hospital personnel. He told me, he said, 'Can't you people see by this woman's clothes she is no homeless person? She's somebody's family.' Good man, that man, even if he is white," P. B. said. "Still a few around." He slumped in his chair.

"P. B., you sleep here, in Aunt Pet's room. It's too late for you to go home. I can't thank you enough for coming home with us to let us know what happened, for helping Aunt Pet." Rosamund yawned. She had laid a sleeping Caryl in her bed as soon as they arrived home.

"Wouldn't have done otherwise. Patricia is a fine woman." P. B. followed Rosamund down the hall.

"I'll call the school to excuse Caryl, and the office for me. You sleep as long as you can, then we'll go back to the hospital," Rosamund said.

Pet had put fresh linen on all the beds that morning. It was late and Rosamund was tired. Nevertheless, she made an effort to smile. "The woman is a marvel," she said.

Pet was still unconscious when Lois called the next morning. "Is there any way I can help? Mr. Shuggs asked, especially, that I tell you of his hope for your aunt's recovery," Lois said.

Rosamund replied, "Thank you very much, Lois. There's nothing I can think of right now. I'll be in the office tomorrow morning. Oh, and tell Mr. Shuggs I appreciate his kind thoughts."

CHAPTER 7

A sturdy man with greying, light brown hair waited at the foot of Pet's hospital bed. His right elbow leaned on the shoulder of a somewhat shorter man beside him. The taller man watched doctors, nurses, and technicians scurrying to cut away hair from the back of Pet's head, apply a cast to her leg, and attach hypodermic needles to thin, transparent tubes stuck into her arms, neck, and leg. Words were brief monotones. A nurse asked, "How do you feel, Missus?" The waiting—and unseen—men, who were not wearing operating-room green, smiled, shook their heads, and snorted at Pet's reply. No one heard them—except Pet.

"How in hell's bells do you think I feel? With my hands, that's how, and you have them tied up in plastic tubes and strings running every which-a-ways."

"Pet, you're getting ready to come over, and you're still scratching at everyone," the taller man said.

Pet opened her eyes; at least she intended to open her eyes. To the medical people, the woman on the table was "out" like the well-known light. The team worked quickly but unhurriedly. "So, you've come to help me, have you? I didn't think it would be today. Figured I'd have my Caryl for a bit longer."

"You'll have her as long as needed, just in a different way. You've been told that," the shorter man said.

"We're your escorts, Pet. You don't really need our help. You're fine," the tall one said.

Pet peered at the shorter, fair-skinned man. "You've been coming into my dreams recently. Who are you?" She glanced back and forth at the two of them several times. "Uncle, your friend resembles you. I've seen him lurking around. Never heard him talk before." Fixing the fair-skinned one with a penetrating Pet stare, she asked, "I said, 'who are you?' Are you family?"

"He's family, Pet. Name is Frank. We want to know if you are ready to

come with us now or later?" Pet's Uncle Munje laughed when a doctor walked through him to inspect the bandage on Pet's leg.

"They wouldn't think you were funny if they could see you," Pet said. "After all the years you've been on the other side, I'd think you'd be used to being invisible to most people. I want to visit a bit longer with my family—and P. B. He deserves it."

"We will be around until you are ready to come." Munje and Frank faded from Pet's vision. She felt their energy still in the room.

The head surgeon heard a soft moan and saw Pet's body shake—then she twitched her mouth as if she were throwing off a bad-tasting medicine. "I believe the old girl is coming around."

He couldn't hear Pet say, "I'll 'old girl' you, first chance I get. You don't know how much time you have, my friend."

Rosamund and P. B. stood and listened when the doctor came into the waiting room. He lowered his face mask and gave them a thumbs up. "We didn't think she would make it. I know we told you otherwise, but none of the team believed it. All of a sudden, Mrs. Thompson's vital signs surged to normal as if she had a charge of adrenaline. Never saw anything like it. Well, once before, when a young mother did the same thing. Seems she decided, in a flash, she wanted to live—maybe it was her three children.

"Aunt Pet is a determined woman. Runs in our family," Rosamund said with pride.

"May we see her?" P. B. wasn't interested in hearing about the doctor's other patient.

"Yes, you may. She's asking to see you." Dr. Beguesse led them into Pet's cream-colored, chilled room. The beige, tan, and brown color scheme did nothing to warm the impersonal surroundings. Red and orange flowers sent by Rosamund's office lent a touch of humanity to the room.

Pet's bed was raised on a slight incline, the usual paraphernalia demanding its pounds of space, flesh, and payment. "I sure am glad to see you," Pet said in a voice not as strong or coherent as she thought it was. "I thank you, P. B. We haven't known each other long, but getting to be good friends can't take long at our age."

The Reverend P. B. was surprised to see how frail she was, when only two days ago she had outwalked him. "You needn't worry about Miss Rosamund and Caryl. Until you get out of here, I'll watch out for them the same as if they are my own."

"I appreciate you doing that, P. B. I'll bake you a cobbler when I get home. You want peach, apple, or huckleberry?"

"Huckleberry, Pet." P. B. rubbed her hand where he could find a place between the tubes and tape. She gave his hand a squeeze.

"I'll leave, Miss Rosamund, and you two can talk." P. B. picked up the brown fedora he always wore or carried. "I'll stay with Caryl."

"You know I won't be coming home." Pet stared into Rosamund's eyes as if she could see to the very back of the sockets. "I want you to know I have enjoyed every minute of the time I've been with you and my girl."

"Don't be silly, Auntie. The doctors say you bounced back like nobody they ever saw before." Rosamund's lilting tone belied her fear. Aunt Pet was nothing if not straightforward. Maybe it was the medicine.

"Of course, I did. What do doctors know about what a person can will herself to do? I want to leave everything neat and tidy, like my kitchen. Now you hear me. My visit has come to an end. That problem at Dectel, with you and Shuggs, will work out fine. You're going to have some rough times but keep working at it. Remember who you are. We come from . . ."

Rosamund completed Pet's statement. ". . . a special family. You can say what you want; you'll be home in a few days. Nobody dies from a broken leg."

"You're right." Pet managed a hollow laugh, a faint imitation of her joyful cackle, amidst the tubes and bandages. "In our family, when we make up our minds to something, we stick by it. For sure, I'll be home in a few days."

Rosamund waited a few moments for Pet to catch her breath. "Are you ready for Caryl? She's waiting. She impressed the doctors, and they're letting her visit you."

"You knew, didn't you?" Caryl asked reproachfully. She didn't wait for Pet's answer. "I've got to learn the dream stuff by myself from now on, don't I? I don't know if I can do it." The nine-year-old mingled knowing and wonder.

"Sure, you can. I'll be with you all the time and so will Uncle Munje and the new uncle I met last night, name of Frank." Pet coughed. Caryl held the little, curved, beige, plastic pan for her to spit into.

"I'm one up on you, Aunt Pet. Both uncles have been visiting in my dreams, but they don't talk to me."

"They will. One generation takes over from another." Pet slipped into thought.

Caryl touched her cheek, bringing her focus back into the room. "Why doesn't Mums dream the uncles?" Caryl asked.

"Maybe it skips generations or chooses, like in a lottery. There are other ways of learning and knowing. I don't know them all." Pet eased herself more snugly into her pillow.

"You're tired. I'll tell Mums to come in. I'll be back tomorrow after school. This hospital is cool. Some hospitals won't let young people in." Caryl would not say 'children.'

Pet beckoned Caryl to come closer. Whispering, she warmed Caryl's ear with her breath. "Don't let your mother on to too much of what you'll be learning. It's our secret for a while. You take good care of each other, you hear?"

"I hear." Caryl held back tears as she went into the corridor to get Rosamund.

"Is she getting better?" Lois asked, making a "tsk-tsk" sound of concern and hopefulness. "You look as if you could use a hospital bed rest, yourself, Mrs. JK."

"Not a hospital bed. My own bed, please," Rosamund said. "Aunt Pet seems to want to leave us. Just when she's found a good friend in Reverend P. B., and she and Caryl get along so well. I don't understand. Life is funny."

"I haven't got anything figured out myself. When you do, let me know." Lois almost let slip the slashed-tire incident. She quickly decided Rosamund didn't need more weight.

Rosamund laid two disks on Lois's desk. "Here are my analyses for the last job Warner requested. Never will it be said that 'we' can't handle it all. I won't fall behind in my work, no matter what the personal issue."

"You have tired circles under your eyes." Lois prepared to transcribe the disks. "Mr. Shuggs has been really worried about you."

"I wonder if it is me or Dectel he's worried about." Rosamund went into her office and closed the door.

Jeffrey parked his four-wheel-drive Trooper two blocks past Lois and Liam's house. He approached their house from a more oblique direction than would be expected if he had come directly from his home or work. Pulling his jacket collar to cover his ears from the cool evening, Jeffrey was pleased with himself. He was confident that no one had followed him.

Liam's wheelchair whirred on the other side of the kitchen door seconds after the bell rang. His pecan brown complexion and Asian facial structure as much Hawaiian or Samoan as African—Jeffrey thought, *who can tell the difference?*—a smiling Liam threw the door open, his strong upper body contrasting with his uncontrollable lower limbs.

"You made it OK? Any problems?" A questioning inflection was in Liam's voice, despite his smile.

"I learned to track and avoid cougars back in the mountains," Jeffrey said, turning his collar down and unbuttoning his jacket. "I doubt that any city 'critter' can do better."

The men sat at the table in the small living room next to the kitchen. The twins came to see the visitor. Liam introduced them. "Try to keep it down, will you, guys? Mr. Shuggs and I have work to do."

"Sure, Dad," Mark said.

"You can count on me," Meryl added. "I'm not a baby like lotsa kids."

Behind his father's back, Mark silently mimicked her words and mannerism, making his father's guest smile and his sister raise a fist at him as soon as they were outside the room.

Liam rolled his chair close to the table, motioning to Jeffrey to sit across from him.

"Are you a family man, Mr. Shuggs?" Liam gestured toward the coffee carafe on a tray atop the table.

"Yes and no," Jeffrey replied. "And, please, I'm Jeffrey, no title needed. My wife and I are living apart at the moment—maybe from now on—we'll see. Our eight-year-old son, Darren, stays with me."

"Some job, man," Liam stroked his chin. "Watching and working with my two, even just after school until Lois comes home, takes some doing. I don't see how you do it, alone, and he's only eight." Liam raised his hand to make high-fives.

Jeffrey slapped an affirmation. "Eight and three-quarters, Darren insists. I've gotten used to being with him; I like it. Darren and I go back home—to the mountains—often. He's a good kid."

Opening a stuffed attaché, Jeffrey loosened his always unwelcome tie. "Let's see what we can find here," he said.

After several minutes of passing papers back and forth, Liam pointed to a line. "I see. This is the day I had the accident, and you found that two days earlier the first large delivery of that chemical—phiofomel—shows on a manifest."

"Yes, yes," Jeffrey's voice lifted. "But, look here. I found a small order, two liters, the twenty-five-thousand-dollar order, five months earlier. I'll bet this is when they first tried it out in the small lab."

Jeffrey scanned several pages of data, forward and backward. "I see a pattern emerging. We are probably in full production on the new model right now. The money spent on the last two orders is a chunk."

"And they swear that my paralysis is genetic." Liam did not sound peaceable. The corners of his mouth drooped into a definite scowl. "What can we do? I don't have a clue."

"Mrs. JK—Jeffrey almost said Rosamund, but she hadn't told him to do so, yet—is close to the brass. If I can persuade her to go along, to be our ally, we might crack open a few heads. If we can't, there's going to be hell to pay, more than your paralysis."

Jeffrey shoved the papers back in his attaché. "I'm going to walk to my car by a different route. After your wife's tire-slashing, we'd be fools to think we don't have a problem. Corporate business is like government. Everything's a security risk. All I want to do is save lives."

Liam shrugged. "I thought it best to let you know about that before we got together, again. I may be paranoid, but I remember the Boy Scout motto, 'Be prepared.'"

"Right." Jeffrey patted Liam's back. "I'll be in touch," he said, leaving by the patio door this time.

CHAPTER 8

Rosamund loosened the clasp of one earring. When she was in a hurry or thinking of other things, she'd turn the screw too tight. She raised her hand to knock at the door of the last room in the hall. Then she remembered Aunt Pet wasn't there. She lowered her hand to the knob, feeling for a moment that the touch of its former occupant was imprinted in the metal. The door opened easily. Rosamund stepped inside and closed the door behind her. She leaned her back against it to steady herself.

"You were right, Aunt Pet, about everything." Rosamund spoke to the empty room. Her vision settled first on the walnut, four-poster bed, its double mattresses—Aunt Pet had shipped hers from Louisiana—looking like an ancient castle painting. She went to the bed and smoothed its quilt. A fragrance, pleasant and familiar, enveloped the bed.

As if compelled, Rosamund turned the silver-framed photograph on the bedside table. Aunt Pet and Joe, her long-gone husband, regarded her, silent and somber on their wedding day, June 19, 1947. That was the date Aunt Pet had written in black ink across the bottom of the picture. It was, of course, Rosamund's imagination that the young couple smiled at her. Rosamund lifted the frame, blew a bit of nonexistent dust from the glass, and put it back on the table. "Just a trick of the light," she muttered.

Back in the hall, the sound of the television in Caryl's room brought a slight exasperated sigh and erased the thoughts and memories that had begun to surface in Rosamund. A soft thud behind the door she had closed caught her attention. She opened the door. Everything looked the same. "I'm getting jumpy. I need rest." Closing the door for the second time, she moved toward a familiar commercial singing from the television. "Caryl, are you ready?"

"I'm ready," the younger, nearly identical voice echoed.

An earring clattered to the floor. Caryl opened her door, as her mother was picking up the fallen jewelry.

"I suppose I shouldn't be playing the TV right now, Mums, but it keeps me from feeling sad."

Caryl held Lola under one arm. She glanced down at the worn stuffed camel. "I am too big for stuffed animals, but she sort of called me from the bed." Caryl held her head up, as high as a nine-and-one-half-year-old young lady could. Her special doll from Aunt Pet sat on the top shelf of the bookcase. Caryl couldn't hold her until later, much later.

"Don't apologize. We feel alike. I'd grab my Lola if I had one," Rosamund said. "The limousine will be here in a few minutes. Let's watch from the window until it comes. The driver will buzz us."

Rosamund and Caryl both turned at the sound of a noise somewhere behind them in the quiet apartment. They went to Aunt Pet's room together. Fear was not a normal emotion for the Jones-Keyes women. On the floor beside Aunt Pet's bed, the silver-framed wedding picture lay face down on the bedside rug. Caryl ran to pick it up and put it back on the table. "Mums, I don't remember Aunt Pet smiling in this picture, do you?"

"I do," Rosamund said.

The doorbell buzzed. "The limo's here." Caryl turned as quickly as she had run to pick up the photo. "We have to get it over with, I guess. I'll bet Aunt Pet would be just as glad if we didn't have any old funeral for her."

It rained all the way to the church on the outskirts of Decatur—a small church in a mixed 1920s old and 1970s newer neighborhood. Once Decatur had been a small town some distance from Atlanta. Now, the small town and the city had grown, one into the other. The street on which the church stood was lined with pines and a magnolia tree here and there. Red brick with white wooden steps, set back from the street so that you could only find it if you knew where it was, the church was solid and welcoming. Aunt Pet had not belonged to this, or any church, but P. B. was a member and he told Rosamund, "it wouldn't be right to have Pet eulogized in a funeral parlor; those places don't have a spirit blessing in them."

P. B. was under a large black umbrella, watching for Rosamund, Caryl, and the handful of mourners who had come to know Aunt Pet in her latest home. Rosamund's parents were on vacation in Hawaii. They could arrive only after the ceremony. Rosamund's brother, Bob, was overseas but sent an e-mail. Rosamund and Caryl were assisted from the limousine and into the church by a sad-faced young man. He had been trained to look as if he knew and suffered with the families he served. Caryl winked at him. When he raised his eyebrows in surprise and disapproval, she whispered to Rosamund. "I wanted to crack him up. He looks ludicrous." Caryl loved to practice her expanding vocabulary. She squeezed her mother's hand. "Aunt Pet was no sourpuss."

Following Rosamund and Caryl, P. B. leaned into the pew and asked, "Do you mind if I sit with the family?"

"I expect you to," Rosamund answered. "I don't know why you feel you need to ask, P. B."

Music played from an electronic source impossible to locate. Rosamund thought that the mournful tones were meant to suggest something beyond earthly reality. Aunt Pet was, without a doubt, pooh-poohing the whole show, laughing at the pompous ritual, just as Caryl said. Patricia "Pet" Anderson was not one for playing unreality.

A stirring in the aisle behind their pew caused Rosamund to look around. Moving into the pew behind them were Jeffrey and Darren Shuggs. The Reverend P. B. Preston glimpsed them from the corner of his eye. He whispered to Rosamund, "Even at a funeral I don't care to see white folks. They've done away with more than enough of us. Don't need to come to view anymore remains."

Jeffrey Shuggs heard P. B.'s words, as P. B. had intended. He felt a blush surge from beneath his collar. Rosamund was uncomfortable. She did not agree with P. B. Preston, anymore.

Friends from Dectel, several from the apartment building, Ma Belle, and even the postman, filled the small church. Rosamund whispered to Caryl, "I didn't realize Aunt Pet touched so many people. And you didn't want her to come live with us."

"I'm chopped liver," Caryl replied. "Excuse me, Aunt Pet." She looked up to the beamed ceiling of the church.

"Apology accepted, I'm sure." Rosamund enfolded a small brown hand in hers.

The soft rain cleared almost the moment the procession turned into the cemetery. The air smelled fresh and clean during the brief graveside ceremonies.

Back in Rosamund's apartment, the last of Aunt Pet's friends were gone: Ma Belle and a few customers from her store. Rosamund went to the end bedroom, again.

Aunt Pet's high-pitched laugh entered Rosamund's mind. She blew a sharp breath as the door opened smoothly over the soft carpet. The picture was on the floor again. "Okay, if you want to be left in private, I accept your wishes."

"Pick it up, Pet." The silver frame lay a few inches in front of the broad shouldered, bronze man. His legs were apart, like a soldier standing at ease. His wrists were flexed backward on his hips. He wore dark leather britches and a clean, rough-dried, homespun shirt, a leather-string tie drooped precisely to both sides of his collar.

"Hello, Uncle. Good to see you in the flesh, so to speak. You look healthier than you do in dreamtime." The young woman in the picture stepped close to scrutinize the man.

"You didn't pick it up," Munje Jones repeated.

"I'm getting Rosamund to know this picture needs to be kept with our family treasures. It's the one good one ever made of me." Pet adjusted her image to more closely match the photograph."

"Rosamund doesn't have the power, but she will remember. Don't worry." Munje, Caryl's second great-grandfather grinned. He knew the girl was the "spittin' image" of him, with her high forehead, her eyebrows growing straight across slightly hooded eyes. Indeed, him all over again.

Rosamund scooped up the silver frame and went to the closet, sensing a growing awareness of what family and heritage had come to mean after Aunt Pet came to live with Caryl and her. She had once thought that Aunt Pet was fanatical with her stories about family. Rosamund realized she had grown to respect those tales.

Aunt Pet had often spoken of a revered ancestor, Munje Jones. Pet said that Munje ran away from a plantation near Alexander, Louisiana, to join the Union army during the Civil War. Munje was Rosamund's great-grandfather. Aunt Pet was Munje's grand-niece, descended from Sariah, the African captive, and a "travelin' Indian." Aunt Pet's grandmother was half-sister to Munje.

"Remembering the twists of family takes some study," she muttered. Inside the closet, behind the rack of shoes, was a worn, burgundy leather suitcase, its straps neatly fastened and tucked. Rosamund pulled the suitcase forward. She recalled its bulging sides the day Aunt Pet arrived from Shreveport. "I wonder if you looked like Munje or that traveling Indian, old gal, or if I do," she said as she opened the case and placed the picture on top of sachet-scented sweaters. Then she carefully lifted and opened a yellowed envelope that peeked from the rayon pocket of the suitcase. Inside were the Civil War discharge papers of her ancestor, Pvt. Munje Jones.

On the other side of the wall, Caryl called to Rosamund, "Mums, I'm really sleepy. I'm going to bed now, okay?"

"Sure, I'm turning in, myself, as soon as I turn out all the lights."

Rosamund slid between smooth sheets. Aunt Pet had been a joy. Strange, how quickly and quietly she had left them. It was as if she had finished one task and simply waited for the next one. "Oh." Suddenly, Rosamund was wide awake. "Tomorrow may be difficult. Aunt Pet, Jeffrey and I will need all the help we can get. Something tells me Mr. Warner may not be as easy a sell as we think, but I'll put it out of mind—expect the best." She relaxed, counting her breaths until she was asleep.

Caryl was not surprised when Aunt Pet appeared in her dream. Aunt Pet told stories all the time—when she was fixing lunch, washing dishes, or walking Caryl to school. Now that she wouldn't be around to talk in person, dreams were the next best way to hear about Louisiana and the old days.

"I think she's too young for the whole story," Munje argued with Pet.

"I'm saying, I've known the child long enough and she is ready. Young folks are not as babyish about the world, the way things are goin' so fast these days." Pet, in a white pantsuit, hovered a few inches above Caryl's bed. "My girl can handle anything we bring to her."

Munje slowly shook his head side to side. "You may be right. I haven't visited in this time, except with you. Why don't we start her during my days in Birley before my pa sold me."

"No, she likes the part about the war. Why don't we begin when you ran away to join the troops?" Pet turned around to see how her new outfit looked in Caryl's mirror. She hadn't had time to decide if she wanted to stay in her 20s or 30s for now. She laughed when she noticed that no reflection greeted her in the mirror. Her laughter was familiar to the sleeping girl who lifted her head from the pillow, then snuggled back into its softness.

Munje slipped into his thought-sending mode. *"I like that story. I hope you're right. I don't want to scare her."*

"I know this time, Uncle. That's why I wanted to join you as her guide." She and Munje mingled. Caryl began to dream.

Black ants. Legs so long you can see daylight under their bellies, a full inch long. They crawled across a log that lay haphazardly on one side of the ditch that Munje chose for his day shelter. Munje held his breath, wanting to still his heartbeat. He thought, If I stay as still as a stone, the ants can't find me. He knew he was safe from sight, among the pussy-willow stalks and trailing grapevines.

He heard the solid metal of machetes hacking rhubarb colored stalks of ripe sugarcane in the morning sun that was quickly rising to noon hot. He did not have to turn his head one inch to know that the overseer, with cocked shotgun and a pistol at his belt, stood nearby, out of range of the shining, juice-dripping, long knives. Munje felt ants crawling over his left arm and hand. At least they weren't those biting little red ones. One ant ventured up his sleeve and found the hole he'd torn crossing blackberry brambles two days before.

Any movement, any sound, other than the slash and crack of the blades and heaving breaths of the slaves, might be carried to the armed man. "Why don't you sing?" Munje sent a silent wish to the slaves. If they sang, his movements would not be noticed. He heard the tearing and falling of cane stalks reminding him of the same sounds he had made and heard every day for too many years, maybe a hundred miles behind him, on Major Alexander's plantation.

For a flitting moment, Munje let Mina's face come into his head. "No, not now," he said. "Keep my mind clear." He dared to whisper, "Oh, sweet dark, please come soon."

The ants explored his arm, upward to his shoulder, onto his neck. Munje held his lips between his teeth, his blood trickling, peering through pussy-willow bars.

"She'll remember most of it, you'll see," Pet said as she and Munje withdrew from the room.

"We've time for a quick cereal or toast, not both. Which?" Rosamund came into the bathroom to brush Caryl's hair.

"Whatever you have," Caryl answered. "Mom, I think I dreamed about GeeGee. All about him hiding from slave catchers, like Aunt Pet told me."

"GeeGee? Oh, you mean your great-great-grandfather that Aunt Pet talked about so much?" Rosamund laid the brush down. Caryl followed her into the kitchen.

"Yep, takes too much energy to say all those greats. GeeGee's shorter. Anyway, it was a neat dream."

"Aunt Pet had fascinating tales, but be sure that you keep clear on the difference between real and fantasy." Rosamund didn't want to encourage Caryl too much in her imaginative excursions.

The toast popped up, just the right brown and crispiness for butter.

Leaving Caryl at school, Rosamund began the daily battle with freeway traffic into Dunwoody. *Too many transplants from small towns, she mused. Take them off the highways and we wouldn't have gridlock.*

She dropped her purse in the parking lot, banging her head on the side rearview mirror when she stood up. "See, Mrs. Jones-Keyes, you hurt yourself when you're distracted."

Was she imagining it or were all eyes watching her when she entered her office area? They must have heard about Aunt Pet.

"Only a little mail this morning, Mrs. JK." Lois handed Rosamund several envelopes. "Are you all right?"

"Yes, thank you. A happy person like Aunt Pet leaves nothing but good feelings. I can't feel too sad. Is Mr. Shuggs in yet?"

Shuggs came through the door fast, taking off his jacket. Corporate culture is uneasy for a man who loves woods and farms. *Ready?* his eyes asked Rosamund, although no words passed between them. He handed her a large brown folder.

She thumbed the pages, scanning headings, pausing to carefully read the last paragraph. "I hope this will convince Warner and the brass," she said. "I'm not sure they'll be easily persuaded. You weren't positive, yourself, at the beginning."

"And you weren't." Shuggs reminded her. "I'm not so sure you are convinced, even now."

"I've given you a hard time, Jeffrey. It's not my way to be suspicious of the way my company operates. I may not be 100 percent sold on your suspicion," Rosamund said, "but I'm willing to go along. We have an hour before the meeting. Shall we go over your presentation one more time?"

Rosamund went for another cup of coffee but changed her mind. She sat across from the man whom she had considered her enemy a few weeks ago. Caryl was responsible for this change, Rosamund remembered:

Caryl had been bumping around in the kitchen when Rosamund came home from work. A shopping bag leaned against the breakfast counter. "What are you up to now, young lady?"

Caryl was startled. "You're early. I'm going to my friend Darren's to make him some chicken soup. He's sick." She looked down at the floor. Aunt Pet knows. Caryl was tall for less than ten. Most took her for eleven or twelve.

"What's the problem? We're friends, aren't we?"

"Of course, Mums, but I know you don't really like some people, and my friend, Darren, . . . he's white. I think you'll understand, but I didn't want to take a chance."

"I'll do my best to keep my fangs sheathed." Rosamund tried to tease a smile.

"Darren and his father only have each other, like you and I did before Aunt Pet came. His mother travels with some kind of music show. His father works late sometimes, and Darren came to school with a cough today. I thought I'd go over and help him feel better."

"To show you I'm not the awful old racist you think I am, I'll go with you, if you don't mind." Rosamund waited for a word from her daughter.

Twenty minutes later, a boy, half a head shorter than Caryl, with blond hair and grey eyes, opened his door. "I called my dad at the office. He said it's OK for you to visit. Miss McRay, across the hall, watches me until he gets home. She has a cold, too, and said she'd keep her germs in her apartment. She knows it's OK that you're here. I explained and she has her door open."

Rosamund had been ready to castigate a man who'd let his son stay home alone. She felt properly chastised. She heated the soup in the microwave for Darren. He and Caryl talked as if they were lifelong friends. Rosamund looked around, noticing how neat and attractive the apartment was. She imagined that men who lived without wives or girlfriends were natural slobs.

"Rosamund, Rosamund, where are you?" Jeffrey brought her back from her reverie.

"It takes only a moment to space, doesn't it? I was thinking of the day I met Darren," she said.

"You were really surprised. I rushed home when I learned that Miss McRay was ill. You didn't know I had a son and lived near you. I was flabbergasted, myself." Jeffrey smiled easily. "Crazy coincidences."

Rosamund blushed. "Being the boss was important for me. Subordinates aren't supposed to bore bosses with personal concerns."

"I'm glad for the change—an improvement, I hope. Now let's get to work." He loosened his tie.

"You didn't like me, as I recall . . ."

Lois rang. "Mr. Warner is ready, Mrs. JK, Mr. Shuggs."

Warner was brusque. An executive neither Rosamund nor Jeffrey knew was with him. "Shuggs, we don't have much time. The only reason you're getting this meeting is because Mrs. Keyes asked that we hear you out. What do you think is a problem in Dectel's manufacturing procedures?"

"Mr. Warner," Jeffrey said, handing the VP and the other man copies of the file, "I . . . I'm concerned that the new solvent our manufacturing facilities are using to speed up the setting time for the circuits is dangerous. It can be lethal over the long run."

Warner's voice was flat. "We have state-of-the-art laboratory personnel and facilities. If there was any problem, they'd know it."

Warner's assistant and echo spoke from his side of the table. "What makes you think you know differently, or more?"

"Letting our own lab tell us everything is like letting the fox guard the chickens," Shuggs said. As soon as he spoke, he knew he'd made a mistake. The managers, the brass, thought him a hick, and whenever he used examples from his rural background, he was laughed at and ignored. He tried to cover. "The latest data I've found, which is according to Dr. Belden, concludes that the new solvent, containing phiofomel, will be 150 percent more toxic than our old formula." Jeffrey hoped to impress them with the name of the scientist, who knew more about new chemicals than almost anyone else.

Warner broke in, "That Belden is a wild-eyed radical. He'd have us going back to processes we used forty years ago. We're able to turn out components much faster than the competition, and at less cost."

"But Mr. Warner, there are studies from Australia and Europe that point to the toxicity. Even the FDA is beginning to question some of the latest formulations. I think we should reexamine before we find ourselves in deep trouble. We'll have millions to pay in damages if we continue." He didn't mention illnesses and deaths. He felt that would have no impact on his hearers.

"I'm convinced that our laboratory reports are accurate. Until and unless they tell me otherwise, you're wasting my time." Warner turned to Rosamund. "I depend on you to funnel to me the best information for Dectel. How did you let this crackpot idea through? No more about this, do you understand, Mrs. Keyes? And, Shuggs," Warner shifted the knot of his tie, "work *for* Dectel, not against it. I hope you hear what I'm saying or you'll be looking for a new position."

Warner, his assistant, and his executive secretary, who'd been punching away on their laptops, ignored Rosamund and Jeffrey as they left the room, rebuffed and bewildered.

"I definitely had him gauged wrong," Rosamund said. "I thought I'd felt him out to be open to hearing us." Rosamund looked out of the window of her office at the traffic below. "How could I have been so fooled?"

"I think he pulled the old smile game to get you into a corner. You've done very well at Dectel, in a very short time. He had me tagged as a troublemaker from the beginning." Jeffrey paced from desk to door, not much room for more than three or four steps in the tiny office.

Rosamund drew a sharp breath. "Jeffrey, something just happened. It's as if I heard a voice inside my head."

"What's the message?" he asked.

"A voice said, 'Slavery ain't over just 'cause Lincoln signed the paper.' Those words are not my style, and it wasn't Aunt Pet's voice. I think we may both have been taken for a ride."

"I don't know about slavery, but I feel chained." Jeffrey shoved the papers back into the folder. "I'm not beaten, yet. I hope you're still with me."

Rosamund felt a familiar knot in her stomach. "Sure, sure, but I've got to sort things for myself. Caryl comes first."

"So does Darren, but we're too young to lie down for dead. We'll talk later, if you want." He left her office, not expecting a good day from that point until 5:30.

Back at Rosamund's apartment, the new after-school replacement, courtesy of Lois, waited with a snack for Caryl. Later, in her room Caryl told Lola, "I didn't say anything to Darren or anyone about my dream, and I don't know if I should tell you. I feel it's just for me, right now."

Rosamund found Caryl, who was finishing her homework. "I have to cancel our rink date tonight. The office was no picnic today, and I have a headache. You'll excuse me, please?"

"You look fagged," Caryl said. "This time, yes. Shall I start a tub for you?"

Caryl jumped up to go to Rosamund's bathroom.

"Not yet, thanks. I just want to lie down with my feet up for a while. We can order in if you want." Rosamund kicked off her shoes, picked them up, and started down the hall, pulling off her earrings.

The phone rang. Rosamund answered. "Not tonight, Jeffrey. I'm tired. I said I have to think this thing through. You may not mind looking for another job. It's not so easy for an African-American woman, especially if she's fired from a Fortune 500 company."

Warner stayed late in his office, telling Miss D'Arcy, his assistant, that he wanted to catch up on his reading. "I'll be distracted at home by the family. You know, teenagers' music and TV," he told her. In the quiet of twenty stories of mechanical hum before the cleaning crews came, he manipulated blue and green monitors in two offices.

Warner copied coded notations into several Dectel files. He grinned, pleased with himself. "My figures work in very nicely," he assured himself. "In fact, perfectly. No one can tell any difference."

He wiped a line of perspiration from his lip. "Always a vice-president? I see the signs, younger men moving faster. I'll get my share. I promise myself." He banged at the console in the senior analyst's office, making noises alien to his daytime persona. "Mickey, they call me. I'll show them a very smart mouse."

Satisfied that he had done what was needed and covered any

stray tracks, Warner surveyed the rooms to be sure all was as he found it. Smiling to himself, Warner exited the cavernous building. He left an open file on his desk, a notice that he had worked late—which was his right and a sign of dedication to Dectel Global. His cool greeting to the cleaning crew was just as coolly received.

CHAPTER 9

"Come, Daughter. I want you to meet an old friend." Munje and Aunt Pet watched Rosamund drop the telephone on its base then pull the covers around her shoulders. She tossed for a few minutes before, sighing deeply, she fell into restless sleep.

A figure of a man, barely old enough to shave, with shoulder-length blond hair and sad eyes joined Munje and Pet beside Rosamund's bed.

"Pet—Patricia, meet my friend, Frank." Munje bowed.

"Now, you just wait a minute. I'm not accustomed to the ways of this 'world,'" Pet paused.

"You've been here three earth days," Frank said. "You'll be fine soon—after all, there's no time; you know that. I'll put on my son Jeffrey's eyes so you'll see a familiar look."

"Your son? What time are we in, now?" Pet scanned the odd uniform. She recognized it as being from the Civil War, the Southern side, 140 years before.

Frank Shuggs smiled. "No time, no time—it's the same as in dreamtime, Pet."

Munje was enjoying Pet's attempt to understand the changes around her. "Everyone and everything is the same: sons, daughters, mothers, fathers—no difference, Daughter. Whatever we choose to 'send' is a choice, and it is all change. Frank and I would like to start our story—for you and Caryl—with our first meeting. It will help you know what we're here to do and what part you'll play in it."

Munje reminded Pet of her husband for a flash. "I thought dreamtime was wonderful, but this time—you call it 'Pass On'—is going to be more than I could ever imagine." She felt both energies imparting something from themselves to her. She said, "Energy, that's what I am, now that I am not with the living."

A field, screaming men, mules and horses, noises like Fourth of July

76 FAMILY LINES

rockets intruded into whatever it was that Pet felt she was. Smoke, noise, and confusion blended in one impression. A young Frank Shuggs in a too-large grey uniform stood behind a small, flat-roofed building. Frank didn't like what he had to do, but his father had taught him to do his duty. He raised his rifle to shoot at a soldier whose horse stumbled in a hole made by a cannonball. Frank knew that this duty differed from shooting bears back in the woods of his North Carolina mountains. The man in blue fell to the ground. Frank cried, "I'm sorry," as he pulled the trigger. He had not missed a shot since he was ten.

Munje Jones, his face as scant of hair as Shuggs', rounded the side of the building. He was trying to find his way to the tent where Captain O'Neil waited for his scouting report. Unaware that he was still behind Confederate lines, Munje was face to face with the soldier in grey. Instinctively, he fired. Munje's black eyes caught and merged with the grey eyes of Frank Shuggs. Something deep inside Munje stirred. It was his first kill; his job was to scout, not do battle. He did not want to look at the face of the dead man, but something pulled his face toward the man he had shot. He saw that he and the fallen man—no, boy—had an unsettling similarity in their faces. In some other place, they might have been friends.

Pet felt the scene in her new energy awareness. The battlefield disappeared. Munje and Frank watched her. "You see?" Munje asked.

Frank nodded, "Pet, you knew that you were called to come to Atlanta to live with Rosamund and Caryl."

"I knew something. Exactly what, I wasn't sure. It's my habit to follow my calls—always have—so I came. Things are not clear for me. I kinda resent not knowing." Pet frowned and tapped her foot.

"Over here, we don't give out too much—else there wouldn't be reason to have both sides. You've been a good learner, Pet." Munje laughed, "Lighten up."

"All right, brothers, let's get to work. What do we do now? Or do I have to do all the work?" Pet peered through a warm mist—pink, grey, and blue—that surrounded them into the room where Caryl slept; Lola was hanging from one hand over the edge of her bed. As the family of ancestors watched, the doll slipped from sleeping Caryl's fingers, falling to the carpet without a sound.

Rosamund felt a tickle move up her nose. Her sneeze awakened her. Her first thought was to wonder if the noise had awakened Caryl; there was no sound from the other bedroom. "Darn, I hate waking in the middle of the night. It'll be dawn before I get back to sleep." She reached for the pillow on the opposite side of the bed, added it on top of hers, and sat up. The events of the workday crossed her mind. "No, I'll work on that later," she mumbled. She pulled a thick photo album from the shelf beneath her nightstand and began to absently turn its pages.

The dark, red, worn book had been brought to Atlanta from the family home in Shreveport, Louisiana, by Aunt Pet. Pictures, clippings, yellowed, faded documents, and neat notations in a variety of inks and handwritings told the chronicle of more than one hundred years. Aunt Pet entrusted it to Rosamund a few weeks before she became ill, saying it was a chance for Rosamund to catch up on family. *She knew she was leaving*, Rosamund thought, letting the book fall open to a much-thumbed page. A sepia, hand-colored image of a man with steady, dark eyes, neatly trimmed moustache and chin whiskers stared out at her, inviting her to enter a different world, time, and place.

"I don't want the weight of all this family stuff on my back. It's enough to take care of Caryl and deal with Dectel." She frowned at the picture. "Leave me alone, please!"

Despite her words, Rosamund felt drawn to the musty odor and heaviness of the album. Perhaps, the dozens of hands that had held it, looked through it, commented on it, and added to its contents left a message she could not deny. "I can't sleep anyway; I may as well . . ." For the first time, she began to really think about the man in the lovingly protected portrait—a sketchy story, perhaps, but becoming more real with each moment of perusal. It drew Rosamund into itself. She read from the yellowed paper:

> Munje (he would never tell his natural name) took the name Jones about 1850. He said he was born in Birley, North Carolina. His father was the master of a plantation and his mother was a slave named Sariah. Munje hated his father for keeping him in slavery. He kept trying to run away, but his father had him caught, brought back, and whipped. His father sold him to a Major Alexander who stopped to visit on his way home to Louisiana after having been to Washington, DC. Munje said his mother, Sariah, told him that her parents came from the West Indies, a place called Trinidad, that her father was a basket maker—a real high position, she said. He worked with the spirit world as a healer. The baskets he made held magic that made people well.

Munje's mother had a husband and a daughter named Ula, but Munje didn't tell us the husband's name. All he knew was that Ula's daddy was Indian. Ula was about two when Munje was sold. Munje found Ula after the war, and our families have kept up relations ever since.

Signed Calvin Jones, Jr. (Grandson) April 15, 1930

For the first time, Rosamund read the entry her father had made. Before tonight, she had only glanced at old photographs, with no real interest. It was OK with her if Aunt Pet entertained Caryl with stories, but the past held little for her. Today's world, its advantages and challenges, demanded total involvement. "Since Daddy took the time to remember all this and write it, I feel a little guilty," she told the picture of a relative of many years ago.

On subsequent pages, she smoothed the fragile, dried pages of the scanty record:

Army of the United States. Certificate of Disability.

Private Munje Jones of Captain Daniel E. O'Neil Company F of the Seventieth Regiment of the United States COLORED Infantry . . . Station: Natchez, Mississippi . . . Discharged this Eleventh day of February, 1865 . . .

She focused on a second brittle page:

Declaration for Invalid Pension . . . Rapides, Louisiana . . . 21st day of October, one thousand eight hundred ninety-three . . .

Many of the faded records were hard to read but became suddenly intriguing. The most interesting, to Rosamund, was a handwritten form: "Bureau of Pensions, Washington, DC, April 6, 1901." Rosamund could imagine a tiny, old woman, her great-grandmother Mina, sitting across a large wooden table, answering questions from an official whose initials at the top were "E. E. D. Ex'r." The date at the bottom read April 10, 1901.

"If the dates are right, the mail was faster than now," Rosamund enjoyed her private joke. She made a mental note. "I'll show this to Jeffrey one day. My connection with North Carolina might interest him."

Where were you born? Answer. Neal Alexander's place near Alexandria, LA.

When, where, and by whom were you married to the soldier? Answer. 1865. Old Preacher Charles Harris.

Were any children born to you and the soldier? Answer. I am the mother of three children by the deceased. Two died as infants. One is living and is of pensionable age.

The most intriguing comments to Rosamund were those given in response to questions nine and ten.

Were you a slave? If so, state the names of all your owners, particularly the name of your owner at the date of your marriage to the soldier, and all the names by which you have been known. Answer. Yes. My owner's name was Neal Alexander, his wife, Martha Alexander. Never had but the one master.

Was the soldier a slave? If so, state the names of all his owners, and particularly of his owners at the date of his marriage to you, and at his enlistment, and all names by which he was known. Answer. Can't tell the names of those in North Carolina. But Major Neal Alexander was the only master in Louisiana. We married after the war, not before.

"I don't know if I could have taken it," Rosamund closed the book. She felt a knot deep in her abdomen. *If I stuck pins in Warner's picture, would it make a difference?* she wondered. *Aunt Pet said that Sariah's father was a basket maker, that he kept mementos of each villager in a basket. When a sick person came for help, he looked in the basket for things to make them well. Sounds like psychology to me.*

Rosamund awakened, not tired as she had expected. She dialed Jeffrey's number. "I apologize for my rude behavior last night. Can we meet for breakfast in the café around the corner from the office?"

"It might be well if we were not seen together for awhile. I don't want to jeopardize anything for you," Jeffrey responded.

"I agree, but not for the reason you may think. We're going to work out a new-and-improved strategy for Herr Warner. I'm inspired by something I read last night." Rosamund's tone was upbeat and firm.

Forty minutes later, in a booth at the café she had chosen, one not frequented by the Dectel crowd—most preferred to be seen in the company cafeteria, family one and all—Jeffrey stirred coffee, two sugars and lots of cream. Rosamund had tea with lemon. "I'm not sure what we will, or can, do. But we will not be beaten by the 'master.'" Rosamund began.

"Master?" Jeffrey dunked his toast.

"Last night, I read the Civil War records of my great-grandfather and an affidavit taken from his wife—about their lives. It seems to me that if people like that could not only survive, but also triumph . . . I'm not going to give in to the same attitude that held my ancestors down."

"I don't relate to the slave metaphor, but if it turns you on, I'll go with it. Now, what?"

"Be prepared for some strange, even disconcerting, actions from me in the days and weeks to come. I'm going to act toward you the way I did before we began to work on this phiofomel stuff. Whatever I do will be a ploy to throw Warner and the brass off from what we're actually doing."

Jeffrey finished his coffee and toast, noting and ignoring Rosamund's disapproving look when he dunked. "I can see you won't be hard pressed to find things to be disconcerted about."

"Just because you're from the mountains doesn't mean you can't have civilized table manners. You did graduate from Wake Forest University." Rosamund gathered her briefcase and purse. "Come by after you and Darren finish dinner and homework tonight, and bring the whole file."

At the office, Rosamund asked Lois to call Warner's executive assistant to make an appointment for the first opening in his schedule. "Ten minutes will be enough," Rosamund said.

At 11:20, Warner began the conversation. "I suppose you've come to explain yesterday."

"Absolutely, Mr. Warner. I was misled by Mr. Shuggs. He told me his information would be of benefit to the company. He's one of our best statisticians. I hadn't taken the time to carefully study his presentation, just took his word."

"I understand," Warner said, hands clasped behind his head, a picture of confidence, control, or both. "Shuggs is a fine statistician, but you're our best analyst. I simply disagree with his interpretation—and so does our laboratory."

"I'll be more careful from now on. You can be sure of it, Mr. Warner." Rosamund left the office, believing she'd done all that she could at this time.

Outside her office, she motioned for Lois to follow her.

"Lois, you and I have an understanding, do we not?"

"All the way, Mrs. JK." Lois impressed upon Rosamund that she was observant—that she could be trusted.

"As of today," Rosamund said, "Jeffrey Shuggs and I will treat one another as if we're angry with each other. But we're not. I want you to help him any way you can. I don't want you to get into trouble, so I won't tell you anymore. Is that OK with you?"

"I am sure that whatever you do is for the best. I'll do all I can to help."

"I really appreciate hearing that. We minorities have to work together." Rosamund cupped her fingers in the sign of quotation marks when she said "minorities."

Lois laughed. "Crazy world. Women, are a minority when we're half the world."

"I've read that we're a little more than fifty-one percent of the entire world's population. Silly, isn't it? All the brown and black people are considered minorities. Put us all together . . ." (she sang) "we spell B-I-G-G-E-S-T." Rosamund picked up her purse to go to the lunch room. Lois Hardy stood in the door, holding her stomach, laughing.

"Dad, I'm glad your mother taught you how to cook." Darren sat across from Jeffrey at the kitchen table.

"What are you hinting for? It's yesterday's spaghetti, that's all."

"Nothing, Dad. It's just that I had something Caryl's mother cooked, and you're better."

Jeffrey dumped the food remains in the disposer. He gathered a file of papers and a floppy, stuffing all into his attaché case. "Do you want to stay or go? I have a little work with your pal Caryl's mother. I'll be back before nine, I'd say."

"I'll stay by myself. *Star Trek, Deep Space Nine* comes on at eight and Caryl isn't a sci-fi fan."

"If I'm going to be late, I'll call." Jeffrey checked the lock and set the alarm. He knocked on the door across the hall to remind his neighbor, Miss McRay, to listen for anything out of the ordinary. "Not that there will be. I'll be out of the building for only a short time."

"It's all here, clear and accurate, as far as I can see." Jeffrey began to trace the details of the problem he'd found. He paced back and forth in Rosamund's apartment. "See, most people think that computers are clean technology. We hear about toxic waste from dozens of industries, especially nuclear and plastics; our vaunted communications industries are not clean."

"I'm willing to buy your premise. What we need is concrete, internal evidence." Rosamund kicked off her shoes, settling into her chair for the work to come. "Cue me, again. What exactly is phiofomel?"

"It's the solvent used to imprint special coding onto magnetic fiber. It's more high tech—faster and takes much less space—than chips. Every manufacturer uses a process developed by Polar, the industry standard. We did, too, until a few months ago. Polar had the most durable, most accurate, and fastest process, until our lab came up with its phiofomel additive. Whoever makes a more cost-effective process that is as good or better gets ahead of the competition, of course. No other company knows that phiofomel can be used to imprint. For years, the industry looked at it only as a finishing application. One of our geniuses stumbled on the breakthrough."

"Any advance we, or anyone makes, will be duplicated in six months or thereabouts anyway. Why the secrecy?" Rosamund studied a blue and red graph.

"Sure, but a six-month lead is worth thirty to fifty million for a couple of quarters. So we go for it. The problem is, once phiofomel is in the works, it's permanent—and dangerous for decades. It's the combination of the chemical, heat and the metallicized plastic, that's the ticking bomb. If we don't stop Dectel, there will be a bonding of antagonistic compounds. The effect will be lethal." Jeffrey pulled at a hanging cuticle.

"Greed is not a pretty flower, is it? Right now, I need to restore my sense of competence after my experience with Warner's not so subtle bigotry."

"What about the danger to others? That bothers you, doesn't it?"

"Jeffrey, someday you may learn that I can say only one thing at a time—linear speech, it's called. I have a full agenda going, always." Her remark was testy.

"Sorry, I'm used to Darren's mother. She means just what she says, and she doesn't go too deep."

Rosamund, still out of sorts, chewed on her pen. "I don't know your wife; I'm naturally put off by put-downs of women, the stereotypes. You know?"

"I hope you meet her some day. Believe me, what I said was no put-down. My wife is a nice person. It's no one's fault we have different interests. Her career is her life, like yours. Hers is physical, not mental. That's all."

"We have too much to do to quarrel. I think we're edgy, tired, and not ready to tackle it all tonight. What say I leave the file with you to study when you're fresh, then we'll make a new start?" Jeffrey was even tempered, until his righteous indignation was summoned.

"Yeah, I agree. Thanks for understanding. You'll get no argument. Give me about forty-eight hours, say, day after tomorrow, Friday. You and Darren are invited to dinner." She rose, stifled a yawn, and placed the file into a table drawer.

"All right, but since you have all this to go through, I'll cook. I'll bring the ingredients here and use your kitchen."

"Well, thanks, again. I'm not really eager to do the kitchen bit." Rosamund let him out.

Whistling across the courtyard and down the street to his building, Jeffrey smiled, remembering Darren's comment about Rosamund's cooking. He'd been smart enough to bite his tongue during that part of the conversation.

CHAPTER 10

Pet, Munje, and Frank, the energy essence of three souls who had chosen to be Pet, Munje, and Frank, congregated in the quiet space of Jeffrey and Darren's apartment. Darren was engrossed in the evening's Star Trek episode, unaware that a protective aura surrounded him.

Pet floated close to Frank. "I want to know how you fit into our story beyond the war thing. There's more, isn't there?"

Quicker than the proverbial wink, Frank caused a scene to appear for her thought waves. Pet was becoming less surprised by the instantaneous world of Pass On. Frank said, "I'm having the time of my lives, Sister. That Dr. Einstein said there might be something faster than the speed of light. There is; it's thought."

A young Frank, the age of Darren, was climbing a steep hill. A closer look and Pet saw that the hill was one peak in a mountain range.

"Doesn't look familiar. Where is that?" she asked.

"My home in the western mountains on the border of North and South Carolina," Frank answered. "That's where I was born and where I lived during the Civil War." Dogwood, walnut, maple, hemlock—trees Pet did not know—surrounded the boy who pulled himself up and through the woods by skilled hand and foot movement.

"Aren't you afraid of bears and cougars?" Pet asked, accepting the sight just as if she and Frank and the woods were on land at that moment.

"Watch," Frank said. A boy sat under a tree, opened a homespun shoulder pouch, and took out a thin sandwich of bread and cheese. Small animals and two birds came close and nibbled the crumbs. "See," Frank said, "when fear isn't on one side, there's none on the other—at least that's the way it was for me."

Munje sensed sadness in his friend. "You've gotten past the remorse of that time. What's happening?"

"Whenever I come back into Earth energy, some of the feeling—just a *little—comes back to me."* Frank brightened. *"There is truth to the saying, 'All things are connected.'"*

Munje's thoughts joined Pet's. *"Frank and I—you, too, Pet—are part of a monad—kindred souls—that comes and goes. Life and transition—the process has been going on and on. We were in a 'lesson' together before, just like we're in now—with you, for Caryl."*

"So that's what my calls are. But, why do you know so much more about it than I do—aren't we all dead?"

"'Dead' is a word with no meaning, Daughter." Munje took on the facade of an old man whenever he called Pet 'Daughter.'

Frank regained his place in the story. *"It's just that you've only been in Pass On, this time, for a few days. It'll all come back to you before Caryl has finished her learning. Darren won't get as far as Caryl, this time. He'll catch up."*

"Yep, and it may seem that Rosamund and Jeffrey aren't actually up on what is gong on. But you can believe they are." Munje sensed a question in Pet's energy field. *"Our story is working out on several planes—Dectel, the children, the grownups, including Lois and Liam—different connections that aren't always obvious."*

"I see another picture." Pet paused as Darren went to the window to see if Jeffrey was outside.

The long-ago Frank was walking past his parents' bedroom. His mother, Lucie, was crying.

"Why did you—how could you, Frank? Making a bastard with one of your slave girls? I saw the child, a boy, at the wash house today. He's got your face and eyes, just brown skin instead of white. Sariah tried to hide him from me, but I made her let me look."

"You were ailing, Lucie, and I'm a man, I am. Besides, slave births don't count. Even the constitution says they're three-fifths a man. This one's just a boy, maybe one-fifth." Frank Shuggs, Sr., laughed aloud. He couldn't comprehend why his wife would be upset. She came from England and didn't understand that slave children meant more money for the plantation. She'd given him Frank Jr. She wasn't hale like his brother's wife. Maybe Scots-Irish women were stronger than the English. African women were the best breeders. Too bad they weren't all the way human. The Bible said so.

Like television displays in a mall store, two scenes played, side by side. On one screen Munje grew, one, two, four, then eight years old. A smart boy, he saw himself and other brown and tan children in the slave houses, the overseer, his father—Master Frank—even townsmen coming to the *plantation at dark, slipping away near dawn. Older children talked. Grownups whispered. There wasn't much laughing.*

On the other screen, Frank Jr. wandered in the woods. He made friends with the animals but with almost no people. The slaves said he inherited his mother's tender nature. Frank Sr. had wanted a son like himself: tough, businesslike. He didn't get his wants.

Frank Jr. stayed away from the slave houses. He didn't want to see what was rumored in the kitchen and outside. He didn't know which ones might look like him, pass by him when the women called, "Time for supper, Ivy, or Munje, or Aristotle, or Pompey."

Munje grew up angry. Frank Shuggs, Sr., had no more slave children. He felt something for Lucie, her being so delicate. Munje was teased by his playmates. He did look like Master Frank, except for his brown color. Stories—probably lies, Munje thought—were talked over the fires at night, about "up North." Slavery wasn't allowed, he heard. Once, twice, three times, he ran away. Even if it was a lie, he wanted to feel that somewhere he could be free to wander in the woods and shoot a gun like his daddy's white son. Frank Shuggs, Sr., told the overseer to do with the boy what he wanted. Each time Munje ran, he was brought back and beaten. Hatred was a constant in his head and body. His mother, Sariah, soothed him. Her cautions he did not take. The fourth time he ran away, Frank Shuggs decided to sell him. "Bad influence on the other slaves," he told the overseer and neighbors, everyone but Lucie. "Besides, they all know he's my whelp. Might give them wrong ideas."

"Uncle, you didn't show me any of this in dreamtime. I could have passed on lots more—to Caryl and Rosamund and her brother, when they were children." Pet's thoughts were not friendly to Munje, who chose to appear as a helpless infant to calm her strong thoughts before they could engulf him.

"You had the family history, the pictures, and writings from your Cousin Calvin and other family down the years. That was enough for then," was Munje's explanation. "Knowing too much too soon can make for too much weight."

Startled and amused to receive such a thought from an infant, Pet lightened up, although she had never been one to be calm too long—in any lifetime.

"Those things in the family album are pretty much right, aren't they?" Pet asked. She knew the stories that had been passed to her, and sometimes, she wondered if they were all true. "I didn't know about Frank's part. You two are half brothers? Now that is a mess of beans."

"No, you couldn't know. That would have set things off, in the long run, getting into another soul's thoughts so intimate like that. With both of us here, we can show you. When we're on the Earth side, we try to pass on what happened as we lived it, but it's easier being here in Pass On. That's the why and what of dreams." Frank morphed into a wise old man for the first time since Pet entered Pass On.

"Munje, when you shot Frank, did you know who he was?" Pet reviewed the battle scene, instantly replayed.

"Only in spirit," Frank said. *"Not that Earthly lives are completely new. Things are partly known and partly sensed at soul level."*

"Jeffrey's coming. The boy's fine. We can go now." Munje beckoned to Pet and Frank to fade away.

"He doesn't know about tomorrow night. Think he'll be afraid?" Frank asked.

"We'll find out then. We aren't privy to everything, you know." Pet was pleased that she knew what was going to happen tomorrow night. She was beginning to catch on.

"Weird story on *Star Trek* tonight, Dad. Characters time-traveling between Earth, just before the Civil War and some planet called Pason, where the same people from Earth live another life. Good stuff." Darren looked up from the couch as Jeffrey came in and threw his jacket onto a chair. Darren closed his notebook, blank pages beneath the pen, before his father could see.

"Did you finish your homework? Your last report card wasn't the best." Jeffrey dropped to the couch and took off his jacket and shoes. "I'm later than I expected. You should have been in bed half an hour ago."

"I know. I think I fell asleep on the couch. I'll go now." Darren picked up his father's jacket and hung it in the hall closet, hoping his helpfulness would change his father's attitude. "'Night," he dropped a kiss on Jeffrey's cheek.

Jeffrey brushed his teeth. He remembered that Darren did not say whether he'd done his homework. "Single parenthood," he blubbered, mouth full of toothpaste. "He has a lot of his mother, the dreamer, in him. Maybe Rosamund can tell me how she does it with Caryl."

Rosamund turned her car from Jimmy Carter Boulevard into the more swiftly moving traffic of the Interstate Bypass. For three days, she had not been able to think of a way to get to Warner, to convince him of anything. Jeffrey had some "facts," but he also had a lot of speculation. As much as she resented Warner's dismissal of Jeffrey's presentation, she didn't want to get herself in serious trouble. An old devil thought surged. *I know Jeffrey's OK, but I can't forget he's still white. When the fat hits, will he burn with me? This convolution is taking heavy time to figure out.*

A white car pulled in front of her and slowed, causing her to tap its rear bumper. The car stopped; so did she. Why did the driver do such a stupid thing? She was in the right lane, keeping up with traffic. She pulled to the shoulder. The other driver did, too. A nondescript, polite man came to the door and said, "I'm sorry, I had to make you bump my car, but there's no damage. I've been trying to get your attention for a number of miles."

Rosamund circled his car. He was right, no damage. She didn't know what to think. Was it a robbery? There was too much traffic for that. "Why?" she began.

"There's smoke coming out of the rear of your car. It could be dangerous." The man seemed ordinary enough, not a pervert or drunk. "What say I go off at the next exit and send a tow truck, just in case?"

"Thanks, but that won't be necessary. I can call on my cellular phone."

The man seemed surprised. "I didn't see any antenna; I didn't know you had a car phone."

"It's a new model. I'm testing it for my company," Rosamund said.

The stranger mumbled, "Oh, sorry," returned to his car and hastened away. The summoned mechanic who checked her car found nothing wrong. Hearing her story, he shook his head. "World's filled with kooks. Be careful, lady. Hate to say it, but it's best to trust nobody these days." Rosamund drove, as quickly as she could, given the heavy traffic. She disliked being late, even when going home. "Aunt Pet said listen to your inner self, and my gut is saying something's not right about what just happened. I won't become paranoid, just careful."

The Reverend P. B. Preston was waiting for Rosamund.

"You're not the easiest woman to catch up to," he greeted Rosamund. "I called about four times. I don't leave messages on answering machines."

"Sorry, about that, P. B. I could have called you back if you weren't afraid of the technology." Rosamund knew he didn't like her remark. He made jokes about cellular phones and e-mail. P. B. saw himself as a modern Atlanta man.

"Now, Rosamund, you know I'm afraid of nothing. I'm just old fashioned enough to think it's courtesy to answer your phone or I can call back. I came to see you and Caryl because I miss Pet."

"I'm just teasing you, P. B. Caryl and I miss her, too." Not thinking of her tiring drive, she went on, "Darren told Caryl, just yesterday, he misses Aunt Pet, too. She was wonderful with the children."

A pause, too long for a give and take reply, P. B. raised his voice. "You act like that man and his boy are like us. They're not. They're white, and you know how I feel about whites."

Rosamund stared at the man, remembering that he was in mourning for his friend. P. B. was white-skinned himself. He could easily be taken for Greek or Italian, wasn't even dark enough to be Mexican or Puerto Rican. "One of these days, I want you to tell me why you dislike white people so much, P. B. I'm pleased and proud to be black, and I don't trust some of them. Jeffrey is working out to be genuine, I think.

"My mother is part black and part white. My dad has a bunch of different ancestors from Africa, Europe, and right here. I don't see a problem."

"If you let me in and give me a hot cup of coffee, I'll tell you." He held the door to the building open for Rosamund.

Inside, the temperature was not yet hot enough for open windows or air conditioning for several weeks. P. B. sat on the couch, where he had waited for Pet to get ready for the movies and the one time he persuaded her to go to church with him. Rosamund put the puzzling encounter on the freeway behind her. "Just what I need, friendly person for a change," she said, setting the tray with cups of hot café au lait on the table.

"I remember just how you like your coffee. See?"

"No reason to pine over Pet. Might as well answer your question." He tasted and smiled approval. "But, that was one grand, brown woman, that Patricia."

"If you don't want to talk about the white thing, we won't." Rosamund didn't really like her coffee with milk, but she had forgotten when she made his cup, adding milk to hers the same as his.

"I don't talk about it much, but you're a smart lady, and I don't want you making any mistakes, like taking up with that Jeffrey Shuggs."

Totally taken aback, Rosamund choked on her coffee. "We work together, and our children are friends. I've told you. I go along with the system because it's the way it has to be. I know who and what I am."

"I surely am glad you remember that." P. B. sounded wistful and demanding—if a thing can be said two ways at the same time. "If I tell you my story, you'll know why I feel so strongly about them like I do.

"I don't like to be taken for white, regardless of my looks. The man who was my father was white. He sweet-talked my mother—she was a country girl—told her he loved her, was going to take her to New York and marry her. She was a Christian, with good home training. That white man—his name was Oliver Wallace—told her they were leaving on the Southern Railroad on a certain Saturday night, but she could prove her love for him before then. There would be no problem. They would be married within the month, up North where it was legal. Mother believed him, gave in to him.

"When Oliver Wallace tried to slip from his house to meet my mother, his pa caught him and sent him somewhere away from Waycross. I was born seven months later. Mother died from a broken heart by the time I was two and a half."

Rosamund watched P. B. appear to shrivel into the couch. *How long can pain last?* "That was a terrible situation, P. B. I understand how you feel. But, it seems that your father cared for your mother. He tried, didn't he? How old was he?"

"He was seventeen. She was fifteen. I've seen her picture, a pretty, little brown girl." He pulled himself up—the usual, self-assured P. B.

"They were babies," Rosamund said." I don't think he could have done differently."

"He could have come back when he was grown up."

"Maybe he did. Do you know for sure?"

"Now that you ask, I don't rightly know. My grandparents sent me to a cousin in Virginia early on, so people wouldn't tease me." P. B. relaxed as if he had a new, releasing thought. "Maybe you're right. He might have tried. . . . I still don't trust any of them."

Rosamund thought, *Them? Us?*

Munje and Frank hovered near the couple, older man, younger woman, toying with their coffee cups. "Score one for Rosamund. She's picking up, even when we don't try," *Munje said.*

"Similar story, different fathers," Frank responded.

CHAPTER 11

A noise in the hallway, a heavy box scraping against the wall outside the front door, interrupted Darren's concentration. Darren welcomed an excuse to leave the table, where his books, paper, pen, and pencil were scattered, and peek through the angled security hole in the door. Two men were pushing what seemed to be a large cabinet covered by a quilted, green cover. He remembered that Miss McRay, the neighbor who stayed with him until his father came home, said the apartment next to her had been rented. Maybe the new people would have a kid, a boy. Maybe then he wouldn't be surrounded by all those tippy-toe grown people.

The movers tugged their load into the vacant apartment. Through the peephole, Darren saw his dad walking toward him from the elevator. He ran back to the table, scribbling in his notebook as Jeffrey came into the room.

Jeffrey whistled his bird-call greeting, "Hi fella. Lots of work today?"

Darren grunted. Maybe he meant yes, maybe no, maybe, maybe. Jeffrey tousled Darren's hair as he passed.

A woman with salt-and-pepper curls, wearing a purple and black jogging outfit, came in from the kitchen.

"How are you, Miss McRay?" Jeffrey greeted the retired teacher who, lucky for Darren and him, lived right across the hall. "Is my guy behaving himself?"

"He's doing fine, Jeffrey. Should be finishing his homework soon. Darren's an intelligent young man, just so curious. He doesn't like to settle down." Her face smiled a conspiratorial, adult communiqué.

"I know what you mean." The corners of Jeffrey's mouth curled downward. "He's a lot like me when I was his age."

"Dad, we're going to have new neighbors." Darren said, not lifting his head from his notebook.

"The building is filling up," Jeffrey said. "Someone moved upstairs a couple of days ago. I hope they're quiet."

Darren looked up. "I hope they have kids."

"Right, you two are used to the quiet sounds of nature." Miss McRay said. "I'm a city person myself. I like city noise. I can sleep through anything—buses, trains, fire trucks. I hope I wake up on time for Judgment Day."

Darren added, "I can take it both ways. In our mountains, we only hear wind, water, and critters." He grinned at his use of the old-timey word. "I'm used to Atlanta noises now."

Jeffrey said, "How about the two of us going home for a weekend soon? Maybe weekend after next?"

"Yeah, before it gets too cold." Darren left his chair and started toward the television.

"Not yet, my man. Let's see how much more you have to do on that homework?" Jeffrey's arm circled the boy's shoulders, stopping him and turning him back toward the table.

Priorities resolved and dinner finished, the two settled down to watch *Star Trek*. When the program ended, Jeffrey led the almost asleep boy to his bedroom.

Darren dreamed of treading through leaves on top of the mountain, where he and his dad would soon be. At first, the noise that awakened him was so faint that Darren thought it may have been the air filter or refrigerator whirring.

At the next sound, he was sure someone was outside his front door. Darren sat upright, listening intently. He got up to go to his father.

Jeffrey awakened as soon as Darren came into his room. "What's wrong, fella? Bad dream?"

"No, Dad. I think I hear someone outside our front door." Darren wasn't frightened. He had spent more than a few nights in the woods.

Pulling on his robe, Jeffrey hurried to the front door and looked through the peephole. Seeing nothing outside, he slowly turned the knob. "Darn, I forgot to put on the alarm when Miss McRay left. I don't see anyone or any sign of tampering with the lock," he whispered to Darren. He stepped into the hall and walked toward the elevator and back.

"Dad," Darren said. "Maybe it's the new folks coming home."

"Could be. We've not had anyone further down our hall." Jeffrey set the alarm. He saw Darren back to bed, got a glass of water, and went to his room—leaving his door open.

Jeffrey didn't ponder the nighttime interruption in the morning—after all, it could have been Darren's excitement over having new neighbors. Living in Atlanta was not the same as living back home, where everybody had kids and family was everywhere. His son was not having a childhood like his own. All the same, he would remind Miss McRay to keep the door locked, and Darren must remember to keep the alarm activated whenever he was in the apartment alone.

Two days later, Jeffrey called Miss McRay. "I'm going to be delayed at the office at least another half hour."

"Jeffrey, I hate to do this, but my sister is waiting to take me to the theater. We planned to leave the minute you got home. Do you think it will be all right to leave Darren for a short time until you get here?"

"I believe so, Miss McRay. You go on. There won't be a problem. Be sure the lock and alarm are on."

Miss McRay made sure that the door was secured and, reluctantly, left Darren.

Curled up on the couch eating an apple, Darren heard the doorbell. He looked through the peephole. A man in a blue jacket, blue shirt, and red tie spoke through the door. "Hello, I just moved down the hall from you. The lady next door is not in. I want to introduce myself. Can I talk to your mother or father?"

"I can't let anybody in. My dad's not home yet. He'll be here in a half-hour. I'll tell him our new neighbor was over. You can come back then." Darren felt his dad would be pleased with the way he handled the stranger.

"Smart boy," the man's voice was clear through the door. "You're doing just what I'd want my son to do, if I had one."

Darren turned away from the peephole, went back to the couch, and dug his fist into the cushion on the back of the sofa. "No boy in the building to play with, yuch."

Jeffrey came in a few minutes later. Darren told him about the new neighbor. "If I remember correctly, when new folks moved nearby, my mother always took a jar of jam or a loaf of bread or cookies to them. Let's see what we have." He rummaged in the kitchen cabinets. "Guess I'll have to pick up something tomorrow," he said.

Frank, Munje, and Pet observed the conversation between Darren and Jeffrey. They had watched the boy remember that he wasn't supposed to open the door and were pleased that Darren was receptive to his intuition that reminded him just as he was about to open the door to the new neighbor. After all, a neighbor is a friend, like Miss McRay, had been Darren's first thought. "We're going to have to sit this one out," Frank said. "The boy is not as tuned in as Caryl."

"So far, everything's working fine. Those goons will have only one try." Munje said.

Pet stood a little away from the men. "How is it that you can reach the boy? My messages seem to be felt only by Caryl."

"Why, Sister, Frank has the old Celtic line in him, as I have half the African and half other parts." Munje was perched on the edge of the table where Darren's homework sprawled—or just about where the table would be if anyone could have seen him. "All of us are from lines of strong connection with spirit. The boy can feel Frank the best. The girl can sense me, and with enough learning, both of them will feel all of us."

At work the next day, Jeffrey and Rosamund barely looked at one another in the outer office and in the cafeteria.

"B-r-r-r, deep-freeze time is it?" Sam chewed his BLT. "I thought you two had gotten to be friendly, especially after our little tête-à-tête in the cafeteria."

"I thought so, too. Guess I was wrong." Jeffrey shrugged.

"Just do your work and get the hell out of here. That's the way Dectel wants it." Sam finished his lunch.

"You're right." Jeffrey placed his tray on the cart.

After work, at the café around the corner, Rosamund and Jeffrey laughed. "Everyone thinks we're sworn enemies, again," she said.

"Again?" Jeffrey raised his eyebrows and pursed his lips.

"When I first came to Dectel, you were not friendly. Now, I know it's your quiet self. Purpose is being served, for now. Learned anything new?" She waited as he pulled a folded paper from his inner coat pocket.

"Dectel intrigue, chapter three. Or is it four? Liam sent me a second, independent, medical report that strongly suggests—I think, verifies—that his paralysis resulted from the fumes in the lab."

Rosamund's skepticism came to the fore. "How do we know we can believe that report and not the company doctors?"

Jeffrey stared at her with disbelief. "Because this report is from a group of physicians who have left government and corporate work. They're fed up with the chicanery they found in their workplaces. And they're reputable and competent—the 'right' degrees from the 'right' universities." Jeffrey emphasized his point with quotation-mark-crooked fingers. "They call themselves Corp Busters—like Ghosts Busters—CBs for short. I have a talk set up with Liam's new doctor, Dr. Ziegler."

"Interesting." Rosamund read the report. "I'm pulling up all the old files I can find in between working on new jobs. Don't be upset by my questions. We're going to get some truly hot queries in the near future. Get used to it."

Jeffrey nodded, folded and replaced the paper, and glanced at his watch, "We'd better get home.

"I forget Aunt Pet isn't with us. When she was at home, I could be flexible." Rosamund placed a tip on the table, shook hands with Jeffrey, and left the café.

They went home by different routes. On her route home, Rosamund thought she saw the white car that had bumped her the week before. There are thousands of little white cars in this Atlanta. I won't conjure up a bogeyman, she thought.

On his way home, Jeffrey bought a small, potted plant to take to the neighbor down the hall. *I think this is what's done*, he thought, picking a few brownish leaves from beneath the foliage.

Jeffrey did not notice a car similar to the one with which Rosamund had her encounter following him. Two men in dark glasses rolled along beside him for a few feet, dropped back, and followed at a constant distance until he turned into his parking lot. The other car did not turn.

In the foyer, Jeffrey found the name "Jensen" on a new mailbox label, but Jensen was not in when he knocked at his door. "Later," he said, whistling his bird call to alert Darren on the other side of his door.

"Who could be calling so late?" Jeffrey mumbled, sleepily reaching for the phone. The clock face shined 1:30 AM.

"Is this Mr. Shuggs?" an unfamiliar voice asked.

"It is," was the reply.

"This is Police Officer Daly. I'm in your parking lot. Can you come down? There's been an accident."

Pulling on pants and a sweater, Jeffrey peered into Darren's room as he hurried to the door. Seeing the boy asleep, he let himself out and went downstairs in the elevator.

Jeffrey surveyed Officer Daly, a young policeman who gave the impression of cool assurance. He and his partner were walking around Jeffrey's car shining flashlights onto and into the interior. The left fender of his car was dented and the headlight was broken.

Daly said, "A resident on the first floor heard a crash, looked out, and saw a white car driving away."

"I don't understand." Jeffrey said. "This lot is well off the street." The corners of his mouth turned downward in their habitual way. "I don't know anyone who parks here and drives a white car."

Daly's partner asked, "Do you know why anyone would deliberately run into your car, Mr. Shuggs?"

"No way. I have no problem with anyone who lives here. Do you think it was deliberate?"

"Can't tell," Daly said. "Might be someone bringing a friend home and had a bit too much to drink, or maybe someone on unfamiliar territory. Your neighbor said the car pulled away really fast."

Reports filled out, Jeffrey found that the car was drivable. "I'll go to work, put it in the shop, and get a ride home," he told the policemen. Back at his apartment door, he was suddenly alert. He thought, for sure, he had closed the door, automatically locking it, when he went downstairs. Now it was slightly ajar. Had Darren awakened and missed him? Inside, Darren was asleep in the same sprawl as before. Jeffrey inspected the living room and the kitchen, opened the hall-closet door, then went into his bedroom. Nothing seemed out of place. Maybe he had been groggy and not closed the door after all, or maybe the lock simply hadn't caught.

"Mrs. JK, Liam says I should remind you and Mr. Shuggs that you need to watch around you. He says there's been a white car cruising our street, and he doesn't think it's teenagers having fun, either." Lois had closed the door to Rosamund's office. She whispered anyway.

"We're being careful, Lois," Rosamund said. The white car flashed thorough her mind. She'd not told anyone about the occurrence on the interstate. It was time to confer with Jeffrey,

Liam, and maybe someone familiar with things that she was not. From somewhere, P. B. Preston's face came to mind. *No,* she thought, *he only worked for the post office.*

"I do not believe in coincidences," the raspy voice of the Reverend P. B. Preston was heard across the telephone line. "I was missing my friend Pet, you, and Caryl and thought I'd invite you to some of my gumbo on Friday night. Can y'all make it?"

"Maybe you don't believe in coincidence, P. B., but I was just thinking of you. I don't think Friday will be a problem. Would you like two more guests?"

"If it's not that white fellow who was at Pet's funeral—and your house, too." P. B.'s rasp rose a notch.

"It's your party, P. B. I'm sorry you feel the way you do about Jeffrey. I hoped you could give me a bit of assistance on a problem I am having at work. Jeffrey's involved in it, too." Rosamund paused for his reply.

"If they can't come, does that mean you can't come at all?" P. B. didn't sound so certain now.

"Of course, Caryl and I will come, P. B. Weekends are good for all of us, and the children have become good friends, that's all." She was disappointed, but she remembered how P. B. felt about Aunt Pet.

During the pause, she heard, "Oh, all right, child. I don't intend to be mean. You caught me unawares. I want y'all to sample my good cooking. I'll have gumbo plenty for five people and lots more for seconds and taking home."

Rosamund didn't tell P. B. how she knew Jeffrey and Darren would be free on Friday. They all had already planned to spend Friday evening together; now, she wouldn't have to cook and witness Darren and Jeffrey's teasing glances. Even Caryl was beginning to compare her cooking to Aunt Pet's—and Jeffrey's.

"A white car, eh? I haven't noticed strange vehicles on my treks to work and back or anywhere else, but I'll keep an eye out." Jeffrey sat beside Rosamund on their ride home. "Why didn't you tell me about the incident before?"

"I simply forgot. Twice, so far, I think I've seen the same car. What is going on?" she asked.

"And my car was crashed by a white car. More coincidence? I wonder," he said, peering behind in a reflexive, yet deliberate, way.

"You'll be happy to know that you won't have to eat my cooking Friday. We're invited to P. B.'s for gumbo, all four of us."

"The man hates me," Jeffrey groaned.

"Not really. I think he's got to come to grips with something inside himself—his own white heritage. You're just an excuse," she said. "Anyway, I had an odd—shall I say, intuitive-feeling or thought about P. B. I think I might let him in on what's going on at Dectel."

Jeffrey sputtered. "He's not FBI or secret service."

"I know." Rosamund cut in. "My feeling has something to do with what Aunt Pet taught me. She suggested that I needed to 'get out of my head all the time' and listen to my intuition—my 'inner calls,' she said. I think this is a good time to begin."

"Your Aunt Pet was a wise woman. There are lots of her kind back in my mountains. I am at a loss as to whether the company is checking us out because we asked a question. I won't say we're paranoid at this juncture. Especially, given Mr. Warner's hostile reaction." Jeffrey gathered his briefcase and umbrella—it had been raining in Atlanta for three days. "Thanks for the lift." He dashed into his building.

The new neighbor, Jensen, was pleasant. He thanked Jeffrey for the flowers. "I'm recently divorced. That's why I don't have much furniture." He waved his arm around the living room. It was bare except for a complete electronic system and two comfortable chairs. "Don't know if I'll stay here long. I'm on a month-to-month."

"I know what you're feeling. My wife and I are living apart right now. Took me some time, but I'm squared away, my son and I," Jeffrey said.

"So, you've got the one boy. He talked to me through the door. Smart boy. Can't be too careful these days." Jensen let Jeffrey out.

"More gumbo?" P. B. asked Jeffrey, lifting the cover and stirring a large copper pot. You've only had two bowls. Isn't it any good?" He laughed.

"As if two bowls didn't prove it." Jeffrey patted his waist. "You are one fine chef, reverend. Would you share your recipe, or is it a family secret?"

P. B. warmed to Jeffrey despite his resolve not to do so. The white man knew about fishing, cooning, and things P. B. had done when he was a boy and young man. "My grandmother started me with a good receipt. I've added my own touches over the years. Each time, it comes out a little different. You're welcome to it."

The children had finished eating and were watching a basketball game. Rosamund, Jeffrey, and P. B. sat around the cleared table.

"P. B., tell us about your work for the post office," Rosamund prompted.

"I can't see why you would be interested in that. I was part of a new program—Domestic Protection, the big shots called it—back in the late 1960s. I found out, after they shoved me aside, that the program was surveillance."

P. B. put his fingers into his shirt pocket, shook his head, and chuckled, "Forgot, again, that I don't smoke anymore. Seems that whenever I get a wee bit nervous—usually when talking about work—I fall back into that old habit. Haven't smoked a cigarette in more than fifteen years."

"See, Jeffrey," Rosamund nearly bounced from her seat, "my hunch, my intuition was right."

"Hunch? Rosamund, what's into you?" P. B. scanned the faces of Rosamund and Jeffrey.

"P. B., Jeffrey and I are looking into a problem at Dectel, and we think the company is not happy about our questions."

"Right," Jeffrey broke in. "We think somebody or somebodies are tailing—surveilling—us. Lord knows why. All I want is for the company to know that if they keep on using a dangerous product they may have the devil to pay down the line."

"Man, don't you know that's exactly the reason they would be following you." P. B. rose from his chair and stood against his pantry door. "I said I was shoved aside. In my case, the Civil Rights movement was just getting off the ground, and I don't think they wanted me around. At first, they thought I was white, but I set them straight. It was P. B. out the door. I still worked for the post office—my regular, up-front job."

"So, if we tell you everything about our suspicions, you ought to be able to tell us if we're paranoid or correct, and maybe help us around the pitfalls. That would be great," Rosamund beamed. She looked toward the ceiling and exclaimed, "Right on, Aunt Pet."

"It's been too long for anything I did to be up to date," P. B. said.

Jeffrey said, "I think basic strategies might stay the same, just the technological details would have changed—at least, I hope so."

Caryl and Darren stood in the doorway to the small dining alcove, "You guys are having fun, and we're not included," Caryl said.

"Jealous, huh. You think only small people, like you, are entitled to fun?" Rosamund asked. "Seriously, your eyes look like hooded owls. We should call a halt to our fun—for your sakes."

P. B. beamed. "I've really enjoyed tonight, my first special day since Patricia left. We'll get together again and hammer this thing through. I'll start on our little problem right away. I'll set us a meeting time and place that will throw your new friends a curve."

"Agreed." Jeffrey grasped the older man's hand.

P. B. placed his free hand on Jeffrey's shoulder.

Rosamund had tucked Caryl in for the night and was removing her makeup. The phone rang.

"Rosamund, someone broke into our place while we were at P. B.'s." Jeffrey's voice was tight.

"No!" she gasped.

"Yes, someone ransacked our apartment," Jeffrey told her. "The police are on their way. Is everything OK there?"

"We're fine. Shall I come over?"

"No, it's better if we aren't seen together. I'm the problem person. What an end to a great evening. We'll talk . . ." Jeffrey's voice trailed off and the connection ended.

CHAPTER 12

"What's missing?" P. B. asked. He, Rosamund, and Jeffrey were in Ma Belle's little grocery store around the corner from Rosamund's apartment.

"Nothing that I can see." Jeffrey rubbed his cheek, his face a mix of confusion, exasperation, and anger. "It looks as if they were looking for something on paper or maybe a disk—something small. Drawers are open and my attaché case dumped, even the little cubbyholes in my grandfather's roll-top desk."

Ma Belle came to the back of the store where the three stood. "You folks look like you could use some privacy. Come on in here." She led them to a small room furnished for relaxation with a table with four chairs, a worn but comfortable sofa, and faded pictures of Louis Armstrong, Fats Domino, and other early jazz musicians hanging, haphazardly, along the walls. A coffee maker took up much of a tabletop alongside dusty electronic equipment: a turntable, radio, and a small black-and-white television—not a place often used or noticed.

"Thanks, Ma. You know how to treat people," P. B. hugged the petite, friendly woman.

Ma Belle smiled, "And le café is free." She left them alone.

"The information that disappeared from the computer at your office, do you have a copy at home, Jeffrey?" P. B. asked.

"No, I have it," Rosamund said. "I planned to review it days ago. I've been so busy that I haven't found the time."

"I see, P. B.," Jeffrey said. "You think whoever broke into my apartment thought I had the files that were deleted?"

"One of the first things I was taught—before somebody decided I was not to be trusted in that post office course—was to find any copies of the contraband." P. B. struck his hands together. "Doggone it, I haven't forgotten, after all these many years."

Rosamund said, "We're lucky—whoever they are—they think you and I are not speaking, Jeffrey, or they might have gotten to me, first."

"We can't count on that too long. We've got to think of a safe place nobody would suspect," Jeffrey said.

Ma Belle brought in clean cups for the strong Louisiana coffee whose odor began to wend across the room. "Hope y'all like the brew. It's my own," she said.

Rosamund forgot she had sworn off coffee. "It'll give our brains a charge. We'll come up with something." She sipped the dark, rich coffee. "Thanks, Ma," she sipped and let out a sigh.

Nearly an hour passed. Jeffrey left Ma Belle's, followed by P. B. ten minutes later. Ma Belle drove Rosamund home in her finned Cadillac that was usually parked behind the grocery. "My son will bring your car home when he gets in, about ten. Is that OK?"

"Definitely. We couldn't do this without you. I hope you don't mind if we don't tell you everything?" Rosamund lowered her eyes. She felt a rush of blood to her face. She was not accustomed to accepting favors from others, especially when they were not family.

"I don't want to know. If I don't know anything, there's nothing I can tell. I'm glad to help out. Your Aunt Pet was a good woman." Ma Belle leaned over to squeeze Rosamund's arm before she let Rosamund out and drove, noisily, away.

Rosamund went into her apartment, two bags of Creole food and seasonings nesting in her elbows. Later, sitting in the dusk, watching the cars below inch their way along the broad city street, she asked herself, "Now, what am I into, Aunt Pet? You have to help me. All I wanted was a job I could manage and the wherewithal to take care of Caryl and me—I don't want to be anybody's parasite, OK?"

"Good mornings," corporate smiles, and chatter crisscrossed Dectel's foyer. No one acted as if there was anything amiss. The brass would be the only ones who were aware, if there was anything of which to be aware.

"Lois, may I see you a moment, when you have time?" Lois was busy with another analyst, one who didn't think women, "minorities," or young people should be promoted until they had proven themselves at least twelve years—as he had.

"Yes, Mrs. JK. In about half an hour."

Forty minutes later, Mr. "Grumpy," the analyst's office nom de plume, was satisfied with the work Lois had completed for him. She went into Rosamund's cubicle, closing the door gently. "Funny stuff going on?" she asked before Rosamund could say a word.

"Indeed. With you and Liam, too?" She filled Lois in on Jeffrey's break-in.

"Nothing so dramatic for us," Lois said. "Just the little white car that seems to be everywhere. I think they want to wear us down, frighten the kids and us until Liam drops the whole matter. Only an idiot wouldn't see a strange car everywhere."

"I thought I'd say something to Mr. Warner, but I suppose he'd say he doesn't know what I'm talking about."

"I've seen movies and read enough Walter Mosley to know that telling certain things to certain folks is not a healthy move." Lois breathed heavily.

"As soon as this new team of doctors' tests on Liam are finished, we'll decide what we can do."

Rosamund continued to turn out a large volume of analyses for Dectel. She didn't want to be accused of neglecting work, and the business with phiofomel involved more waiting than doing.

"I haven't dreamed of Aunt Pet in nearly a week. I could really use some insight from her after the past few days." Rosamund handed Lois a sheaf of papers. "Finish these for me, will you? I'll proof them before I leave today."

Darren and Caryl sat side by side in the school cafeteria. It was too cold to play outside. The large room had the atmosphere of a club: fun murals, music the students liked, and tables and chairs scattered where kids would enjoy hanging out. Clusters of children stood, sat, talked, or watched others play game-boards and board games.

Darren gazed at the nearest groups. No one seemed close enough to overhear him. "I think my mom is trying to get my dad in trouble," he whispered.

"How come?" Caryl asked.

"Last night when we got back from Reverend Preston's, somebody had broken into our apartment. Maybe my mom is angry and she came to find something to hurt my dad."

"Your imagination is humongous," Caryl said. "Your mom wouldn't have to break in. She has a key. You told me. I think something bad is going on at Dectel. I overheard my mom and her secretary, Lois, talking. They thought I was reading. I was, but I can feel when people are talking about trouble."

Darren slid to the end of his chair. "I guess you're right. My dad's being extracareful. Always telling me to keep the lock on the door and the alarm on. It didn't do any good last night."

Darren spoke slowly, still whispering, "We can help your mom and my dad by keeping our eyes and ears open, like your Aunt Pet told us."

"I believe you are growing up, Darren." Caryl patted his hand in a near-maternal gesture.

*"They're doing fine."**Pet smiled at the children from an empty table nearby—so the monad's energy wouldn't frighten any child who was astute to its presence. "Uncle, Caryl is picking up on feelings faster than Darren. I know he's a little younger but can he be sped up? He might need that inner knowing pretty soon."*

Munje and Frank drifted in from the Dectel office—only a step away in Pass On. "We're spending so much time with Rosamund and Jeffrey— there's a lot to catch up. The Dectel thing is bigger than we were first told. Those goons hired by the brass don't understand that the company wants to throw a scare, not really hurt them." Frank smiled at the children and touched them lightly. Caryl glanced up, feeling the breeze on her hair.

"We're not God, Daughter," Munje said. "We're working lessons here, just like in Earth life. We're learning, too, with more inner guidance."

"We know that the break-in last night netted zilch—see how up to date I am?" Frank and Munje rolled their energies into one another in playful exuberance. Munje continued his thought wave. "We have to find a strategy for the real encounter, to help the children and their parents. Nothing must happen to cause real damage, but between both—the Earth life and the spirit life—our job is to work a solution."

Rosamund drove out of Dectel's parking lot. P. B. sat in his car halfway down the block. He waited until the small white car began to follow her as she merged into the misnamed "rush-hour" traffic.

Two men were following Rosamund. The driver constantly flicked ashes from a cigarette as he drove. P. B. did not see the passenger's face, but the driver—ordinary looking except for a nose with a large hook—turned several times to speak to his passenger.

The light changed to green. Rosamund continued, and before the white car could move, P. B. deliberately cut the car off and stalled. As he had planned and hoped, the driver stopped and ran into P. B.'s car. "Old man, can't you see?" His face flushed; his fist was in a ball, as if to hit the older man.

"I'm sorry. The sun got in my face—sun's low this time of day." P. B. said. "I didn't see the light change. I was scared, so I stopped. I'll pay for your damage."

The passenger came to look. "Don't bother," he said. "Come on, forget it. We've got a schedule to keep."

"OK, OK. Nothing's hurt, anyway. Let's go, Sam.... And you, watch how you drive, old man, sun or no sun." The men returned to their car.

P. B. smiled to himself, starting his car, "One named Sam, one with a broken nose—been in a fight." He jotted down the license number. He gazed down the street, knowing that Rosamund had reached the expressway by now. *They can't catch her in a million years in that traffic,* P. B. thought. "Old man, you say. You creeps better watch out," he threw at the vanishing automobile.

Jeffrey scanned the card and dialed the number at the top of the letterhead.

A man's voice answered. "Evan Thomas here." Jeffrey asked how Darren was doing. Should he come in for a conference? Darren's teacher said, "You don't need to come in, Mr. Shuggs. I know you have a tight schedule."

Jeffrey said, "I hoped Darren's problem was under control. He's been much happier in the past month or so."

"Right," Evan Thomas said, "his friendship with his classmate Caryl has given him needed confidence. She's good for him. Has anything happened to change things—with his mother?"

"She called him on the weekend. There's something else. I don't want to talk about it on the telephone. I'll stop by—at your convenience." Jeffrey didn't like to think of a phone tap, but it made sense.

"I'm going to take it back." Darren held a *Star Trek* comic." I don't know what made me do it," he said, looking down at his shoes.

"Maybe it's what that psychologist doctor on *Oprah* yesterday called 'relapse.' You caught yourself this time, and you aren't trying to lie out of it." Caryl wanted to yell at him, call him stupid, but her insides told her, 'don't do it.'"

"Yeah, I know. Will you go with me—wait outside the door—while I tell the teacher?"

"Sure," she said, feeling grown-up.

"My dad would be glad I'm doing the right thing this time." Darren walked his basketball walk—like the big guys.

CHAPTER 13

In a pink-bronze haze—or if Jeffrey were in his mountains, he'd say "backlit clouds"—the energies of Pet, Munje, and Frank lingered, unseen by all except children and the childlike.

Rosamund parked her car at an outcropping near the summit of Stone Mountain. She wanted to be alone to clear her head. Unknowingly, but like her ancestors, Rosamund had been drawn to a high area for contemplation and meditation. She saw a smooth rock about fifty feet away. Climbing to the small knob, she wrapped her long, paisley skirt around her legs and leaned her chin on her folded arms. Across the valley, a cloud appeared stationary, although a gentle wind steadily moved nearby clouds. Rosamund saw the sun reflected oddly. The stationary cloud was not white like the others but hues of pink and bronze.

Watching the cloud, Rosamund began to feel sleepy—not a tired sleepy but a relaxation that suffused her. She smiled with an easiness she had not felt before. She casually observed the shifting contours of the cloud. As if she were drawn into, becoming a part of, the cloud. "Yes," she whispered. "I can do it—there is a way."

A breeze caressed her cheek. She glanced at her watch, stood, and stretched, thinking, *thank goodness for Georgia weather.* Ohio was never this warm in early December. Her lunchtime over, Rosamund went back to her office. *Another day or two of being careful and the extra pound gained from P. B.'s gumbo-fest will have lost its sting.* She turned the waistband of her skirt, smoothing a nonexistent bulge.

"Look, when we focus on helping her see through her problem, when she is receptive, we can do our work." Munje segued back and forth, shape-shifting: *his Civil War self; his Caryl self; his young, peasant mother self in Mali*

110   FAMILY LINES

thirteen centuries ago; and his elderly Druid self just before the pilgrimage of Patrick to Ireland 600 years ago.

"Why do you change your energy so often, Uncle?" Pet asked.

Frank replied by moving into Munje's space field, "It's natural, Daughter," *he said in his own voice and Munje's form.* "It's fun and good to remember how complex and complete we really are. Why don't you try it?"

"I'm more hesitant than you. We are different, aren't we?" *she asked, tentatively merging into a version of a young Darren, then of P. B.*

Munje watched Rosamund sitting on the rock at Stone Mountain. "Wouldn't she be surprised to know that she hid behind that rock once before and watched Atlanta burn?"

He linked with Pet. If Rosamund had turned around, she would have seen the pink-bronze cloud expand eastward and meld with the white cloud beside it.

Caryl watched the clouds bump and merge from her classroom window. "Neat," *she exclaimed.*

"Our work is very important," Munje continued. "Dectel needs a little shove—no, a big push—to get back on track. Ignorance is, probably, the real cardinal sin. It isn't that Warner, the brass, or anyone is bad. They simply haven't opened themselves to accepting the results of their actions."

"Down there it's called greed. I remember it well," Frank added.

Jeffrey stood at a cafeteria window waiting for Sam to join him. Sam worked on the floor above, and they ate lunch together once in a while. Sam seemed to want to be friendly. Jeffrey wondered. *We don't have anything in common except working here.* Jeffrey noticed that the wind had picked up; the clouds were stretching from cumulus to cumulo-cirrus. *If Darren and I don't get to the mountains soon,* he thought, *the snows will begin. I don't want to take him on a snow overnight, yet.*

"Yo, man," Sam's attempt at hipness was nothing if not ineptitude mingled with insincerity. He clapped Jeffrey on the back. "What are we feasting on today, hog maws or chitlins?"

Most of the time, Jeffrey ignored Sam's jokes. "I never ate either in my life. Seems like the cafeteria doesn't carry your favorites."

"You know I'm joking. I thought you'd get it, what with your work with your boss." Sam took a tray from the pile and waved Jeffrey in front of him.

"You don't get it, do you? That kind of joke went out with bell-bottom slacks. No one I know enjoys your kind of humor." Jeffrey shook his head in dismay. "I'd wash my son's mouth with soapy water if he said anything as crude—and cruel."

"Touchy, touchy. I apologize. It's hard to read you, Shuggs. You look like a mountain man; you sound like a mountain man," Sam put his tray on the table, shook his head, and feigned sadness, "but you sure don't act like one."

"In my part of the country, it's called 'home training.' I recommend it. My son gets a steady dose." Jeffrey smiled and added, "Pal."

Finishing lunch, Sam and Jeffrey caught an elevator. "Hold it, please," someone called. Hurrying into the elevator, Rosamund looked away from the men. She stood to the left and side of her companions. Jeffrey nodded politely and averted his eyes. Rosamund stifled a smile, thinking, *he's playing it very well.*

Jeffrey got off at his floor. On the floor above, Sam stood aside to let Rosamund and two other employees off. Upon exiting, he turned in a different direction, down a hall away from the large reception area, toward a private door with no name on it.

"Has he said anything we can use?" Ed Warner said from his huge desk. The driver with the large nose, who had followed Rosamund, and Sam—whose last name was Hudson, but few remembered he had a last name—sat on the other side of Warner's desk.

"Shuggs is a bore," Sam said. "He talks about his kid, his mountains, and nothing else."

"We don't have all year to find out where he hid the data and what he plans to do." Warner turned to the driver. "What about you? You didn't find anything in his apartment? Have any of your men found anything?" His high-pitched voice escalated. The room was soundproofed, or he would have sounded like a whining baby to Miss D'Arcy.

Big Nose shook his head. He was dying for a cigarette. "I have cars tailing them all the time. So far, nothing I can put my finger on. She goes her way. He goes his. That Hardy guy, he went to three different doctors in the last two weeks."

"Don't worry about him," Warner broke in. "He's a mosquito in the wind. He's not smart enough to be any trouble."

"You want us to stop his surveillance, then?" Big Nose asked.

"Yes. Shuggs is our problem. I'm not sure about Jones-Keyes. She said she's not involved with him—maybe she's not. I don't trust them—affirmative-action types. Take Hardy's wife. She might be smarter than we give her credit." Warner paced, head lowered, and tugged at his chin. He wheeled to the men so quickly Sam jumped. Big Nose was not fazed; he'd had weapons pointed at him. "OK, here's where we are. Forget Hardy. Sam, keep on Shuggs. And you," he pointed to the man with the prominent nose, "maintain your watch on Jones-Keyes. I'm adding pressure on her here in the office. I could be overly cautious and have nothing to be concerned about."

Sam and the man from Dectel's internal security left by an entrance the office staff did not know existed.

In her office, Rosamund thumbed through the new assignments Lois had passed on to her. Two of her jobs had been returned. *Nitpicking,* she noted. She felt a twinge that she was not being assigned the high quality of reports to analyze that she had several weeks before. "I wonder what is going on," she said to nothing and no one.

"Setting you up for heavy criticism," Pet said. "You're right, niece. There is a way."

Frank and Munje were lying on their backs beside a stone that looked much like the one Rosamund had sat on, but with mountains ringed all around, not one mound like Stone Mountain. They were a hundred miles north, in the place where both had been born nearly one hundred fifty years before. Munje, the boy, first ran behind the pigsty. He looked around and, seeing no one, darted to the woodpile, then to a ditch beside the logging road. "This time, I'll get 'way. Don't mind what Mama say. I won't stay no slave to my own pappy."

The boy inched on his belly in the dry leaves. Soon he was in the woods, among the pines, oaks, hickory, and hemlocks. He covered himself with leaves to wait the night through. This time, like all the others, the men found him and brought him back to the farm.

Frank Shuggs, Sr., sat astride his horse, watching the boy pull against the ropes that held him. "Give him another licking. I'm tired of wasting good man time on him. Next trader by, he's sold." Without so much as a glance into his brown son's eyes, Frank Sr. strode back to the farmhouse. His son Frank Jr. was being tended by his nurse, Sariah.

The mahogany dark young woman, heavy with her second child, didn't noticed Frank until he stepped onto the porch. She stopped singing the tune she'd learned in the slave quarters. Big Frank barely gave his son a look. "At least, the place will pass on legal, now," he had said to his lawyer regarding Frank Jr.

"Hard man, our father," Frank's energy sent to Munje.

"And he's still at it—Warner, this time," Munje responded. "Time, time, who's got the time?" Munje sang. "Happens in the flicker of an eye."

Pet added, "Takes some a heap of learning time, doesn't it?"

"Seems forever," Frank breathed a sigh, sending a small bank of clouds tumbling into a cirrus across from where the Pass On energies hung out.

"Enough already!" a thought message wafted to them from the up-ended cloud.

"Sorry, didn't know you were there," three message patterns returned, simultaneously.

"Always on the job." The cloud realigned itself.

The call to Rosamund had been Warner's, not his assistant's or Lois's. Rosamund passed Lois's desk. *I must be doing something right—or something wrong—the head cheese personally summoned me.*

At Warner's door, she was told to go straight in.

"Good afternoon, Mr. Warner. How is your day going?"

"Fine, fine, Mrs. Jones-Keyes." Warner's squeaky voice distorted the strains of Mozart from the speakers behind his desk.

No Muzak for the brass, she thought.

"You know I don't waste time, Rosamund . . ."

Rosamund was surprised by his use of her first name, a first for him. Her mind became alert for something unpleasant.

"I'm almost ashamed to have to say this, after the outstanding assessment I gave you a few weeks ago."

Pricks of serotonin, or adrenaline, or bile fired, yet she sat quietly. Warner's smile was a mask, painted for effect—screaming phony.

"I don't understand how your productivity has fallen in such a short time. Are you well? Is something wrong at home?"

Rosamund remembered Aunt Pet's admonition, "Take it easy." Breathing deeply and slowly, she waited. Warner blanched. Her demeanor, a lack of anxiety or fear, was unexpected. Rosamund replied. "I can't imagine why you say that, Mr. Warner. I have completed all the analyses assigned to me ahead of schedule."

He almost sputtered. "My record varies—I was informed that your quality has eroded."

Rosamund settled deeper into her chair and crossed her legs, her fingers lightly laced. "If you wish, Mr. Warner, I can bring you my file, which has times of entry and completion for each job: Unito, ABAC, CU . . ."

Warner stopped her. "You don't need to name each one."

Encouraged by his hesitation, she spoke boldly. "I noticed the level of reports to which I was assigned when I first came to Dectel. I surmised that the company must have a testing procedure for new people—giving them really tough assignments to see if they can survive, achieve at a high level. Then, when the test is done to Dectel's satisfaction, the trial is over and less-demanding projects are assigned. It's like a probation. Am I correct?"

"I suppose so . . . of course. You managed to survive . . . achieve . . ." His voice wandered.

"Thank you, Mr. Warner. I'm relieved. Mr. Warner, do you mind if I go back to my desk, now? I know you are very busy, and a new job has arrived on my desk."

"Right, right," he said, almost recovered. "Keep up the good work."

Back at her desk, Rosamund whispered to Lois, "You were right. It was a blowoff. As a reward for the warning, I invite you and the women in reception, Rhoda and Kekisha, to dinner at the Plaza Tower on Friday."

Lois was smiling broadly. "I didn't know that the company had forced Dr. Langston out, and a black engineer before him. Rhoda and Kekisha watched the whole thing."

Rosamund was elated. "I want to thank them for telling you to warn me to keep absolutely full and accurate records on every assignment. If not for you sisters, my rear would be in Antarctica."

Lois giggled. "The girls didn't say 'rear.'"

Jeffrey and Rosamund met for an almost regular conversation at the secluded café not far from Dectel. She told him, nearly bouncing with enthusiasm, of her meeting with Warner.

"The new helper can't stay with Caryl on Friday night. Would you—could you and Darren help us out? The kids get along well. I was so psyched by how Warner wilted that I forgot and made a date for Friday night." Rosamund rearranged the papers she'd crammed into her briefcase. "Ugh, homework. Don't we ever graduate from school?" She grimaced.

"We have different rewards; we pay for school. We get paid when we graduate. Hey, let me congratulate you for your masterful handling of Warner."

"Masterful? What about 'queenly' or 'goddesslike'? Thanks, anyway. I don't want to anticipate what may be next."

"Touché. I'll learn. Sure, Darren and I can spend Friday evening with Caryl. What time?"

"Sevenish," Rosamund said. "I'll be home by ten. Is that all right with you men?"

"I doubt that Darren has a more pressing engagement; sevenish it is."

"Oh, oh, isn't that your lunchtime buddy?" Rosamund caught a familiar face at a table near a far window.

Jeffrey placed a tip on their table. Sam Hudson did not lift his head from his magazine. "No friend of mind. He's a pest. If he doesn't see me, I won't see him. He can make his own assumption. We're not at the office. So long."

Rosamund slung her heavy purse over one shoulder and grunted at the heft of her briefcase. "Bye."

CHAPTER 14

Sam Hudson watched Rosamund and Jeffrey leave the café. He smiled like a man who's found the brass ring. The waitress passed his table to retrieve her tip from the table behind him. He wasn't her type. Sam looked around for a telephone, spying one near the entrance to the restrooms. Flicking a quarter, he savored his slow walk to the instrument.

"When I least expect it, lady luck comes to me," Sam said into the receiver. "Old Squeaky was wrong; the black woman is involved. She is friends with Mountain Man. They just ate two BLTs on whole wheat, no mayo."

He listened a few seconds. "OK. Twenty minutes."

The waitress returned to Sam's table when she saw the outer door close behind him. "Cheapo," she mouthed. "Told you, Martha," she shrugged at the waitress clearing the table across from her. "Twenty-five cents for the $9.95 special—and good service. Big shot from the big company. Huh."

Twenty minutes later, Sam Hudson and another man were in a company car in the Dectel lot. "The information Warner wants is probably in her place," Sam told Jensen—Jeffrey's new neighbor, the driver with the big nose, and head of security at Dectel. "We can get in when no one is home."

"They must be stupid—don't seem to be worried by any of our hints," Jensen drawled.

"I've seen folks like them before. Educated types. They believe they haven't done anything wrong, so they don't worry. Does Shuggs know that you are his neighbor?" Sam asked.

"Sure, I've met him, but he doesn't connect me with the company—never seen me there." Jensen polished his eyeglasses. "Our tap turned up nothing, just calls between their kids. Found out they go to school together."

Next morning, Lois announced, "Mr. Shuggs is on line three."

"JK, would it be all right if Caryl came to our apartment tonight? Darren has a new computer game he wants to show her."

"Yes, certainly. No problem. I'll bring her by on my way to our little party," Rosamund said to the speakerphone.

The office phones were monitored. Jensen called Sam, "Tonight, after seven."

Pet wanted to be on her own. The men's energies were a little heavy to her, sometimes. "Going to see my girl—alone," she told them.

Pet lounged in the Buddha figure that sat on the back of a file cabinet. Rosamund had bought the ancient figure on impulse at a yard sale during a morning jog. Pet had tuned into Rosamund's conversation and the surveillance. "Rosamund, child, get your antenna up," she said. "Be careful. Watch it!"

She summoned Munje and Frank, who had been re-creating Revolutionary War battles. Munje was a Loyalist, then—much to his chagrin.

"Don't know if she picked up, Daughter," Munje said. "This is a new one we didn't anticipate."

"I told you when you first came over, Patricia, we still have limitations in Pass On—different but limitations just the same." Frank said. "Let's hope you got through to her."

"Rosamund might be past the age for learning," Frank said. "It's the little ones who learn best—they keep more of their knowledge from previous times."

"Let's go, Puddin'." Rosamund called to Caryl from her bedroom. "Jeffrey's changing of our schedule puts us under a hurry-up. I wouldn't tell him; he's doing us a favor."

"Mr. Shuggs wouldn't have been upset if you had told him."

"Regular psychologist you're becoming," Rosamund teased her precocious daughter.

"Not so, Mums. He's a nice man. Darren has a good father."

Caryl's voice carried a longing. *A father would be good for her,* Rosamund thought. At the front door Rosamund turned around. "Wait, Caryl." She opened the drawer of the leather-covered table in the bay where she did bills and night work for Dectel. She pulled a small envelope from the drawer and stuck it in one of the pockets of her purse.

"Mums, you're not working tonight? It's p-a-r-t-y," Caryl scolded.

"I don't know why I'm taking this—a feeling came over me, said to take it with me." Rosamund took a similar envelope from her purse and dropped it in the drawer along with a couple of notepads and two pens. "Now, I'm lighter," she closed the drawer and set the alarm. They ran for the elevator that was letting off a neighbor.

"Hello, Miss DeLong." The Jones-Keyes pair greeted the tenant from the end of their hall. They reached the elevator, pushing the door open as it began closing on them.

"Sorry I'm late." Rosamund tousled Darren's hair.

"That's okay," Jeffrey said. "The kids and I had fun."

Not long after, a tired Caryl stifled a yawn. "Night, Mums. Don't wake me. I'm sleeping late tomorrow."

"Sleep well. It's Saturday," Rosamund said.

Caryl felt her way down the hall to her room.

"Need a seeing-eye puppy?" her mother asked.

Rosamund absent-mindedly unfastened an earring. It clattered to the ground. Bending to retrieve it, Rosamund noticed a piece of paper in the corner of the closed desk drawer. It was the yellow corner of a notepad. "I completely closed that drawer," she murmured.

"What, Mums?" Caryl called from her room.

"Talking to myself, Puddin'." Rosamund didn't want to frighten her. Taking a tissue from her purse, Rosamund gingerly opened the drawer. The envelope and pens were as she had left them, but something wasn't right. The drawer had been opened. The contents of the envelope she put in the drawer was a subscription form for a journal. She'd laid a Luther Vandross CD and an Octavia Butler paperback on each side of the envelope. They were slightly askance.

She reached into her purse for the other envelope. The disk for the phiofomel purchases were inside.

Pet, Frank, and Munje circled the dining-room chandelier.

"I said she wasn't too old to learn," Pet hummed, imitating the fluorescent light above the desk.

"I can't call." Rosamund paced the floor. "This has gotten scary. I'll see P. B. first thing tomorrow." Rosamund went to the end of the hall, into Aunt Pet's room, and sat on the side of the bed. "What am I going to do?" She stroked the coverlet. "If I sit here, maybe something will come to me. Oh, baby, Caryl, I don't want harm to come to you. What have I got myself into?" Closing her eyes, she leaned back on Pet's bed, the pillows holding her in a sitting position. Pet's old suitcase was on the chair where Rosamund had left it when she found the family history documents. Soon, Sariah Rosamund was asleep.

"Let's go home, today." Darren stood over his father's bed, rubbing sleep from his eyes.

"Today? Why today?" Jeffrey sat up in bed, rubbing his eyes.

"I'm tired of the city. I have our sleeping bags, Coleman stove, filled water bottles, and a bunch of power bars." Darren proudly showed his dad each item.

"You remembered almost everything. We'll have to pick up a few other items on our way. All right, pal. We can do it." Jeffrey pulled on his robe and went to shower.

Rosamund called Jeffrey from a pay phone. No answer. She made another call. "May we come over, right away, P. B.?"

The urgency in her voice was more than enough for P. B. "Do you want me to come over there?"

"No, no. You might be seen," she said, whispering into the telephone.

Taking a cab, Rosamund and a bewildered Caryl were at P. B.'s in less than a -half-hour.

"Serious business." It was P. B.'s turn to pace.

"They didn't get the file. They may be getting desperate."

"It's time for a counterattack—no subtlety. Is there someone else at Dectel that you and Jeffrey can take into your confidence? This is too much for you young folks to handle."

Rosamund blushed. "No, P. B. I don't want to crawl to some white company man—besides I don't know one we can trust, except Jeffrey. Warner is, obviously, against us. Now that they know I'm working with Jeffrey, we should get our facts—information—

our ammunition together and confront the problem, win or lose."

"I like your spirit. I have a few contacts I can call on—I've never given up a friend." P. B. reached for and held her hands. They were icy cold but steady.

"I don't know where Jeffrey is. He's probably gone 'home' for the weekend. He's been talking about it. What a surprise he has waiting when he gets back."

"You've had your surprise already," P. B. said in as light a tone as he could muster.

CHAPTER 15

"*Fighting, scrapping, war, hurting, arrows, swords, guns, missiles, lasers, or worse—it is still hurting.*" Pet spiraled. She wasn't above a mountain or in any known space. The ambiance was aimless and oddly nonspecific.

"*Over here, Patricia.*"

"*Where are we, Uncles?*" Pet eased closer to the source of the sound.

"*We're inside the coding memory where the phiofomel is applied, the root of the mess our young people at Dectel are wrestling with.*" Munje was a dark green probe weaving into and around the inner works of the Dectel secret. "*No, I take that back,*" he said. "*The root of the problem is greed. That's all.*"

Pet attached her energy to Munje. Frank brought up the end of the spiral. He signaled. "*Glad you picked up on that thought, Brother. It's not the thing; it's the thought.*"

"*Let's give Dectel a rest until Jeffrey is back in the city. I have another story to show you, Pet.*" Munje's message whistled from the far end of the green curving line.

"*Saying is doing, Uncle. I'm ready for the next. What is this one?*"

The Pass On energies were moving through gun smoke in a swampy marsh. "*If I were alive, I'd be coughing,*" Pet said. She focused on a flat-topped mound that appeared between swirls of gun smoke and lines of troops in grey and blue. "*Uncle, that's the Indian burial ground across the square where I was born, in Louisiana, but there's a war going on.*"

"*Indeed, I was a scout for the Union army the spring of '63. General Grant had landed at Milliken's Bend on the Mississippi River. I followed two Confederate scouts back to their camp after I found them snooping over our way. See,*" Munje pointed a silver stick, "*there are dense woods to the left. Two half-Indian, half-black boys sneaked up from the river, south of town. I knew how to track from when I was a boy, just like Frank.*"

"This was after you and I met," Frank added.

"If you call shooting a meeting—but you're right," Munje said. *"Anyhow, all by myself, I heard the Rebels talking strategy for the Vicksburg battle. I worked my way back to our lines and told Captain O'Neil. He told the company that I was a hero. Never got a medal, though. The captain was taken down days later at Vicksburg."*

The panoply of the 1860s' action played clear to Pet—Munje on his belly, the dark swamp, tents around small fires. *"You don't sound happy about your bravery,"* she asked, puzzled.

Frank said, *"We have been through enough lives that little escapades like his—and mine—show the futility of fighting—if it's war or business. I'm happy to see any part of war 'cooling down' or 'chilling', as the kids in present time say."*

"Cooling down? How?" Pet reached to touch a young soldier lying on the ground, a wound in his side. The boy-man felt a lessening of his pain and breathed easily before he transpired.

Frank and Munje's essences were one. Frank's energy was high pitched, like a violin string. Munje vibrated like a low note on a bassoon. The effect was a chord, blending to soothing harmony. *"Look at the way Rosamund and Jeffrey are working together to stop the silliness at Dectel. He was a Southern man who didn't like female bosses. She was a sorta black-power type. Now, they're on the same wavelength."*

"I see," Pet said. *"Slavery isn't a color or a national thing; it's a mind thing. The trees are gone from my old neighborhood in Louisiana, but the burial mound is there. And Warner's game is the same as any master-slave."*

"You've got it, Daughter." They easily slipped free of the tiny square that held the phiofomel-treated component.

P. B. held Rosamund's cold hands. "Drink this hot tea—and Caryl, you curl up on the couch and rest while your mother and I figure out things." He spread a knitted afghan over the girl, who drifted to sleep in a few moments.

"This is serious, isn't it, P. B.?" Rosamund turned the cup in her hands, warming her fingers. "If whoever was in our apartment had not been careless, I would not have known that anyone had broken in."

"You have the making of a good investigator." P. B. praised her. "An important skill is to notice everything before you look for evidence, and be sure that you have replaced every little crumb just as you found it."

"The mystery and detective stories I read when I was growing up must have helped." Rosamund managed a tight laugh. "Dad and Mother worried that my reading tastes were trash."

"Not so. Never can tell when something you know might be useful." P. B. refilled her cup. "Here's what I've found, so far. I was thinking to tell you and Jeffrey at the same time, but you need to hear some good news. Your big-shot VP, Mr. Edward C. Warner, is trying to pull a fast one on Dectel—for himself and his best buddies. Mr. Man owns a controlling interest in the single laboratory that manufactures the purest phiofomel in the world."

"I thought everyone in the business knew about phiofomel. What's this about the 'purest'? I'm confused," Rosamund went to the couch, where Caryl had thrown off her afghan. She tucked the multicolored cover around her legs.

"You have to ask somebody who knows more than I do," P. B. shook his head. I did some digging—called in a favor from an old buddy—because this is way over my head. It seems a lot of things look like they're secret, foolproof, but a sharp person can find a way to get what he wants, if he wants it bad enough."

"You did this for me, P. B.? You don't really know me that well. I don't want you to get into any trouble on my account." Rosamund's eyes widened.

"You look just like my Patricia when you raise your eyebrows like that. I can't get that fine woman out of my mind. It's like she's whispering in my ear that I should do what I do. I'm almost willing to say that she knows what I'm finding out. Smart woman that Pet." P. B. nodded and held his cup high with satisfaction. "No, I'm in no danger. I'm sure."

Caryl stirred on the couch. She sat up, yawned, and stretched. "Aunt Pet says, 'Right on,' Reverend P. B."

"What?" P. B. spilled his tea.

"I was dreaming," Caryl said. "Aunt Pet talks to me in my dreams. I heard her say, 'Right on,' then I heard you say you're not in danger." Caryl swung her legs to the floor. "I feel rested now, Mums. Can we go home? Lola fell behind my bed when I hurried up. She doesn't like standing on her head."

P. B. and Rosamund chuckled.

"I don't think anything more will happen. Somebody's frustrated as h—," he caught himself, glancing at Caryl.

"I know about four-letter words, Reverend P. B. Mums and

Aunt Pet told me that sometimes the only way to shake somebody up is a bad word. Bad words are okay to say as long as they're used . . . appropriately? Is that the word, Mums?"

P. B.'s. chin dropped. "This is a smart young lady you're raising here. Runs in the family, I see."

"We'll go home now. I'll call you—I'll be careful of what I say if I need to call. My line is surely tapped, as well as Jeffrey's. We'll work out something, probably at Ma Belle's. Okay?" She put on her jacket and tossed Caryl's to her.

On Nantahala Mountain, Darren stirred hash over the campfire. A chipmunk came near, stood on its hind legs, and stared at the man and boy.

"Dad, he's not afraid of us. The park squirrels don't come so close," Darren whispered.

"Animals can tell if you're a friend. Sometimes people are frightened and don't know the critters won't harm them. I'm glad you 'made me' come on up here, Darren. I didn't know how much I missed fresh air and quiet." Jeffrey propped his camp chair against the side of his truck and relaxed. The sky was clear of city lights. "Look at all the stars," he said.

"This is the way it was all the time you were a boy, isn't it Dad?' Darren turned from the chipmunk, which had decided to travel along. "Tell me a mountain tale, one your grandfather told you."

"Do you want a family story or a made-up one?" Jeffrey pulled a blanket around his shoulders. Darren snuggled into his, against the side of the Trooper.

"Family's best. The one about Great-Uncle Frank, when he ran away and joined the war when he was a boy. That's my favorite," Darren said.

"Son, lots of times, old tales are sad tales. I don't know if anyone can tell a happy war or love story." When Jeffrey said 'love,' his voice broke.

"You're thinking about Momma, aren't you?" the boy asked.

"What does an eight-year-old boy know about love?" Jeffrey teased.

"Eight and three-quarters. I love you—I know it is not the same—and I love the mountains. I don't know how grown-up man-and-woman love is. . . . I know about feelings, and I have sad ones when I miss Momma, too."

Jeffrey saw his own childhood face, except for Darren's mother's mouth and the way he moved his head when he talked. "Sometimes, the things you say make me wonder if childhood exists anymore. Babies grow up too fast." He remembered the call from Darren's teacher, the on-again off-again taking things from other kids. The teacher had said that Darren took small things, "pilfered" was his word, in part because of his fear over the absence of his mother. Jeffrey decided he wouldn't mention her tonight.

"So it is, then," Jeffrey went on. "According to my great-aunt..."

"Sariah, named after a favorite nurse the family had." Darren broke into the story.

"Who's going to tell it? You asked me." Jeffrey reached to rumple the boy's hair.

"Just keeping you straight," Darren dodged the gesture. "I'll be quiet from now on."

"You be sure to do that. My great-great-grandfather—according to genealogists, he'd be my second great-grandfather and your third great-grandfather—owned a good-sized farm, a plantation—in the middle of North Carolina, near the town of today's Burlington. I guess it wasn't big enough to be a real city back then. Big Frank had two sons: Frank Jr. and another son born five or six years after him named Jeffrey Patrick. Jeffrey Patrick was my great-grandfather, your second great-grandfather.

"Frank Jr. and his father didn't get along. Frank Jr. did not like the mean way his father treated his workers."

Darren put his hand on his father's leg. "Dad, you don't have to pretend with me. I know those workers were slaves. We studied slavery history in school."

"OK, fella. Frank Sr. was not a nice man as far as I can tell. Granddaddy said that young Frank saw Big Frank hitting a slave girl with a walking stick. Frank Jr. grabbed the stick and broke it against a big ol' pecan tree. He never spoke to his daddy after that. Frank Jr. left home as soon as he could. He joined the Confederate army. It wasn't because he was for slavery. He wasn't. All his family had been born in the South since they came here from Europe, and he knew he was a Southerner. He was killed in a battle, somewhere in Louisiana—sent in the wrong direction. His mother, Lucie, grieved so she lost her mind. She locked herself in a room, leaving the raising of her other boy, Jeffrey Patrick, to the slave nurse-well, she was free after the war—who stayed on with great-great-grandmother."

"And my third great-grandfather was strangled by one of his workers—slaves—during the time General Sherman was fighting General Johnson around Greensboro, right, Dad?"

"I'm not ever going to tell you that story again. You know it as well as I do."

"I get pictures in my head when you tell it that don't come when I think it," Darren let his blanket fall aside. "Dad, I like hearing the stories. They help me know what I can do, better," Darren said.

"Time to turn in. We're spotting from early morning until time to go home," Jeffrey said.

The two climbed into the rear gate of their truck and were soon asleep. The chipmunk edged near to take the leavings from their supper.

Fifty feet away, two men watched through infrared glasses. "He didn't bury anything. Guess we're off the scent," said the man who had accosted Rosamund on I-285.

"Warner believes they have something and are going to spring it soon. We're being paid good money. I'm not going to sweat because the guy hasn't given anything up." The thin, nervous, balding one picked his teeth. "I want more than fast food, beans, or soup. They're asleep, how about going down the mountain to find some good country cooking?"

Jeffrey heard the sound of a truck going down the mountain. He slipped out of his sleeping bag and tiptoed quietly outside to the covered rear wheel. He removed a copy of Liam's medical report, went to a large oak tree, pulled out a waterproof packet, and put his sheaf inside. Thoroughly wrapping his addition to his childhood treasures against chipmunks and inclement weather, he went back to his bed in his truck. Darren stirred, turned, and slept.

The morning was colder than expected for the time of year. Jeffrey and Darren packed the truck then spent two hours spotting migrating birds.

"We have time to stop by our cousins in Ola on our way home. Would you like that?" Jeffrey asked the boy, who was trying to not shiver.

"Sure would. Do you think Cousin Lottie has any hot chocolate in the house?"

"My teeth are clicking, too. Let's dash," Jeffrey said. "The family is waiting for us. I called them before we left Atlanta."

"I like cousins. I don't care if they are third and fourth. I wish I saw more of them." Darren climbed into the high seat. "Heat, quick, please," he pleaded.

"You have a lot of toughening to do, city boy." Jeffrey glimpsed the unfamiliar truck not quite shielded by the sparse foliage. He gunned his motor loudly. To be sure to let you know I am here, he said to himself.

Darren and Jeffrey ate lunch, with hot chocolate, among their mountain kin and drove on to Atlanta.

Hours later, a tired Darren jumped down from the truck. "Warmer here than up on Nantahala," he said, taking off his outer jacket.

Upstairs, he telephoned Caryl. "We spotted four birds I never saw before. My dad knows them all."

"My mom says she is going to buy some cumin for lamb stew. Want to go with us? She says for you to ask your dad if you can go." Something in Caryl's voice said, "Don't fool around. Be serious."

"OK, I'll ask."

"Dad?" Puzzled, Darren made the request.

"Rosamund hates lamb with a passion." Jeffrey responded, as puzzled as Darren. "Oh, oh, something's up. Tell her, yes, you can go with them."

Jeffrey waited downstairs until Rosamund and Caryl drove to his building. Jumping in the car, Darren told them about his weekend. At Ma Belle's P. B. waited in the cozy room. Ma Belle showed the children dried herbs hanging from hooks and jars of savory plants with names like Bedstraw and Flapper dock.

Before the children became bored or too rambunctious, Rosamund came to the front of the store. "I have what I came for, we can go now," Rosamund said. She gave a small bag to each of them. "Darren, give your father this package of dried mango. Tell him it is fresh from Jamaica."

Back home, Darren gave the bag to Jeffrey. Inside were strips of mango tied together. Rosamund's report of the night before and a request to meet with her and P. B. at Ma Belle's at 7:30 was taped inside the bottom of the bag.

Jeffrey called Miss McRay. Would she watch Darren for him? She brought her latest mystery novel. "Don't worry, Mr. Shuggs. I'll see that he gets to bed on time if you're not back."

Going out the service entrance, Jeffrey glanced around for strange cars. He took a circuitous route to Ma Belle's, just in case. He went into the corner convenience store and bought a magazine. At Ma Belle's, P. B. and Rosamund waited in the little back room.

"My God, what is wrong with those people?" he asked. "We're only trying to save lives." Jeffrey didn't have room to pace, so he drummed on the table.

"You're the cool one, aren't you?" P. B.'s manner was meant to be a teasing check on Jeffrey.

Rosamund was no longer frightened; she was angry. "The nerve. Sneaking into peoples' homes. We're not criminals, dope dealers, or receivers of stolen goods."

Ma Belle appeared with the coffeepot. "Child, you're forgetting. The worst creeps don't come in po' folks clothes. I lived—and fought—through the Civil Rights days; the biggest shot can be your worst enemy. Button-down shirts and fancy offices don't mean nice or legal." She put the tray on the table, along with hot water for Rosamund's tea.

The unlikely cohorts pulled their chairs close to the table. For several minutes, no one said anything. "Let us put on the table what it is we know," P. B. said.

"I know that my home has been violated and Warner is trying to fire me, "Rosamund slapped her fist on the table.

"I was followed and watched the last two nights," added Jeffrey.

"I don't believe they know I am with y'all. I can move freely," P. B. sounded confident. His face was less so.

"I'm going in to work tomorrow with my widest grin and laid-back look, then I'm going to dig through every file and document in the international system. I will find the tie-in of phiofomel to every person and place it exists." Rosamund had a gleam in her eye. "My 'Jones' is moving into high gear."

Rosamund went on, "Lois told me that Dr. Belden has contacted Liam. The doctor heard of the accident. He wants to observe Liam, see if what happened here at Dectel's lab is similar to other cases he has observed."

"Great. Warner ignores the good doctor's cautions. With Belden in our corner, and Liam's new doctors' reports, we may have enough to go back to the brass," Jeffrey's grin was wider than any P. B., Rosamund, and Ma Belle had ever seen.

P. B. warned, "When the cat is cornered, he fights harder. Don't expect these guys to lie down for dead."

"I know they won't give up easily," Rosamund said, "but with all the evidence we will have, they will pay attention. What we are doing, really, is trying to protect Dectel."

Jeffrey patted her shoulder. "I hope you're right. After being followed on a weekend respite, I think my neighbors and family know more than 'hillbillies' are supposed to know. Smile and be friendly, but keep a distance from rattlesnakes. You don't want one in your bed."

Rosamund allowed herself a laugh. "Homespun wisdom is refreshing, Jeffrey. P. B., do you have any ethnic insight for us? The next forty-eight hours may be crucial."

"Not really, Daughter." P. B. hesitated. "Why, where did that come from? I've never called you 'daughter' before, have I?"

"Uncle, how do you find your way into thoughts that aren't family? How did you do that 'daughter' transfer?" Pet asked, in the steam rising from the coffeepot.

"I didn't really intend to do that, Daughter," Munje blushed—if steam could be said to blush.

"We forget, too, that we are connected, one energy with infinite possibilities.

"I kind of like it, P. B. If you don't mind. You're like family to me. My dad isn't down here, and you make things feel close, and you're helpful." Rosamund looked at her watch. "I need to get back to Caryl. The housekeeper agreed to stay on until I returned. I don't want to spoil her time off."

"I do, too," Jeffrey shook hands with Ma Belle and P. B. "You people are great. We all have to be careful. Bears aren't as treacherous as some of our own kind."

"Our own kind? I don't want to be one of the Warner kind," Rosamund pulled her heavy purse to her shoulder.

"Is 'our own kind' racist?" Jeffrey asked.

"Once it would have been, but now it is not. I mean evil, like in w-r-o-n-g."

"We'll continue to leave separately." P. B said. He closed his briefcase. "Rosamund, you take the front door. Jeffrey, upstairs, across to the shoe store, down, and out their side door. My buddy, the owner, is expecting you. I'll stay here until Ma closes. That way, we can't be connected by snoopers—if they are cruising." P. B. enjoyed planning. "And I am dead serious," he concluded.

At Jeffrey's apartment, Miss McRay gathered her book and purse. "That new neighbor, Jensen, bothers me. When you go out or in, Mr. Shuggs, he opens and looks out his door. After you left tonight, I went across to my apartment to get my glasses. There he was peeking down the hall, watching you get in the elevator."

"Keep your door and this one locked at all times. He may only be nosy." Jeffrey felt a ping in the back of his head.

CHAPTER 16

Trying to hide her nervousness, Lois announced, "Mr. Warner wants you, Mrs. JK."

Rosamund sighed, "Fur and fat are tearing up the fans. Okey-dokey. I wonder what now."

"Don't know," Lois said. "The tension in this place is tight as a guitar string." Lois shaped envelopes into a neat stack on her desk. "I have to see the office manager. I'll be back shortly."

Rosamund and Lois touched hands, but not high-fives. Rosamund hummed as she made the trek to the executive office. She acknowledged Warner's executive assistant at the desk that was more impressive than Lois's and hers together. Today, it looked as massive as Warner's. Given the minimum of a smile and a mumble to go on in, Rosamund sent up a silent request for stamina, strength, and a cool tongue.

Edward C. Warner was staring out of a window that overlooked downtown Atlanta, miles from the prestigious Dectel suburban location. Distracting himself by observing the scene below, he pushed out of mind the remote possibility that the black woman would discover his part in the phiofomel deal. She may be smart, but not as smart as he.

He turned when his door opened. "Good morning. Have a seat, Mrs. Keyes," he said. He remained standing, the expanse of green glass behind him, each of his thumbs twitching on the slit of his pants pockets. Warner's weight seemed to have increased during recent months. His coloring suggested that he did not seek the favor of the sunny days of the mild Georgia winter.

"I have an assignment for you, in Chicago," he blurted, with a bare nod. He rushed on. "Telecommunication is great technology but face-to-face contact still has use. We want you to represent the corporation at a confab between Dectel and JCN. You're a keen analyst; I've said that before. You can interpret the climate and nuances at the meeting to Dectel's advantage."

Personnel with backgrounds and training in group dynamics or psychology would have been better suited to this task than Rosamund would be. She masked her surprise and concern. If she protested, it would imply that she was afraid, or worse, incompetent. A twinge of her ambition to topple the barriers of corporate culture surfaced. She ventured a question, nevertheless.

"Thank you for you confidence, Mr. Warner. NetLink is a great idea, and representing Dectel is a wonderful opportunity. Are you sure that my particular skills are appropriate for the confab?"

"Of course," Warner brushed aside her question. "You are articulate, personable, and you know the purpose and need for the project. Imagine, instant audio and visual digital, multiple access anywhere in the world, and at a reasonable cost—not a year or two but months." This meeting is the final deliberation for our consolidation. You leave in the morning. Miss D'Arcy has your travel packet." His tone said dismissal. He looked toward the window. "Beautiful view from up here," he said as Rosamund left his office.

Edward C. Warner knew he had moved to top-level management by his shrewd judgment of people, their needs, and ambitions. He believed there was no reason to think he had lost his touch in the executive suite.

Warner's executive assistant handed Rosamund a dark blue, leather envelope with a gold-embossed Dectel Global logo. Inside were her airline ticket and hotel and limousine reservations. Her itinerary listed the confab to begin at 1:30 p.m. First class all the way, she noticed. Right out the Dectel door for her, perhaps. Rosamund smiled at Miss D'Arcy, certain that the perfect image of corporate propriety knew something that she did not.

At the door to her own office, Rosamund found Lois holding a tissue to her face. Nearer, she saw the tissue was not being used to dab at a superficial blemish. Lois's eyes were teary and red.

"Come in here. What is wrong?" Rosamund maneuvered Lois into the private space.

"I've been let go," Lois spoke in a hoarse whisper. "The office manager says the company is retrenching. I'm low person in the department-you'll be assigned a new secretary shortly after you return from the conference. I received my two weeks' notice."

"The screws are closing," Rosamund said, handing Lois a fresh tissue. "Without you here, they hope to stop the inquiry into Liam's accident. Sending me out to fail is corporate smarts. Jeffrey is probably out, too. If not already, soon." She forced down the little voice that said, "Even the white male."

"No warning," Lois said. "My last evaluation was two weeks ago. I have a superior rating. How can I face Liam and the twins?" Lois had stopped crying. Her face was puffy but composed. "You think they're doing the same to you?"

"I do. Warner wants to avoid a discrimination charge. My role at the confab in Chicago, tomorrow, is designed to make me look bad. I'm no expert in negotiations." Rosamund gave a little cry. "Oh, darn, I haven't time to arrange for Caryl."

Lois' composure shifted to indignation. "They know you have a daughter. You could have been given more time. It isn't as if they planned for you to leave town today."

"You're right. I hadn't thought of that." It was time for Rosamund's indignant side. "Don't worry. Liam will understand. He's in tune with the possibilities. We will survive—yeah, we will overcome."

"Don't worry about Caryl." Lois held Rosamund by her shoulders. "I'll take her tonight and as long as you are away. Meryl will jump with joy at having a sleepover guest. We didn't have our joint picnic yet; the girls will have a chance to begin to know one another."

"If women are to make it in this crazy world, I guess we have to learn to neglect our children the way men have always had to do. I'm leaving early, and approved or not, I'm going to have my hair and nails done. I will, at least, make a well-turned-out corporate statement," Rosamund laughed.

Lois managed a faint smile.

Inside gigantic Chicago O'Hare International, Rosamund found the temperature was no colder than Atlanta. Once outside, her luggage deposited by the driver, she felt the renowned Hawk, the Windy City's trademark. The gleaming bronze façade of the Hyatt Regency loomed before her when the limo descended the slight hill to the entrance.

Ensconced in her suite, Rosamund opened the draperies above a never-ending stream of automobiles and trucks. Outside, to the north, a pink-bronze cloud hovered. "If I were a less-rational person, I'd think that cloud followed me from Stone Mountain. It's probably a reflection from this building."

She had more than an hour before the meeting. Too wrought-up to eat lunch, she decided to go down for a cup of tea. She ran a comb through her hair, "Good cut André gave me. He saw I wasn't a cheerful camper."

A red light on the hotel telephone flashed; an internal mechanism buzzed at the same time. It was her compatriot, the Dectel chief of European operations from the headquarters there, the one she was to meet. His plane had been delayed by the stacking up of planes landing at O'Hare. "Typical," he said, impatiently. He and she would not have time to compare notes before the meeting.

The penthouse conference suite was intended to impress, and it did. The buzz around the oval table struck Rosamund as forced friendliness. In a second, smaller room, assistants to the conferees fussed over piles of paper. The assemblage tried to match the impressive dimensions of their surroundings—and what was expected of them.

Dectel's chief of European operations and two lawyers arrived at 1:25 p.m. Friedrich Woestmann lambasted the airline and the airport, opened his attaché, and transformed himself into the focused executive.

Faces were a blur: nearly identical suits, ties, haircuts, and cologne. Rosamund gave herself an internal reminder. *One day I'm going to remember that all this is meaningless, but right now, my butt is on the line.*

Introductions, formalities, the procedure was a choreographed tableau. Rosamund stifled a giggle. A line from Gilbert and Sullivan teased, "I am the very model of a modern major general."

The JCN representative was the epitome of Wharton assuredness. "Mrs. Jones-Keyes, we understand that Dectel is prepared to provide state-of-the-art audio interfaces compatible with our in-place video orbits," he said. "This is our agreement. My people have one question, what is the status of your newest generation Speed-o-Lite transmission?"

"The current generation is in final test production," Rosamund said. She consulted the notes she had studied en route from Atlanta. "We anticipate full production within six weeks."

A man with a JCN badge entered the room after the introductions were made. He sat opposite the JCN spokesman. He said, "Is there a problem with the new transmitter? We were led to expect full production as of today?"

Rosamund's questioner was a dark brown man in his forties. He looked vaguely Asian. His accent was pure American.

"There is no problem," Rosamund added. "We are being prudent. That is all."

"Really? My information differs." The man's attitude was suspicious, inimical. *What?*

"If you have someone snooping into an operation, you may find all kinds of rumors that give a faulty picture," she heard herself say.

Silence swooped around the room. Rosamund was reminded of the odors from a paper factory she used to pass on her way to school. The JCN representative, his lawyers, Dectel's European chief and lawyers, and the assistants lingering in the anteroom like servants waiting to serve dinner stopped all movement for a beat. Rosamund had affronted no underling. Aklud Gebadd was the CEO of JCN and was unaccustomed to being spoken to by anyone without deference. Everyone in the room knew who he was. Rosamund did not.

Sri Gebadd roared with laughter. "I'll be damned. The new one has guts. How do you know I have spies? But doesn't everyone? If my investigators are giving me inaccurate data, I want to know."

"I apologize for going off like that," Rosamund countered. She sensed something heavy going on around her. She was confident of what she knew. She said, "I am a senior analyst at Dectel. I take pride in the thoroughness and accuracy of my work and my analyses show production well within target date."

The Wharton JCN addressed the questioner by name. Rosamund recognized the name of JCN's chief executive officer. Taking his cue from his CEO, the moderator recessed the meeting for one -half-hour. Rosamund was embarrassed. She left to recover from her faux pas in the ladies room. Woestmann stopped her on her way back. "Are you aware that NetLink's three-year progress could be dead in the water from your words?"

"I am defending Dectel. Doesn't that count?" She was exasperated. "I didn't know who he was. Doesn't honesty count?"

"Honesty is not at issue," Woestmann insisted. "You play the game by the rules, or you don't play. Mr. Warner is senior vice-president in the U.S.; he is not CEO. Perhaps, sending you to speak for Dectel Global, USA was a mistake."

"I think that is exactly what Mr. Warner intended," she said. Rosamund wheeled and left him before he could say more.

The subdued hum of voices had returned to the conference suite. Sri Gebadd was nowhere to be seen. Others at the table averted their eyes when they met Rosamund's line of vision. During the short recess, the lawyers had agreed to postpone final signing until full production of Speed-o-Lite was a fact. The men congratulated one another on a splendid job. Nothing was lost; they would meet again when Dectel delivered the new product.

"NetLink is the communication medium into the next century without doubt," Mr. JCN announced.

Rosamund did not remember his name, something nondescript, like his appearance. A vice-president, she heard.

Rosamund returned to her suite. She called Lois and Caryl. Her plane would arrive at Atlanta's Hartsfield International at 10:30 in the morning. "I'm going to find a little restaurant somewhere in the recesses of this monster hotel," Rosamund told Lois. "I'm a pariah in these parts. I'll spare you the gore until I see you."

On the services list, she found a tearoom. She felt the men would choose a beef eatery. The tearoom was sparsely filled. "Weekend tours and honeymooners are mostly our customers," the waitress said, taking Rosamund's order.

Rosamund was comforting herself, glad that she had a cushion in her savings account. The small insurance Aunt Pet left would come in good while she sent out her resumé. She mused, "I can't expect severance from Dectel," spearing the quite good salad she had ordered.

"Miss," the waitress stood over her. "Miss, you're thinking awfully hard aren't you? I spoke to you three times."

"I'm sorry. My thoughts were miles away. What is it?"

"The gentleman over there asked me to give you this note." The waitress gestured toward a table shielded by a large plant in one corner of the room.

Rosamund blanched. Sri Aklud Gebadd inclined his head in

an almost regal way. The note asked if he might speak with her after her meal. She wrote beneath his signature, "Yes sir." She ate deliberately, hoping she gave no sign of her discomfort.

Gebadd finished his meal and waited until she was given her check. He approached her table. "I apologize for my intrusion. May I sit?"

"Of course," she said. "I apologize, again, for my response to you earlier."

He sat down. "You cannot appreciate how refreshing it is to be confronted by a genuine person who makes a genuine comment. My compliments, Mrs. . . . Keyes, is it?"

"I prefer the combination of my family name and my husband's name, Jones-Keyes," she said with candor.

"Excellent. In many cultures respect for the maternal and paternal lines are maintained. Americans are maturing. May I order you a coffee or tea?" he asked.

Rosamund was unsure how to respond to the important man's relaxed manner. "No, thank you. I have all I can manage at this time. You said, 'Americans'? You sound as American as anyone."

"My father was a United Nations representative for much of his career. I spent many years in New York. You seem surprised to see me in this restaurant. I am a vegetarian. The regular restaurants have vegetarian dishes but they sometimes prepare them in the same utensils as other food. I can taste the difference. In a place like this, the salads and pastas are safer, shall we say. Also, I like slipping away from my sycophants whenever I can." He laughed, a pleasant sound that attracted the attention of the few customers.

Rosamund leaned back in her chair. She respected the man. "I am glad you have no hard feelings about today."

Gebadd checked his watch. "Here is my card with my private number. If there is any way I can be of service, please let me know. I admire your attitude.

"I will be in Atlanta in a few days—not to Dectel, on another matter. Given time, may I call you? You can show me the Atlanta others can't or won't."

"I am new to the city myself, but I have found a spot or two that may interest you." She gave him her card.

Gebadd and Rosamund left the restaurant together. One of his assistants was pacing the lobby. Gebadd frowned, shrugged, and went toward his hunter.

"You handled that very well, if I do say so," Frank and Munje bowed to Pet in the uniforms of Roman legionnaires.

"It was good to lend the child a helping hand, so to speak. She has the family backbone, right?" Pet said.

"Well, she sounded more like you than Rosamund at that monster table, but she was herself at dinner," said Munje.

"Beg, borrow, or take, where the energy comes from makes no never mind. The important thing is to be open to accepting it when it does come." Pet flirted with the persona of Catherine the Great. *"Nice,"* she said.

Back in Atlanta, Liam, Jeffrey, and two previously unknown men rode a MARTA train on their way to a secluded house in Dunwoody.

Jeffrey addressed the man seated beside him, who wore a bow tie and was near his own age. "I don't like this hide-and-seek scenario, but, you understand, Liam and I are being followed by investigators from Dectel. We haven't used the train before—all of us getting on at different stations—we hope they are thrown off the track."

The older man, Dr. Belden, sitting across the aisle, said, "Oh, no, we are enjoying the process. The corporate tradition has done all it can to deny our findings. We may, this time, be able to demonstrate the validity of our work."

Jeffrey was confused that Belden kept saying "we." Then, he recalled a minister who talked that same way; the minister had said, "If I use the 'royal we,' it minimizes the tendency to slip into ego arrogance."

Liam's wheelchair fit into a niche at the end of the coach. "Not so long ago, I would not have been able to join you. What with ramps and motorized lifts—I appreciate for the new technology."

"Even if one facet of new technology has hurt you?" the younger man, Liam's new doctor, Ziegler, joked.

Belden said, "May we suggest that technology is not the problem? It is the unthinking uses to which so-called advances are put. The thing, itself, is neutral, we believe."

"I'll buy that," Jeffrey said, standing as they neared a station. "Here we are. A friend from my home will drive us where we are going. I don't trust anyone from Dectel, except Rosamund."

Jeffrey's friend and Dr. Ziegler stored Liam's chair and assisted him into the van. Jeffrey returned to the station's entrance and scanned the street on both sides to assure himself that they had not been followed. Feeling sure, he joined the others in the van.

A short time later, they were ushered into a large, contemporary house set into the curved, wooded streets of the fashionable suburb.

The wife of Jeffrey's friend took them into their family room and brought a tray of sandwiches, cookies, coffee, and pop. "The bathroom is through that door," she pointed. "If you need anything, let me know. I'll be nearby." She took her toy poodle for a walk.

"I have some tentative ideas. Let me know what you think of them." Jeffrey said, his face animated. "Finally, justification." He rubbed his hands together, then remembered to defer to the senior member of the group.

"We're up against powerful forces." Belden began, his countenance and voice totally involved in his topic. "Do not underestimate them. Dectel will fight any effort to stop whatever we try to do. They will not give in to loss of market." Belden's resonant voice lowered, "We know. We've tried to bring sanity—responsibility—to corporate policies before. We have been made into outsiders. BAC, Inc., fired us ten years ago, and no one has hired us since."

Belden was not bitter, merely resigned to the reality of his predicament.

Doctor Ziegler opened his briefcase. "Liam is, without doubt, impaired by phiofomel. The amount of the chemical he received in one exposure is equivalent to what a person working with the components would have to receive over a period of eight to ten years. The accumulated exposure to a roomful of workers, or in a private residence, would reach, according to my calculations, damaging proportions over time. In the case of an infant, child, or older person with lessened resistance, the effects might be seen in three to five years."

"I don't understand why the company is willing to take such a risk with people's lives," Liam broke in.

"Here it is," Jeffrey said. "I have a friend who once worked in surveillance for a governmental agency. He found evidence that Edward Warner, Dectel's senior vice-president, has a financial interest in the company that perfected 'pure' phiofomel. Ironic, the term 'pure.' It simply means industrial contaminants have been removed, so it is 'pure' for use in our communication components.

"The stuff has been used differently, so nobody tried to clean it up before. Big time money is in the offering." Jeffrey paused, a new idea had suddenly come to him. "Rosamund is at a conference right now that will send the price of Warner's new stock into outerspace. That's your 'why,' Liam."

Their hostess knocked on the door. "Need anything more, gentlemen?"

"You make great oatmeal cookies," Liam said. "May I have your recipe?"

Frank wandered from his monad energies. He saw the white car, two doors down the street, hidden by a curve outside the house in Dunwoody. "Well, Liam's tag has been stopped. Jeffrey evaded his. Ziegler is not in the surveillance net, yet. But Dr. Belden is a longtime threat. His 'spy' is more experienced. Let me see what can be done." Frank encountered Pet, Munje, and other energies in their monad on the edge of the ocean off the coast of New Orleans. "Palaver time, family," he said.

Jeffrey's friend drove the men to a different MARTA station when the meeting was finished. Ziegler and Belden sat at one end of the crowded coach. Jeffrey stayed near the niche where Liam's wheelchair fit. The motion of the train calmed him as he reviewed the afternoon's events. He felt they had accomplished something significant. They knew who was following them and why. The medical evidence should be pretty well irrefutable. In a few days, Dectel's board of directors and CEO would be sent the pertinent information. "They've got to listen this time," he said, unaware that he had spoken aloud.

"What did you say?" Liam was dozing, but he was startled awake by the intensity in Jeffrey's voice.

"Nothing important," Jeffrey bent to his ear. "Personal communication, that's all."

"Me, too," Liam grinned. "All about payment."

Rosamund landed in Atlanta on time, located her car, dropped her bag in the trunk, and drove to Dectel. Most of the building was recovering from lunch. "Did all go OK?" she asked Lois.

"Not a hitch. Your Caryl is fun. She and Meryl made a great fit. She charmed Mark. He barely tolerates girls, even his twin sister. I dropped Caryl at school on my way to the office." Lois appeared not to be worried about her impending layoff.

"I can't postpone the inevitable. I'll bet Warner has a full report on yesterday. Let's get it over with. Let him know that I am here." Rosamund's eyes were drawn to the photograph of Caryl on her desk She gave it a thumbs up, waiting for the call from Warner.

CHAPTER 17

Edward C. Warner and a man Rosamund had not seen before were waiting for her, this time in the small conference room. The one time Rosamund had been in there was when she was hired—scrutinized by several of the brass.

"This is Dr. Bill Northcroft, from our Denver facility, Mrs. Keyes." Warner seemed to be in a good mood. "Bill's down to give our operation the once-over."

Northcroft extended his hand. "I've heard of you Mrs. Keyes, one of our bright stars."

Wary of the pleasantries, Rosamund said, "Thank you." She waited for either of the men to take the lead.

"How was Chicago? Your first trip?" Northcroft continued.

"Why, no. I have friends from college who live there. I've visited on occasion."

"The South side?" Northcroft asked.

"My former roommate lives in Glenview; do you know the area?" Rosamund asked. He had named the neighborhood in Chicago where most African Americans traditionally lived.

A slight twitch in his voice let Rosamund know that he knew she had detected his racist assumption. "Not really," he said quickly.

Warner leaned back into his seat. "Now, to the confab. What have you to report?"

Rosamund chose her words carefully, "JCN wants to wait until the next-generation Speed-o-Lite is in production. I told the conferees that NetLink will be an actuality within one to two months."

Warner pulled his chair closer to the table. Abruptly, he said, "Woestmann says you angered the Muslim. We don't want an international incident, you know."

Rosamund was astonished at Warner's bigotry, but more at his willingness to show it. Was the man losing it? "I found Mr. Gebadd to be a fair man," she said. "He was not in the least upset. In fact, he said he appreciated my honesty."

"I wouldn't trust his words." Warner said. "That kind is skilled at saying one thing and doing the opposite."

A warning rumbled inside Rosamund. She was tired—the tension of the confab and lack of sleep—she ignored the little pull of caution. "If you have that opinion of the chief executive officer of a major international corporation because of his heritage, I can't imagine how you view me." The moment the words were out, she knew they were not "copacetic," as her father often said—"not cool," Caryl would say.

Northcroft came to life. "Mrs. Keyes, I think you are experiencing a bit of heightened stress. The report we have regarding the confab is that you embarrassed Mr. Gebadd. Everyone at the table saw it. Apparently, the man covered it well, but under the circumstances, we think you should take leave of absence until this thing is resolved."

"Resolved? There's nothing to resolve. I told you Mr. Gebbad was not offended." Rosamund felt a wave inundating her as if she was drowning in a bad dream.

"We can't take that chance, Mrs. Keyes." Warner came back. "We're going to have to put you on medical leave for a while—you'll stay on full salary until a full evaluation is completed."

Staring first at one then at the other—Warner, a punitive overseer; Northcroft, a stranger suddenly manifesting control over her life—Rosamund was unable to speak. She listened to them outline the conditions of her leave—her dismissal. Warner's squeaky voice penetrated.

"Dr. Northcroft agrees with me that you are under a great deal of pressure. Time off will give you a chance to rest and relax, and you'll remain on salary. You will be contacted as to the conditions of your return to your duties here at Dectel."

No longer smiling, Warner went to the conference-room door, opened it, and stood aside to let Rosamund pass.

How she found herself at her desk, she didn't know. Lois had gone; her desk was pristine and clear. Rosamund thought, *Dr. Northcroft, is he a psychologist or some kind of therapist? They want to say I'm crazy?* Automatically, Rosamund gathered her personal effects:

Caryl's photograph; a multicolored, crystal, good-luck pyramid on the bookcase; lotion; and a hairbrush from the bottom drawer of her desk. No one was in the outer area. Odd that everyone would go to lunch at the same time, even the girls from reception.

Rosamund made her way home. She wandered from room to room, trying to steady herself, glad that Caryl was at school. The passage of weeks had erased the faint fragrance of Aunt Pet from her room at the end of the hall. Rosamund moved back down the hall to Caryl's bedroom in a daze. The double-headed doll that Pet brought Caryl lie horizontally, its skirts askew, revealing its duality. The Indian half rested against Caryl's favorite, Lola. The African half leaned against a framed photograph of Caryl's father, Carl. Rosamund smoothed the bedcovers, picked up a sock dropped on its way to the hamper, straightened Lola, and put the two-headed doll on the top shelf of Caryl's bookcase.

In the kitchen, with a cup of tea circled by both hands, Rosamund tried to reconstruct the events that had slammed into her so suddenly and forcefully. The digits on the microwave clock showed nearly three hours before the end of the school day. Rosamund finished her tea, "Ma Belle," she said. She grabbed her keys and coat. Minutes later P. B., Ma Belle, and Rosamund were hunched around the small table at the rear of the exotic store.

"If I know the way those people's minds work, they think that getting you out of the building will end their worries. Right, Belle?" P. B. asked.

"Yeah, they don't know how bad treatment festers in our people. We got built-up marrow in our bones for bad treatment," the Creole woman said, a hint of mystery in her speech.

"I'm getting over the shock; I'm mad now," Rosamund said, squeezing the words from behind clenched teeth. She removed first one earring then another, as she shared the story of her encounter with Aklud Gebadd. When she finished her story, she absently put the small gold rings back in her ears.

"I think you have an ace up a sleeve that they don't know has an arm." P. B. almost shouted. "They don't know us, child, no they don't."

Ma Belle clapped her hands, then slammed them on the table. "P. B., you the whitest black man I ever heard. If there ever was an example of the truth of the soul and not the body, you are it, mais certainement."

"It's good to be acknowledged, Miss Belle," P. B. said. He executed a courtly bow. "We have got to get our chickens in a row," he said.

"Don't you mean ducks, P. B.?" Ma laughed.

"Don't care for ducks, too greasy. I'm a chicken man, myself," he laughed with her.

Rosamund was smiling. P. B. and Ma Belle gazed knowingly at one another. Laughter relieves body, mind, and spirit, regardless of trouble.

Ma Belle turned on the small television on a shelf in a corner of the room. "It's almost time for my dose of soaps," she said. "You all keep on strategizing. Don't mind me."

The five-minute-before-the-hour newsbreak began with the usual altercations from the wire services. Rosamund and P. B. stopped in mid-sentence at the words, "Dr. Ralph W. Belden, renowned chemist, was found dead at the bottom of a ravine in North Georgia this morning. The scientist had been a critic of American business in his advocacy for more stringent testing of chemicals in the manufacture of high-tech materials. Belden was fired from his position as top researcher at BAC, Inc., in 1985. The authorities are investigating the possibility of foul play . . ."

"Damn," Rosamund and P. B. uttered simultaneously.

"Tap or no tap, I've got to call Liam and Jeffrey. May I, Ma Belle?" Rosamund asked, already reaching for the telephone.

"Who's Dr. Belden, cherie?" Ma Belle moved the telephone to a more convenient spot on her cluttered table.

P. B. said, "He's the scientist who knows the truth about that poison Dectel says won't hurt anyone."

"I see. Sounds like the police don't need to investigate 'if' there's foul play. Does his death mess up what you folks are working on?" Ma Belle glanced at Rosamund; a frown crossed her normally cheerful face.

"Not by a long shot, I say," P. B. responded. "We're working on several fronts. No good strategist leaves his flank unprotected."

Rosamund returned to the table. "Liam can't make it. Lois isn't home to drive him. I reached Jeffrey on his cell phone. He will be here as soon as he can—he's on a job at the subfacility in Marietta."

A mile away, Caryl and Darren were leaving the computer lab for their classroom. Darren had not exhausted his excitement from his weekend in the mountains. "My dad and I tell stories together. He starts it, I tell the middle part, and he finishes it. Dad likes to pretend he's not going to tell me anymore, because I already know the story, but he's kidding. I know it."

"Neat," Caryl said. "Do you have a favorite story?"

"I have more than one. The one we told last time was about my second great-grandfather. He was raised by a nurse who took care of him when he was a baby. His mother 'pined away.' That's the way folks talked back then—they meant she was sick, I think. The nurse's name was Sariah. Isn't Sariah a funny name?"

"Not funny to me." Caryl slipped into her seat just before the teacher began to speak. "That's my mother's name. It's been in our family for years."

"For true? We'll have to tell your mother and my dad about that." Darren stopped talking. Mr. Thomas, was staring at him to get him quiet.

"Getting close, we are." Pet said to Munje and Frank.

"Like a jigsaw puzzle, one piece at a time."

"A grand puzzle it'll be when all the pieces are put together. Everybody is slipping in their piece," Frank said. "Look over there." A modest cabin sat, almost hidden by laurel bushes and dogwood trees in spring red and white bloom.

"I cannot stay," a tall, bronze man with flowing black hair held behind his ears by a strip of soft deer leather sits cross-legged on the ground before an ebony-colored teenaged girl. Their knees touch. Her hair is plaited in a pattern of rows that reveals the shape of her delicately rounded head. She holds a baby. The man lifts the child from its birch cradle and unwraps a berry-dyed blanket. He holds the infant in one arm and follows the contours of the child's body with his other hand. His eyes close. "So to remember her," he says.

"Can we not go with you?" the girl asks. "Ula is a good baby. She hardly cries, and she stops as soon as I give her my breast."

"It breaks my heart to leave you, Sariah. My ototema, my brothers and I will be killed if we stay. Other ototema, people of the wolf, are waiting for us a long walk from here." The man is He-Who Walks. He is dressed for a journey. He tells Sariah, "People of the cougar must find those who, like us, do not want to wait to be killed by the men whose families came from over the sea to Mother Turtle Island."

"You will have other children after you leave me, won't you?" Sariah asks.

"I do not have a crystal to say what will happen." He opens a pouch from around his neck. Inside is a mixture of sweet-smelling grasses. He reaches in the pouch, then uses his thumb and small finger to form circles on the forehead, abdomen, and buttocks of the infant. The child makes soft sounds as her father marks her.

"This medicine will teach her in dreams of my people, her father's people. It will be in her as the blood is in her—your line and mine, together." The tall man of the Catawba wraps his arms around Sariah and their child; their heads touch. "In the great Pass On, we are always together. It is important that you and I have met and mingled."

He-Who Walks and Sariah do not cry at their parting. He lifts his roll to his back and joins his brothers, who waited in the woods.

Pet was transfixed before the scene. "My great-grandmother," she sighed so forcefully the loggers who were working on the side of a hill had their orange protective helmets blown off.

"A grand mother, indeed," Munje echoed.

Frank glanced forward and backward from his vantage point in timelessness, "We couldn't do anything for Belden. He understands."

Jeffrey came into Ma Belle's from his secret approach. "I heard about Belden on the car radio." He tossed his jacket onto the worn couch and dropped into a chair at the table around which Rosamund and P. B. sat. "There's more funny stuff going on than I can imagine. I'm ready to swear that the guy in the car that tried to follow me here is the same guy who moved into my apartment building. Fellow named Jensen, with a broken nose. I'm pretty sure I lost him."

"Big, broken nose?" P. B. perked up. "I'll give you a dollar for a dime if he's not one of the guys in that car I stopped the day they tried to follow Rosamund." He took out a brown envelope he carried in an old briefcase. "Look here, Jensen works for Dectel Security. That's Jensen, Hudson, and Gray on surveillance, as far as I've been able to find."

"Wait a sec. Give me first names," Jeffrey said.

P. B. held the paper closer to the light, "Computer-paper letters don't come out dark enough—ah, here—William Jensen, Samuel Hudson, and Anthony Gray. There could be more, but . . ."

Jeffrey stopped him, "Sam Hudson, the little weasel! Filthy, double-dealing, slime—pretending to be friendly. I never liked the smell of him."

"We know two of them. Good." P. B. made notations. "What about you, Rosamund?"

She shook her head no. "Just Sam Hudson. Only because I've seen him with you, Jeffrey. Gray might be the one who tried the interstate ploy with me. My guy didn't have a broken nose. I wonder which one of them cut Lois's tires."

"Or followed Darren and me to the mountains," Jeffrey added.

"We have two faces to match with names; this should be a help," Rosamund said. "We have to figure our next step. Omigosh, are our kids safe? For the first time I'm *really* scared. I was concerned, but I'm scared now—for my daughter and Darren."

Ma Belle had been standing inside the door for several moments. She had taken care of her customers. "This business is thicker than jambalaya," Ma Belle said. "All because of a little bit of chemistry. Mon Dieu, I made 'A' in chemistry in high school. I don't remember it being such a big deal." She pushed the power button on the television, "I don't need soap operas. Real life has more suds."

CHAPTER 18

"We are dealing with people who play for keeps." Jeffrey paced in the small room. The man who loved the out-of-doors seemed, to his friends, out of place in the confinement. "Rosamund, you and I are adults. We can take what we get, or we pay the consequence. But I want to get our kids out of this town for a while."

Rosamund studied her calendar. "I can get the school to excuse Caryl early and send her to my folks in Ohio. What do you think, P. B.?"

"I think you think right, "P. B. said. "It would relieve the pressure on you two, and it would keep the kids out of harm's way. How can we get them out of Atlanta without being noticed?"

Ma Belle chimed in. "I can manage that. You get them ready. I'm descended from pirate people. I know how to disappear grown folks and little children, for sure."

"Jeffrey, I'll talk to the children's core teacher about homework while they are away," Rosamund said.

"Good idea. Thanks." Jeffrey said. "I've only spoken with Mr. Thomas by phone. He sounds like a guy who cares about kids. I'll call him to verify it's okay for you to get Darren's assignments," Jeffrey's face was strained. So was his voice.

Rosamund called the school for an appointment with Mr. Thomas. He told her to come over after school. He coached then and would watch for her in the gym. Rosamund found Thomas as he was dismissing his basketball players.

"Mrs. Jones-Keyes, the parent of my budding Madam President. What can I do for you?" the still-in-great-form, athletic coach asked.

"Madam President? I expect her to be a new pioneer in psychology, you know, after Jung and June Singer."

"That's a new thought. She can combine statesmanship and therapy . . . we could use both." Mr. Thomas wiped perspiration from his upper lip.

Up a flight of stairs that carried the odors of years of small bodies, they followed the glass-topped line of doors down a corridor to Mr. Thomas's office.

"Caryl is going to go to my parents' in Ohio, tomorrow, and I would like to have directions for home and makeup work for her." Rosamund handed him a note that Jeffrey had hastily written. "Mr. Shuggs asked that I do the same for Darren—we're neighbors. Darren is going to be out of the city, also. He called you, I believe." Rosamund didn't notice that her hands were nervously rubbing together.

Thomas sensed her uneasiness. "I don't mean to pry, but is there a problem? The children have been doing well, as always. Darren, especially, is more relaxed than I've seen him all year."

"I can't tell you anything, only that it will be safer for them to be away from the city right now." Rosamund steadied her hands, giving Mr. Thomas her professional façade.

"All right. I can't say that I am reassured. I respect your privacy." He began writing. "If there is any way I can help—any way—please call on me. I am fond of all my students, and these two are among the best I've ever had." He removed several pages from a notebook and put them into two large envelopes. "Have you notified the principal's office?"

"I did, on my way to see you. All the arrangements are legal," Rosamund took the envelopes. Mr. Thomas's handshake was firm and comforting.

On the way to her car, Rosamund remembered his well-groomed nails. *No slob,* she thought. She smoothed back her hair that she was letting grow out. The movement lifted her eyes toward the second floor of the school building. Mr. Thomas was looking down from his office window. Unlocking her car door, she smiled up at him.

"Mums, I will be absolutely ecstatic to see Granddaddy and Nana, and if you won't tell me the reason I'm getting out of school a whole week before break, that's OK with me. I trust you." Caryl packed her favorite toys and two books, to read on the plane, in her backpack.

"It is best this way, Puddin'—and thanks for trusting me. I know you're itching to know—trust me." *Indeed. Who else?*

"Can't I just call Darren to tell him, and my best girlfriends, Misty and Jennifer?" Caryl, who had grown nearly two inches in the past few months, asked.

"I'll see that they know you're away as soon as it is s——. I mean as soon as . . ." The doorbell rang. Rosamund hurried to answer it. Jeffrey's neighbor, Miss McRay, was outside her door. She was flushed from her brisk walk.

"I feel I'm in one of my mystery stories," Darren's after-school sitter said. "Here's a note from Mr. Shuggs. He said I was to be sure no one followed me, so I went to a movie—only stayed fifteen minutes—the film wasn't good."

Rosamund took the note. "Would you like a cup of tea or coffee, Miss McRay?"

"Thank you, no, my dear. Even though the movie wasn't good, I'm going back. The cashier is a friend of mine. I told her I'd be back shortly. She'll let me in."

Abruptly, the diminutive, energetic woman waved good-bye, wheeled around, and left Rosamund standing with her mouth agape.

Jeffrey's note read: "I didn't have the privilege of a face-to-face firing. My 'pink slip' came by messenger. I am 'insubordinate' and 'tardy.'" He included a telephone number, one that belonged to his wife's layover apartment in Nashville. "I'll be in touch after Ma Belle has taken Darren to my cousin Lottie's."

Rosamund finished packing for Caryl. Ma Belle would take Caryl to Asheville for her flight to Ohio. Her son would drive Darren to North Carolina to his cousins. In the rush of preparations, Rosamund had told Ma Belle, "I feel as if our children are going on the Underground Railroad—like slavery time." She permitted herself a joke. "There weren't any airline tickets, were there?"

Cloak-and-dagger plans finished, Rosamund stared at the television set, the evening news talking heads going on and on. She barely touched her dinner. The after-school helper was informed that although Caryl would be away a week early she would be paid.

"Aunt Pet, I'd love a warm slice of your gingerbread and lemon sauce right now." Rosamund said, holding the photograph of Pet on her wedding day. She had moved it from the bedroom to a table alongside a chair in the living room. She absently flicked from channel to channel. On a noncommercial station, two commentators were listening to a woman wearing large, black-rimmed glasses and a decidedly unfashionable suit.

"Dr. Belden was on the verge of presenting data on the dangers of a chemical that is used in the production of communications components. The chemical is highly toxic," the woman said.

"What is the chemical?" the male interviewer asked.

"I'd rather not say at this time. We hope that Dr. Belden's murder will not stop the work he was doing." The woman was nearly in tears.

"You mean 'alleged murder,' don't you?" the woman commentator asked.

"You can be politically correct if you wish. I have no such constraints. The doctor was murdered as surely as you and I sit here." Her teary demeanor disappeared. Belden's colleague, whoever she was, was emphatic.

"Right, Sister, the wash will be hung out to dry." Pet's energy was above the table on which her wedding picture sat. She was alone. Munje was following Caryl outside her airplane window. Caryl dozed: a brown man in a football player's uniform caught a ball. The team wasn't the Atlanta Falcons; the name on the front could be Angels, but his face was the same as the soldier she had dreamed of many times.

Frank's energy floated over the back of a pickup truck. He looked into the rear window. Darren and his cousin, Frank, Lottie's son, were excited by the unexpected visit they would have together.

In the Atlanta apartment, Pet smiled as she imagined Rosamund, Aklud Gebadd, and Mr. Thomas, whose name was Evan. "Nothing wrong with having two helpers in a body's life," she mused. The warmth in the room made Rosamund check the thermostat.

In a few days, we can turn the heat off, Rosamund thought. The news program ended. She turned off the set. There was nothing worth watching until ten o'clock. She took her tray to the kitchen and cleaned her dishes. At her worktable in the living room, Rosamund put the final disk into her computer. "The man had to slip up, just once, and I'll find it," she said, her brow tensed, her bottom lip between her teeth, and one earring on its way to the ceramic saucer on the desk.

Jeffrey and Dr. Ziegler were in P. B.'s car beside Hartwell Lake, on the Georgia side of the divide with South Carolina. The men were dressed as fishermen, caps obscuring their eyes.

"Too bad Liam can't be here. He said his wheelchair might attract attention." Jeffrey said. "It is probably better if one of us is never with all the others, in case we encounter problems."

"We can't have fatalistic thoughts like that, man," P. B. said. "You're with a preacher, and I've asked for protection from our enemies."

"Sorry, Reverend. I think of you as an investigator these days; I forget your other side," Jeffrey told him.

To his other companion, Jeffrey said, "Dr. Ziegler, I'm sorry about your colleague, Dr. Belden. We have more reason to take this thing all the way to the wire, now."

Dr. Ziegler was shaken. "Having to acknowledge that educated, well-placed people will kill a good man to protect a dollar's worth of material goods is not easy," he said, taking fishing gear from the trunk of the car. "Belden wasn't a punk; he spent his life in scholarship."

"Scholarship and things like honesty and decency are not marketable." Jeffrey checked to see if everything was out of the trunk.

"What do you have for us, doctor?" P. B. asked.

Dr. Ziegler unfolded a paper he took from his coat pocket. "Da Legra of Italy reported six unexplained cases of paralysis among workers in a subsidiary of Dectel. The company produces link components for the merger between Dectel Global and JCN. Those corporations are almost equal giants in the field. Do you see what I see?" Ziegler handed the paper to Jeffrey, who read it and gave it to P. B.

"The breakdown appears to have begun earlier than we calculated. I don't know exactly what has happened. Maybe the chemical coating is stronger than they planned, or the heat buildup is interfacing more rapidly, or it may be something we never anticipated. We may be getting a large part of our problem solved for us—naturally."

"Dr. Ziegler's legal people want to combine Liam's case with the ones in Italy and elsewhere. That will not be easy. The big boys have ways to scatter the focus on their culpability." Jeffrey was thinking aloud.

"I'm in over my head," P. B. said. "Low-level shenanigans I can work with, but I can't follow you into deep scientific byways."

"Don't play yourself cheap, P. B. You are invaluable." Jeffrey squeezed the older man's shoulders, their eyes mirroring friendliness. "A problem is best solved when different skills come together. I know from watching the ways animals, birds, wind, sun, and water function together in my mountains."

Dr. Ziegler said, "I definitely agree. Our working together is a first-rate example of an early NASA moon-rescue exercise. People from a number of backgrounds and training get to choose a specific number of tools—say a rope, thermometer, pail, and -so -on—from a long list. Their job is to plan how to get them, safely, to a rendezvous with a rescue vehicle after they are lost on the moon. When the group uses only one kind of expertise, say an engineer or pilot, they don't do as well as when they listen to a farmer or a child, too."

P. B. laughed. "I never thought of myself as an astronaut. That would cut some big shots down to human size."

"Maybe we're all astronauts, exploring space in our own ways," Ziegler warmed to the concept.

Jeffrey bantered, "Why, Dr. Ziegler, I believe you have a touch of the metaphysical in you."

"I wouldn't go that far," Ziegler blushed. "But, we certainly are a long way from knowing all we need to know. That's what science is really about, not knowing it all."

"We may as well try our luck in the lake as long as we are here," said P. B. "A two-hour drive shouldn't be only for business. All work, you know."

"Rosamund nor I have jobs at this point. Does anyone think we can catch enough fish for meals until we have new employment?" Jeffrey tied a colorful fly to his line. "I'm sure Warner set Rosamund up for a fall. I wouldn't be surprised if he set the company up for one, too. I haven't figured out why. Rosamund is searching for a tie-in with a record at Dectel that makes sense."

P. B. spoke proudly: "If anybody can find it, that lady can."

In the comfortable Decatur house east of Atlanta, Lois and Liam were on the verge of having a serious argument. Lois paced the floor between the dining area and the kitchen. Liam sat in front of the television. He lowered the volume. "I want to call the station. You know the only way anything gets open and changed is when the media get hold of it." Liam held the remote loosely in the hand that retained the most muscle strength.

"We don't know if they'll even care, and suppose those gangsters Dectel has watching us blow us away? Do you want to take that chance?" Lois retorted.

"Look at us, now. I can't work. You've been laid off. What future do the twins have? I don't believe in sitting on the side, doing nothing. We'd die on welfare—which I'd never take. I've got to get you and the children some kind of way out of this." He wheeled his chair toward the dining area. "Please, say you'll go along? We don't have a way out."

"Let me think on it," Lois said. "I'll be back soon." She put on walking shoes and went outside, letting the door slam.

She was back soon. "All right, love, if you want this so bad, I'm with you. Seems the night sky tells me to go along with you."

The person at the television news desk listened to Liam's explanation: that Liam knew Dr. Belden and that he, Liam, was paralyzed by the chemical Dr. Belden knew about, and, yes, Liam was let go—on disability—by Dectel Global after his accident. The journalist would come with a crew in the morning. If the story was worth anything, it would make the evening news.

Liam had not finished dressing when the new station's truck rolled into their driveway. Two men and two women were in the Hardys' living room with camera, lights, and sound equipment as quickly as one might expect firemen to arrive at a fire.

"Mr. Hardy, are you a veteran?" one of the media guys asked. A microphone hung from the lapel of Liam's suit coat. He insisted on dressing for the interview.

"Yes, sir, I am," Liam said.

"How do you know you aren't a victim of Agent Orange?" the man interrogated.

"Because I never went to Vietnam. I was born in '59. My service was 1978 to 1982. I was stateside, except a short tour in Hawaii." Liam was annoyed by the man's quick assumptions.

"That's good," the reporter warmed to his questioning. Liam made a sympathetic character in his wheelchair. "What does Dectel Global attribute your paralysis to?"

"They say it's genetic. No one in my family was ever paralyzed, especially not after passing out in a laboratory full of chemical odors." It was Liam's time to warm to the exchange. "I say it's a cover-up."

The camera moved closer to Liam. The next "question" was a comment. "Companies are having problems with workers pretending disabilities. Maybe they think you're playing that game for millions in compensation."

"Man, I can't play with my children or dance with my wife. Nobody in their right mind would play such a dumb game. Let me tell you something. I think Dr. Belden was killed because he knew the facts about that chemical."

The camera spotted the reporter, "Mr. Liam Hardy, a veteran, accuses Dectel Global of being responsible for his paralysis. We will ask Dectel to respond to his charge. Does the death of Dr. Belden have a tie-in to Mr. Hardy's disability? Stay tuned for this late-breaking story of corporate and individual tug of war."

The media man signaled to the technicians to stop taping. He removed his microphone and smiled at Liam for the first time since coming in the door. "OK, Hardy, I don't know if any of it will make the six -o'clock. If my producer thinks there's anything to your story, you'll see it. Don't think I mean to be tough. The station and the audience expect us to be detectives—it's called investigative reporting. I have to take that tact. No hard feelings?"

"Now that you've explained, no hard feelings." Liam and the journalist made high-fives.

The camera and sound men were in the truck calling for the reporter to hurry. They had to get to the next action as quickly as they had burst in at the Hardys'.

"Are you nuts, calling me on this phone?" Rosamund announced to Jeffrey's carefree 'Good morning, Mrs. JK.'

"They can't do any more than they have. Hell, we're both on the dole—at least I am. Let's have lunch at the little café."

"Why not? We can't go to Dectel's cafeteria. Our badges have been confiscated. Maybe we'll run into some of our coworkers. I mean, former coworkers."

Rosamund stopped by Caryl's room. The quietness, the unslept in bed were disconcerting. She wondered if Jeffrey were doing the same. She dressed and went to walk in the park.

Rosamund had stayed awake until after two last night. She had not found what she needed from Warner's file and was more tired than usual on her return from her walk. She set the alarm to give her time to shower and meet Jeffrey after a short nap. She took her notes and the disks into Caryl's room, where Aunt Pet's gift doll set proudly on its shelf. Lola was in Caryl's backpack, but given Caryl's community of dolls and stuffed animals, no one was lonely.

"I'll feel fresher, later. This time, I'll find it, "she said, closing the door behind her.

"Never too old to learn, in this time or another. Take notice, Uncle." Pet sent a gleeful message to Munje, who was simulating his skill at fishing.

"Lessons, lessons, will they ever cease?" Munje's fly cast snagged on a simulated bush.

CHAPTER 19

The private entrance to Warner's office opened and closed three times. Each time, Warner brusquely motioned to the newcomer to sit. Sam Hudson, Bill Jensen, and Tony Gray were quiet while Warner completed his conversation.

"What are you going to do to chase the authorities away from us on this Belden mess?" Warner glared at Jensen and Gray. "I said shake him up, scare him off, not kill him, you idiots!"

Gray, thin and solemn, shrugged. His eyes settled on Jensen. "It was a mistake, Mr. Warner. We only meant to scare the doctor. He ran off the mountain like he wanted to go, like he wanted to implicate—put the blame on somebody. I saw his face, almost peaceful-like, the moment he went over the side."

"Don't blame me," Jensen defended. "I wasn't in the friggin' car."

"I wasn't blaming you," Gray said. "You're in charge of the operation; you set it up."

"It's no difference to me who is to blame. What are you going to do about it, now?" Warner lowered his voice. He didn't want Miss D'Arcy to hear.

"I don't know how you could be implicated, Mr. Warner. There're lots of people, in lots of places, who wanted Belden off their cases." Jensen knew he wasn't in trouble. He wasn't a hired goon. He was legitimate, head of internal security for Dectel.

"That's a happy thought." Warner's face made a lie of his words. "I can't afford to have anyone else hurt. Just that evidence Shuggs or Jones-Keyes stole from this building. Once I'm in the clear, I want the matter wiped clean. You'll all get a nice holiday in the islands. No hillbilly or jungle bunny is going to bring me down."

Sam said, "We picked up an exchange between Shuggs and

Jones this morning. They're having lunch at the deli around the corner from here. I'm going to offer him my condolences."

"Do you think Shuggs connects you with this job?" Jensen asked.

"No chance. Do you think he knows who you are?" Sam asked.

"I'm clean," Jensen said.

"I believe the mountain man is beginning to like me," Sam said, as he left for the restaurant.

"The woman saw me. I'll stay clear," Gray said.

Warner glanced at his watch. "Get on with it, Sam. The rest of you be ready to defend yourselves if the police find anything. Tell the other men as well. I don't know you, never saw or heard of any of you"

Rosamund arrived at the restaurant before Jeffrey. She heard someone call to her from a nearby booth.

"Rhoda, Kekisha," she said and bent to hug the women from reception with whom she had celebrated her escape from Warner's wrath.

"We're tired of the Dectel cafeteria menu," Kekisha said. "I had no idea you'd be here." Kekisha's eyes filled with tears.

"We heard what happened to you. We're so sorry." Rhoda was a large amber-colored woman whose embrace swallowed Rosamund in soft, warm folds. "The word is that you'll be back, but when?"

Kekisha was pencil thin. She liked to refer to her appearance as "teasing tan." She and Rhoda were an odd pair. Kekisha wanted to have her breasts enlarged and teased Rhoda about "borrowing" from her ample supply. "Do you know how soon you'll back?" Kekisha asked.

"The strangest thing happened since we last saw you." Rhoda gestured for Rosamund to sit beside her. "Miss D'Arcy and the office manager summoned everyone in the department to take some kind of stupid personality test. That's why we didn't know you were gone until just before everybody left. Personnel leaked the news." Rhoda always knew Dectel's inner workings, the behind-the-scenes of statistics and analysis department and most of the Atlanta office.

Rosamund looked around the busy room. "I'm meeting Mr. Shuggs." Being with the women made her feel good. Good things were happening to her in Atlanta amidst the shocks that were bombarding her.

"We heard Shuggs got the shaft, too," Kekisha said.

"Yes," Rosamund said. "I'm glad to know why no one was in the office when I left. I thought you all were avoiding me."

"Not in a dozen lifetimes," Rhoda declared. "All the sisters in the sec pool and the programmers have been praying and wanting you to show those honkies. We're proud of you, girl. Don't you know? The few Hispanics they've let in the door are rooting for you, and some whites, although they don't broadcast it."

Rosamund's eyes brimmed. "I didn't know. I love you girls." She took the tissue Kekisha pushed toward her. Jeffrey was standing beside the booth when she lowered the tissue from her eyes. She saw that the women from reception were uncomfortable with his being there. "Don't worry," Rosamund smiled at one then the other, "this man is almost a soul brother. He puts away a mean gumbo."

Tension eased. Rosamund and Jeffrey took the booth behind the women.

"Just food, no business." Rosamund signaled "time-out."

"No argument from me," Jeffrey responded. "I'm tired of intrigue. The children are safe. The police and the media are chasing down the Belden story; I'm all for enjoying an hour or two—and I'm hungry."

The waitress took their orders. When she left, she murmured something that sounded like "cheap." Sam Hudson was coming toward Rosamund and Jeffrey, a cup of coffee in his hand.

"Mind if I join you?" He smiled, slid into the booth beside Jeffrey before a word could be said. "I heard about your bad news, old buddy. You, too, Mrs. Jones-Keyes. There's got to be a mistake."

Jeffrey began, "You're damn right there is, and . . ."

Rosamund kicked him under the table. "Thanks for your concern. Somebody's dirty linen will be washed and hung out to dry, soon," she said, giving Sam a disarming smile.

Recovering composure, Jeffrey took his cue from Rosamund. "Sure, Sam, it has to be a mistake. In the meantime, Mrs. JK and I are eating our last meal out for a while. We both need to watch the bank balance until things straighten out."

Sam asked, "Do you have a family, Mrs. Jones-Keyes? I know my pal, Jeffrey, has a fine boy."

"I have one, myself," Rosamund jabbed an artichoke. Despite her intentions, it was not easy to sit across from the man.

Sam stopped slurping his coffee. "A boy, I thought you had a girl."

"How do you know she has a girl?" Jeffrey glared.

Sam reddened. "Don't know. Maybe somebody mentioned it. I was just making small talk—you know how it is."

Rosamund kicked Jeffrey a second time. "I meant one child. Sam is psychic, aren't you, Sam?" She managed a laugh.

"Yeah, yeah, psychic, that's it." Sam gulped his coffee. "Gotta run. See you around, Shuggs, ma'am."

The waitress came to clear the booth, "That guy is the cheapest creep to come in this place."

"So that's it. I heard you say something when you took our orders." Rosamund was searching her purse for her wallet. "I thought you meant one of us."

"Not you folks. I've seen you in here lots of times. You're good." The waitress scooped the dime tip Sam left. She would come for Rosamund and Jeffrey's after they left. She knew it would not be paltry.

Rosamund gathered her purse and new knit cap. "Very important part of the action," she said, adding to the tip that Jeffrey had left for the waitress.

Kekisha and Rhoda paused by the booth.

"If I can help you, ask me, you hear?" Rhoda bent to whisper. "There's no love between Dectel and me."

"I'll remember. Thank you." Rosamund gave them another quick hug. She and Jeffrey left the restaurant behind the women from Dectel, their allies.

Rosamund and Jeffrey went down the block to a tiny art gallery. "It isn't the High Museum," she said. "But it is a respectable respite to digest lunch."

"We don't need verification on Sam Hudson after his slip-up," Jeffrey said, writing on a pad.

"He's in the situation up to his follicles," Rosamund said. "We have to find his connection to Warner, and what he is looking for."

"With the kids away, and twenty-four hours a day to get ourselves cleared, we have time to break this horror story," Jeffrey said. "I can't get a reference with this dismissal on my resumé." For the first time Jeffrey was dejected, and it showed.

"I want to get back to my homework. How about Ma Belle's tomorrow at four—is that okay?" Rosamund said.

"Right," Jeffrey said.

At home, Rosamund retrieved the disk she had stored in the African half of Caryl's doll. She took her phone off the hook and began to methodically peruse Warner's records from Dectel. Two hours, later she left the console to rest her eyes and stretch.

She put an exercise tape in the VCR. A few minutes into the routine, her doorbell rang. Grabbing a towel to wipe her face, she went to the door—thinking it might be Jeffrey, or Miss McRay, perhaps P. B.—although she wasn't expecting anyone.

The security hole revealed a face she did not recognize.

"Who is it?" she asked cautiously. "Who do you want?"

The man was in a chauffeur's uniform. "Mrs. Rosamund Jones-Keyes, is it you? Mr. Aklud Gebadd asks to see you. He is worried. You were not at your office."

Rosamund was not going to be taken in. "If Mr. Gebadd wants to see me, tell him to come up here, so I can see him." Warner and other Dectel people knew of the meeting in Chicago.

"Yes, madam. I will." The man turned and went back to the elevator.

Not believing what was happening Rosamund picked up the telephone then placed it back in its cradle, remembering the tap. She glanced around for a weapon—nothing except an ornamental walking cane from a visit to a theme park. She waited, feeling trapped in her own home but glad that Caryl was safe in Ohio with her parents.

The doorbell rang again. On the other side of the door stood the now-familiar Aklud Gebadd.

"I don't believe this," she said, opening the door. "I feel stupid, insisting that you come in person, I . . ."

Sri Gebadd interrupted her confused run-on. "I was told when I called your office that you were no longer with Dectel. Your personal number was busy for more than two hours. I became concerned."

Rosamund regained her equilibrium. "Please come in; sit down. Is your driver with you? I want to apologize."

"After he brought me to your door, I asked him to wait in the car," Gebadd said. "Something is terribly wrong. Tell me what has occurred. Has it anything to do with the meeting in Chicago?"

"Yes and no," she said. "First, let me make us some tea, then we can talk." Rosamund looked at the most powerful man she had ever known—nor had anyone like him known her.

In the kitchen, preparing tea, she recalled what Aunt Pet had told Caryl when Caryl was in awe of a famous rap star. "Everybody gets in their pants the same way," Pet had said.

At that moment, Rosamund snapped back to herself. Aklud Gebadd was a thoughtful man who was concerned for her safety. That was all there was to his coming to her apartment, she told herself.

In the living room, Rosamund put the tea tray on the coffee table. Gebadd placed the photograph of Caryl back in its place. "Your daughter is beautiful. Her eyes tell of intelligence and wisdom," he said.

"Now," he said, sipping kukicha tea, "tell me what you will."

The gist of the story was unraveled for Gebadd. Explaining the phiofomel problem to him gave Rosamund opportunity to see things from a different perspective. She said, "Telling you the story helps to give me a better grasp of what Jeffrey knows a lot better than I do. I know, now, what I need to look for in my analysis of Warner's records. I haven't found the hidden trail, yet."

"It appears to me that Mr. Edward Warner will have to be extracted from the wall he thinks he has built around himself," Gebadd said. "I have people I trust at JCN. After all, I, too, am being played the fool."

"All this because I insulted you," Rosamund ventured a laugh.

"When honesty becomes an insult, we have lost our humanity," Gebadd smiled in return. "This is enough business. You promised to show me a different Atlanta than downtown, tall buildings, and fancy eating places. Do you feel up to it? With all the turmoil whirring around you, I think you can benefit from respite and relaxation." He stood and held out his hand to Rosamund.

"Is it safe for the chief executive officer and president of JCN International to wander around Atlanta without entourage?" she asked. Rosamund didn't know people who had chauffeurs at their call. A hired limo, yes, but not personal and permanent.

"Only rock and cinema stars are at risk. No one knows people like me, unless, like Iacocca, I choose to do my own commercials." Gebadd enjoyed her concern.

"Give me time for a quick change. I know just the place to

begin." Rosamund was relaxed and pleased with the way the day was ending.

P. B. Preston's "contacts" came through for him once again. He was shopping at Ma Belle's. He showed her a paper from his always-present briefcase. "Look, Belle, the cars that stopped Rosamund and wrecked Jeffrey's car are both registered to a dummy company set up by a "C. Varne," but paid from a numbered account in the name of Edward C. Warner—not very imaginative, I say."

Ma Belle bagged P. B.'s purchase, waited on another customer, then asked, "You all be coming here tomorrow evening? I want to make something special for you, my praline cake. Is it coming up soon, celebration time?"

"Don't know, yet. I never count my chickens before they hatch." He carefully folded and replaced the form for the dummy account in his breast pocket. "These are some deviling white folks. You make that cake, just the same. Good or bad, we can sweeten the way."

Lois answered the telephone. "That's three television stations and the *Atlanta Journal-Constitution* who want to interview you," she told Liam. "I don't understand. Why so much attention now? They didn't care when you were first hurt." She sat at the dining table where Liam was putting together an electronic game for Meryl and Mark.

"I think the public is getting-on to industrial accidents, toxic wastes, all sorts of hidden, secret stuff for a long time." Liam put down his screwdriver and reached for Lois's hand. "It's not me, honey. I'm a minnow. Could be, I'll be a catalyst for people's pent-up frustration."

"Mrs. JK says she's going to have the data on Mr. Warner's part in our trouble very shortly. Will that bring this trouble to a close?" Lois asked, her smooth brown face leaning on Liam's hand that covered hers.

"It will," he reassured her. He didn't want to let her know that he could only hope it would.

Rosamund had Gebadd's chauffeur drive through the part of the city where the historic black colleges and universities and the

M. L. King Memorial were located. She told him what she knew of Spelman, Clark, Morehouse, Morris Brown, and Atlanta University, showing him the new medical college and the interdenominational seminary.

She said, "I've lived all my life in the Midwest. I don't know much about these places, only what my parents told me. They suggested I look them up when I moved here. I would like for Caryl to choose one of these schools when she is ready for college."

"Are all religions taught at the seminary or just Christian denominations?" Gebadd asked.

"To be honest, I haven't a clue," she said. "That's an interesting question. When things are back to normal, I'm going to find out."

Gebadd's chauffeur had no difficulty finding his way around the city. Rosamund said, "There is much more to see, but it is getting dark. Perhaps, another time."

"Definitely, another time," he said. Gebadd had been watching her enthusiasm for the sights.

"With you, time passes so quickly. I did not notice. Tonight I will put my people on the trail of the man who does not appreciate a highly competent and dedicated member of his organization," he said. "I will call you, if you do not mind."

"No, you can't call. My telephone calls are intercepted." Rosamund was surprised by the quiver in her voice. "I will call you from a pay phone."

Gebadd studied his watch then began entering notations his car's electronic console.

She watched him, wondering what the device was and how it worked. Her cell phone was a can and string compared to the technology in Gebadd's car.

He noticed her interest. "I have made transfers to all my calendars in every JCN facility around the world. My people know where I am at all times. They will know not to schedule anything for me in the times I have blanked out."

"Wonderful," Rosamund said. She almost uttered Caryl's favorite, "neat." "By the way, Mr. Gebadd, would you like to meet the man who has been paralyzed, Liam Hardy?"

"Enough 'Mr. Gebadd,' please. I am Al to you. Yes, as soon as it is convenient, I want to meet the young man."

At her apartment building, Gebadd told his driver to record

the license number of the car that had followed them from the time they left Rosamund's apartment.

"I have already done so, sir," the man told him.

"Good job, Khalil."

Inside her living room, Rosamund leaned against the door for a full minute before she recovered. "I think I'm in over my depth, Auntie," she said to the photograph in front of her. "I'm not the best swimmer in the world."

"You're good enough and better, so far as I can see," Pet retorted. "I've said all along. Everything will be just fine."

"No, you didn't say that," Munje whirled around her.

"You said, 'There's a way,'" Frank reminded her.

"Whatever." Pet popped herself beside Aklud Gebadd on his way to his hotel—to enjoy the pleased expression on his face.

The blinking light on Rosamund's answering machine caught her attention. Taking off her shoes and earrings, she heard, "Mrs. Jones-Keyes, this is Evan Thomas. I hope everything is good with you. Your phone was busy most of the afternoon. Don't forget, I am available when you need me."

"Drops of rain or buckets of sleet—too much," she said to the machine, saving the tape with Thomas's home number.

CHAPTER 20

Rosamund awakened early with a sharp awareness of having dreamed of dancers in the shape of the alphabet playing a game of tag with the numerals 0 to 9. For over two hours, she scrolled lines of data, seeking a pattern—a clue—to the puzzle of how Warner had manipulated funds and materiel.

"Did it!" she almost exploded. She pushed back in her chair so forcefully she was propelled into a file cabinet—more than a foot behind her. "Mr. Shrewd hid his transfers in numerical anagrams of his and his wife's initials," she said.

She carefully wrote the codes and their translations:

> E. C. Warner's Hidden Accounts:
> DOT - 53
> Deo - 35
> Ero - 40
> Meo - 40

DOT = transfers to DOT from Dectel.
Deo = transfers to Dectel and independent operators off payroll: Hudson, Jensen, Gray, and other operatives.
Ero = transfers between European subsidiaries and DOT.
Meo = transfers between Dectel and Central and South American subsidiaries

She knew there would be codes for Asia and Africa, following the same system, and they could be easily accessed, now that she knew what to look for.

She was elated. She wanted to call Jeffrey and Gebadd—she didn't think of him as Al; he didn't look like an Al—but how to get to a phone without being seen? She remembered her neighbor, Miss DeLong. She would ask to use her telephone.

Miss DeLong was not home. The only thing to do was leave the building. She had plenty of time before she would meet Jeffrey and P. B. at Ma Belle's.

"Shopping," she said, snapping her fingers. "Women are expected to shop." Rosamund grinned with relief for having made the breakthrough. "On the crest of the hill," she hummed while she dressed in a fun outfit, one she would never wear to the office. Singing softly, Rosamund almost skipped to her car.

At Gwinnett Mall, shoppers were in a happy mood. At first, she kept looking behind her to find the source of their pleasure. Her reflection in the expanse of mall glass gave her the answer, her outfit—cinnamon, red, and green wide-legged pants, cinnamon scarf flowing around the neck of a matching top. Her long-legged, energetic stride and good looks brought a sunny response from shoppers.

Rosamund bought a burgundy leather belt in a specialty shop, asked for the ladies room, and made her call from the phone around a corner, outside the restroom.

"You are a marvel," Gebadd said from his private line. "I don't believe you need have any more fear of those 'goons,' as you call them. Will you meet me for lunch at Coaches Six?"

"I can," she said. "I can't call Jeffrey, but I can get in touch with P. B. Preston. I told you about him."

"You did." Gebadd said. "I have my aide already following your decoded pattern. My car will arrive for you at one o'clock."

Rosamund left her car in the parking lot of the mall to be retrieved later. Customers were curious watching the young African-American woman escorted into the beautiful car by a liveried chauffeur. Glances at the license plate showed it was not a rented livery.

Lunch was delightful. Gebadd had reserved a table in a private dining room. He toasted Rosamund. "My compliments to a most astute analyst and the most persistent young woman I've ever seen in the corporate world. Last night, you were not sure that you could find the hidden accounts. Within an hour or two of awakening, you have found them. Excellent!" he sounded nearly as happy as Rosamund.

Rosamund had no idea how he would react to her explanation, but she went on, "When I sleep on a tough problem, after having given it my best, a solution always comes. You know, like an 'Ah ha!' First, I have to work my brain to its limit before a clear insight. My Aunt Pet believed in the power of dreams and insights from the ancestors in your dreams. I used to take her homilies with more than several grains of salt. Now that she's dead, I don't know. She seems to be more with me now than ever before." She raised her glass, "Thank you, Aunt Pet."

Gebadd gave no hint of disbelief or ridicule. "I would be the last person to deny your truth. It works for you. Something brought us together, and I am delighted. Ancestors and dreams work for many people."

Rosamund was unsure how she wanted—or ought—to accept his last words. Gebadd was from a very different world—and was probably married. She didn't ask his marital status. She had gone from her parents' home, to college, to marriage, to widowhood in one seamless, flowing sequence. She was comfortable with men in a business context. A shy youngster, she had been slow to date. She met Carl the year she finished university, both on their first jobs.

She preferred that Al Gebadd be a business friend, the way she thought of Jeffrey. "Today is too much for me, and it is not over yet," she said. "Will you go with me to meet my friends? We can compare notes, and how we are to move forward."

"I will be happy to meet with all of you, later. I need to find out what my people have uncovered, as quickly as possible." Gebadd resumed his friendly professional attitude. "May I come to your apartment—we will not use the telephone—after your meeting, say at eight tonight?"

Rosamund sensed that he might be confused by what she felt was her withdrawal. She smiled and spoke more warmly, "Yes, please do. We will all be there. I'll be glad when life returns to normal—whatever normal is. I'll get on home now and to Ma Belle's."

"Ah, the secret passages. If it were not so serious, it would be a child's game," Gebadd held Rosamund's hand longer than a handshake.

Four o'clock arrived and Rosamund drove boldly to the front entrance of Ma Belle's little store. She made a show of taking her string shopping bags from the trunk of her car, shaking them out for the people in the white car peeking around the corner to see. She walked briskly in to Ma Belle's shop.

Jeffrey came through the back way minutes later. P. B. came from his apartment, inspecting the baskets of produce on the sidewalk. He stopped at the outdoor display, picked up two mangoes, and juggled them; whistling, he went inside.

"Slow down, girl," P. B. said. Rosamund was almost dancing, talking fast to Ma Belle. "You're bubbling like a hot spring. It's good to see you out of the dumps." He listened as Rosamund told Ma Belle the latest. "Ha," he said. "So Mr. Warner has a bunch of coded accounts to move money around? We guessed that much."

"Right," Rosamund said, her face animated. "But, just how he'd done it was the puzzle. He used anagrams of initials—his and his wife's—to create a sequence that does not interface with Dectel programs. His accounts didn't fall into any usual sequential pattern but were close enough to escape a cursory detection. That's what finally caught my attention."

P. B. grinned. "Told you, Ma. The man has no imagination. He did a real obvious thing. Rosamund couldn't find it at first, 'cause she was looking for something more sophisticated. Am I right, Rosamund?"

Rosamund shook her head, "Don't give me credit that is not due, P. B. He could have come up with something more difficult to locate—and I guess I was thinking that way. We can be glad he's not as smart as he thought."

Ma Belle chimed in, "Greedy, just like I said."

Jeffrey and Rosamund compared notes. He said, "Dangerous, too. We still have a way to go. Don't forget poor Dr. Belden. Whoever had him killed is not going to lie down and play dead, remember? Rosamund, you think we can trust Gebadd? He's one of 'them.'"

"I don't believe I'm naïve," she said. She thought for a moment before going on. "Gebadd said Warner was playing him for a fool, too, or he thought he was. Yes, I think he's trustworthy. How far, I don't know. But where Warner is concerned, he's with us."

Jeffrey wasn't completely convinced. "We have to trust him. He has access to the inner circle, and his clout is total. Show him these medical reports on phiofomel." He gave Rosamund a number of papers. "Watch his face to gauge his commitment. Is it to revenge or to money—or to saving lives. Okay?"

"I nearly forgot. Jeffrey," P. B. said. "Your new neighbor, Jensen, is head of security at Dectel. Gray is an Atlanta private investigator with a shady past. He's brother-in-law to Jensen. And your buddy Sam Hudson works in security at Dectel. I think Warner sensed a fellow rat and enlisted him. The man wants to move up the corporate ladder, big time. He'll do anything. He's not too bright. You know that already."

"I've a feeling we're missing a piece or two," Rosamund said. "What about Belden's tag—that's what you call him, right? He was in the picture before we met Belden."

"Right," Jeffrey said. "We need to know who hired him."

"And what happened to him," Ma Belle said.

"If he killed Belden, he's probably in the Bahamas by now," P. B. added.

"Al will meet us when his people find the right matches with the stuff I gave him this morning." Rosamund did not notice she call Gebadd, "Al." Ma Belle and P. B. gave knowing looks to each other.

Munje, Pet, and Frank were around, as always. "Is Gebadd what he seems?" Pet asked.

Frank tried on a Gebadd persona, then a Warner. "He doesn't 'feel' like Warner. He is not one of 'them,' as Jeffrey says. What do you sense, Brother?"

"He could go one of several ways," Munje pursed his energy lips and grimaced, "defending his business ethic, his personal ethic, or going with his heart. Shall we watch the scenario unfold or tap into the wider storehouse?"

Pet swirled and dipped above the heads of the small group at the table. "I did, already, but I won't tell."

"I don't want to know," Munje said, "not yet. The highest good is at work."

"But, so slow," Pet retorted. "I know, I know, timelessness is the word. I'm still working on patience."

"Patience?" Munje asked. "We're seeing an example of patience under our spirit noses," he giggled.

The room at the rear of Ma Belle's little store, La Bonne Bouche, meshed to an outdoor scene, a dark young woman with wide-set, sad eyes beneath straight, full brows and long lashes walked back and forth beside a riverbank. Her movements were deliberate and fluid. She searched the warm, humid field behind her to see if the other women had taken the clothing they had washed to be hung behind the slave quarters. Mina had made sure she washed a large amount. Her mother and the grandmothers had no reason to demand that she do more work, today.

178   FAMILY LINES

Mina felt she could see Munje as he swam the river, crawled up the other bank, and began his search for the Federal army. On the quiet of the deserted riverbank, she lifted her arms to send a prayer to Olodumare, the father spirit of her ancestors. He was her egungun her mother had taught. She sent a prayer to the Jesus that Mistress Alexander read of from the book. If one god could not protect her Munje, for sure, two would.

The old woman, called Mandy by the mistress and master and Kai in the privacy of the quarters, told Mina of the African goddess Oya. Oya was the caretaker of the river. Mina asked of Oya, "Give my Munje protection from the guns of the enemy and bring him safely back to me." She picked five stone celts from the clear water's bottom, raised them to the sky, then put them in her bosom pouch.

A woman's voice called, "Mina, stop wasting time. Come help with supper." Mina gave a last glance toward the clouds being blown eastward. "There is a way," she whispered.

Munje, in tattered slave garb, was miles away, thinking of Mina. She felt the warmth enter her back and infuse her. Spirit Munje changed to an older Munje in farmer's clothes on a white horse in front of a simple, sturdy farmhouse. He bent to kiss Mina. She held a baby. A small child stood beside her. They waved to Munje as he rode away.

Munje's energy took on a distinctly golden hue. "After the war, I rode all over western Louisiana and eastern Texas, up and down the river, from Shreveport to Pineville, Jefferson, Marshall, and Greenwood, showing my brothers how to register and vote. Mina is the one who brought me home, her and her faith," he said.

Munje beckoned to an energy in the gathered monad. Mina came to the center of the circle. Frank motioned to a gentle energy in the group. Lucie's energy joined Mina's, a calm presence with the smell of spring flowers after rain.

"Glorious," Pet breathed, scattering clouds, birds, and tree limbs as she always did.

Frank and Munje laughed, and in the grocery, Rosamund looked at the sun streaming through the clouds.

"Learning, Uncles, learning fast." Pet said.

The twins ran into the house, "Mom, why are those vans and cars outside?" Meryl asked Lois.

"Yeah, those people look like spacemen and women with wires and earphones," Mark said.

Lois stacked disposable cups beside her coffeepot. "Your dad is a celebrity," she said. "Those people are from TV and radio."

"Is Dad going to get his legs fixed so he can walk again?" Meryl asked.

"I don't know about that, but the people who are responsible for his being in the wheelchair may have to answer for their part," Lois said as she placed napkins beside the cups. She filled the sugar bowl and put it on the counter.

"You mean, he'll get a job or some money to pay the bills, don't you, Mom?" Mark grabbed a cookie from the tray. "Thank you," he remembered to say.

"You're not welcome," Lois said. "We may not have enough for all these people."

Reporters from the networks and a local channel were quizzing Liam. The cable newsman shoved a microphone almost up Liam's nose.

The man practically screamed, "The police found a letter left with Dr. Belden's lawyer. He accused Dectel; DOT, Inc.; and a company in Italy of having him followed and harassing him. What do you know about his accusations?"

Before Liam could answer, another reporter jumped in, "Your name was in Belden's letter. What do you know about that? Did he know you?"

"If you fellows would listen the first time, you would know that I already told the reporter from CNN all that stuff. Yes, I met Belden." Liam wondered how much of what he was going to say would be heard and how much would be cut for a later breaking "newsbyte." "I'm just one of several workers who are paralyzed from accidents. People already died in Italy. Let me tell you something you ought to know; my wife and children have been followed, her car tires slashed. I've been followed. Somebody wants me to shut up and all the trouble to go away. But I didn't make the trouble. Neither did those poor patsies in Italy—and who knows where else."

Lois watched her husband, smiling proudly with every word he said. She leaned down to Meryl and Mark, holding them on each side of her. "You can be proud of your dad, kids. He's a brave man."

"We know," Meryl said. "He's smart, too." She put her arms around her mother and kissed her neck—as high as she could reach.

Eleven-year-old Mark didn't want to be a baby or a girl. He was nearly tall enough to put his arm around his mother's shoulders.

The reporters continued interrupting each other, not listening to Liam's responses. The video cameras churned continuously. Abruptly, it was quiet. As if on cue, to make their deadlines for the five-o'clock show, the horde left—cookie crumbs on Lois's carpet and an empty coffeepot.

The children went outside to play. They watched the rolling in of cables and the mad scramble to hurry up and stop.

Meryl said, "I hope Caryl comes back soon. She's fun, even if she is nine."

"Nyah, girls!" Mark said.

"You're jealous because she can beat you at all your video games," Meryl said, running away from her twin, who tried to pull her hair.

Warner and Sam Hudson looked glum watching the television screen. Liam looked directly into the camera, accusing Dectel.

"We can't show our hand," Warner said. "The media love to attack what they call 'white-collar crime.' Hudson, you're sure you covered your trail, aren't you?" Warner tapped his foot nervously.

"It's not over, is it? You can salvage the stock, can't you?" Hudson looked much less the fun guy he pretended.

"I've made as many transfers as I can. I'll wait to see if that hillbilly and the nigger were able to do substantial damage." Warner stopped tapping his foot. "Nobody is going to pay radical environmentalists any attention. Once the media has its newsbyte, it'll blow over in a day, I'm clear. Don't worry."

Sam Hudson left. The outer office began to clear. Miss D'Arcy came to Warner's door. "I'll be leaving in ten minutes, Mr. Warner. Is there anything I can get for you before I go?"

"Everything is fine, Miss D'Arcy. I will see you in the morning." Minutes later, he stood in the large green window admiring the view. Warner smiled, thinking, *The day one of them gets the best of me, it will be a rainy day in the Sahara.*

Closing his attaché, Warner heard footsteps in the outer office. He turned as Dectel's CEO and two other directors of the corporation opened the door to his private office. Warner smiled at the men. He knew the heads sometimes met after the staff had left.

Chapter Twenty

A conference call always set meetings, and they would go in the CEO's penthouse office suite.

"Alan," Warner called the CEO's name. "Robert, Abner, to what . . ." He stopped in mid-sentence by the entrance of Aklud Gebadd—Warner recognized him from pictures—and two people, a woman and man he had never seen before. Edward C. Warner froze.

Dectel's CEO, Alan Townley, said, "This is important, Ed. Let's go up to the conference room."

The little group went to the room where Warner had been hired and where he always felt like an insider. Solemn and quiet, everyone took seats around the oval table.

"You know the details, Mr. Gebadd," the CEO said. Alan Townley deferred to the man who was the one person in the room with power equal to Townley's.

Warner spoke to Aklud Gebadd. "Now, if this is because that black woman insulted you, Mr. Gebadd, I have taken care of that little matter. She is no longer with us. I apologize for her behavior."

Gebadd waited until Warner finished, fixed him with a noncommittal stare, then smiled broadly, "On the contrary, Mr. Warner, that black woman, as you call her, did me a favor. She has also done Dectel and JCN a tremendous favor that is incapable of repayment."

Townley added, "Warner, your lack of foresight and loyalty have come close to ruining us all. What in God's name has come over you?"

"I don't know what you mean, Alan," Warner stammered.

"Oh, but you do." Gebadd nodded toward the man who had accompanied him. The man opened a shiny portable overhead projector and aimed it toward the screen that opened at one end of the room. He laid a transparency on the lighted platform. Warner was dumbfounded to see his coded account numbers highlighted by color and notations. To the initiated, the tale of his involvement became clear. Gebadd's assistant filled in the rest.

"You would have gotten away with your plan without anyone being wiser, if it had not been for the black woman you've put on leave of absence." Gebadd looked around the table, pausing to smile at the brown face of the woman who accompanied him, his head of protocol.

"Let me explain?" Warner asked. "I was trying to get increased market share for Dectel, that's all." He stopped, surrounded by an environment of silent, unsmiling faces.

"I do not see it that way," the man Warner called Abner spoke. "You deliberately ignored cautions brought by one of your staff—a young fellow named Shuggs—whom you also fired." Abner was president of the Dectel board of directors. "We could not maintain market share or viability—maybe not even survival—with the lawsuits that would come with a phiofomel scandal."

"I was only trying to help," Warner protested.

Gebadd said, "Help whom? NetLink would have been the equivalent of a plague if you had your way."

Townley moved within inches of Warner. "For your information, I have recalled any and all components we have produced and halted production. And, as for your scheme to control DOT, Inc., you're in conflict of interest. Civil and criminal charges are being brought against you," he said.

Robert Miles, head of the San Francisco office, had said nothing until then. "There's no need to discuss anything with you. You know what you did—somewhere down inside. We're in business to succeed, just not at any price."

"Ed, were you involved in Belden's accident?" Townley asked.

"No, not actually," Warner was colorless. His hands hung at his side. He felt as if he were holding a block of ice in each hand. "The men I hired for surveillance said Belden went off the mountain of his own accord."

"That's for the legal system to decide," Gebadd said. "I learned that Belden was also being observed by agents for a European company, but their man was sick the night of the accident. Anyway, the Europeans were interested in hiring Belden for his knowledge of industrial chemicals, not to harm him. His surveillance was for his protection."

Townley looked at the vice-president. "Ed, clear out your things. Don't try to leave Atlanta. It's your turn to be watched."

Warner tried one last time. "You don't understand," he began.

"I think we do," Townley said. Everyone at the table nodded agreement.

Pet wafted through the light from the overhead projector until it was turned off. She joined Munje and Frank in the descending light through the green window behind the oval table. "*Great party, isn't it?*" *she sent to the members of the monad, who each had their part in the unfolding events.*

"*It gets better, I think,*" *Munje sent.*

Frank intertwining with Lucie, Sariah, and He-Who Walks, hummed Pet's tune, "*Around and around she goes, and where she stops, nobody knows.*"

"*Thief,*" *Pet called.*

"*One for all,*" *Frank returned.*

Rosamund's phone rang. It was Gebadd. "Where can I meet with your little band of Robin Hood's merry men and women."

"Aren't you taking a chance, calling on this line?" Rosamund asked.

Gebadd said, "We don't need to worry anymore. The line has been cleared."

"If that's true, I'll call Lois and Liam, Jeffrey, P. B., and Ma Belle. When can you get there?" she asked.

"Check with your people and let me know. May I come to your home at eight as you and I planned?" He had hoped for a private visit with Rosamund, but remembering her response at lunch, he wasn't sure.

"Why not? I think I have enough chairs—if we use the ones from the dining table."

"What would we do without practical-minded organizers?" A light-hearted reply traveled the instant distance. Rosamund laughed. At the other end, Gebadd smiled.

Rosamund tidied her living room. "I've been so busy I haven't dusted in days. Oh, well." She hummed as she scurried around, "When the red, red robin comes bob, bob, bobbing along . . ."

CHAPTER 21

P. B. and Ma Belle arrived at Rosamund's before eight o'clock. Their arms were loaded with bags overflowing with food.

Ma Belle let out a low groan when she placed her load on the kitchen counter. "I've heard about your cooking skills, cherie," she said to an astonished Rosamund. "If you all goin' to be spending a lot of brainpower tonight, you need blood to the head to do a good job."

P. B. opened the refrigerator door, pushed the few items aside on one shelf, and put his load in the space. "Nothing much, Daughter. Now, you go get yourself pretty—prettier. Belle and I will whip up a few tidbits in two shakes of a cottontail. I don't mean to hurt your feelings, but I can sure tell that our Patricia is missing."

Rosamund sputtered, "Everyone will have eaten dinner before now. What . . ."

"Shush. Out of here. Sit and put your feet up." Ma Belle waved both hands, saying, "Get along with you, now."

Outmaneuvered, Rosamund retired from her kitchen. She went to Caryl's room. Under the skirt of the two-headed doll, she searched for the flat, plastic disk. It had slipped further into the padding. Digging, Rosamund felt an odd shape. She pulled out a purple, velvet bag. Untying a gold-colored drawstring, she emptied the contents onto Caryl's bed. Several small objects tumbled out. Rosamund fingered five stones, smooth as if they had been washed by ages of tumbling water. Before she could closely examine the pieces of shiny metal, the doorbell rang. She scooped the objects into a pile on the bedspread and took the disk with her.

Jeffrey handed her a bottle of wine. "I saw Liam on the six-o'clock news. He did great. I brought this to celebrate his triumph. We may not have ours."

"No pessimism tonight, if you please." He followed her to the kitchen. P. B. and Ma Belle were arranging canapés and finger food for dipping.

"Party?" Jeffrey asked.

"We don't need a reason to have a good time." P. B. twirled a mesh bag of cheese.

Rosamund left to answer the doorbell again. Gebadd gave her a second bottle of wine.

"You have excellent taste," he said, admiring the blue skirt and sweater she had changed into after their lunch.

"Thank you for noticing. This is more practical for tonight."

"Practical?" his voice questioned. "Rosamund, you are more business focused than I imagined. Tonight, we have cause to be joyous." He gave her a second admiring gaze.

Jeffrey came from the kitchen. He extended his hand. "Mr. Gebadd, welcome to the world of serfs and slaves."

Gebadd took Jeffrey's greeting to be a joke. "Mr. Jeffrey Shuggs, indeed." He smiled and shook Jeffrey's hand, holding it in both his hands. "I've been so looking forward to meeting you. Rosamund has shared excellent words about you."

"You, too," Jeffrey replied, not as enthusiastically as he had been received.

"Al, please, make yourself comfortable. I'll be back in a moment." Rosamund indicated that he should stay in the living room. "Jeffrey, come help me in the kitchen."

Out of Gebadd's hearing, Rosamund asked, "Do you want another kick in the shin?"

"For what?" Jeffrey asked.

"You know damn well. You're being nasty to him," she replied.

"When they get that big, they don't listen to what anyone says," Jeffrey shrugged.

"The man is brilliant. Nothing eludes him. Wait before you judge, will you?" she pleaded.

"I'll try to remember my 'home training,' and the occasion." Jeffrey sounded and looked tired.

She sensed his mood. "I don't mean to be cruel.

I'm not my best, myself."

Ma Belle and P. B. brought a tray of hot canapés and another of chilled assorted vegetables and dips. The wine was poured and toasts offered all around.

Rosamund passed the disk, "For good luck," she said. "If we all touch it, maybe our thoughts will bring Mr. Warner to his just desserts."

"He is on his way already," Gebadd said.

Everyone turned to him, drinks in mid-air. He summarized the events in the conference room at Dectel. Rosamund, P. B., and Ma Belle gave him warm thanks and congratulations. Jeffrey was the last to do so.

"I thank you for being in a position to do what those on the bottom rung can't do, Mr. Gebadd." The corners of Jeffrey's mouth were in their often-questioning position. "There are still some pieces of the problem I do not think are cleared up. What about Liam? What about Rosamund's, Lois's, and my jobs?"

Rosamund was upset. "Jeffrey, you were the one who brought phiofomel to my attention." She sought to restore the upbeat mood. "Aren't you happy that it is off the market, that Warner has been stopped?"

"Of course," he said, "but we were followed, harassed, had to send our kids away from home for safety, had our homes invaded. I feel sort of left out." He sat, heavily, on the sofa.

P. B. sat beside Jeffrey. He placed a hand on Jeffrey's knee. "Mr. Gebadd couldn't have done what he did without the information you and Rosamund found. You were first to spot a problem. You guys are the front-line troops, Jeffrey."

Rosamund said," You're right, P. B. Isn't he, Mr., uh . . . Al?"

Gebadd closed his eyes and held his hands almost prayerfully. In the kitchen, the teakettle whistled. For a long moment, no one spoke. Gebadd raised his head, opened his eyes, and settled his gaze on Jeffrey. "I comprehend your feelings, Mr. Shuggs." He had a deep voice that could be called melodious. "You uncovered the horrible situation. You risked your life. You have been unfairly treated and you do not trust me; I understand your reason." Sri Gebadd was hardly more than two inches taller than Rosamund, but his bearing was that of a man much taller. He stood and went to a round table on which family portraits rested. He picked up the one of Caryl and smiled at the childish inscription, "I love you, Mums."

"This little girl reminds me of the many children I have seen." He gently replaced the picture. "Whatever you may think, Mr. Shuggs, I could never do anything that would bring harm to her or others like her. Phiofomel would do that."

"Jeffrey, Mr. Gebadd is our friend. He's on our team, an important part of it." Rosamund settled back in her chair. "We might never have been able to get through the corporate wall if not for him. We were all needed."

Jeffrey covered his face with his hands. Rosamund went to him, massaging his shoulders. "I didn't realize the stress you've been under."

She looked at Gebadd. "He's overwrought. You'll see."

Ma Belle had gone to the kitchen during Jeffrey's outburst. She brought a cup to Jeffrey. "Here, son. Sip this. It's a soothing tea. You'll feel better."

Jeffrey took the cup. "I apologize to all of you, especially you, Mr. Gebadd. My momma would tan my carcass if she heard me just now. I need to go home, be by myself for a while. Excuse me . . ." He did not look directly at anyone and was gone before the others could stop him.

"Let him go," P. B. said. "The boy's under big strain, not just the company business. It's not easy raising a boy by yourself—I know women do it all the time—but for men, it's not the same." P. B. addressed Rosamund. "He doesn't have close family like you do, and he worries about his son."

"You think that's what's at the bottom of his anger?" Rosamund asked.

"Not the bottom, a part of the whole picture." P. B. looked at Gebadd. "Do you think so, Mr. Gebadd?"

"You may have the key, reverend." Gebadd spread his arms in a hands-up gesture.

"Jeffrey is a grown man," Ma Belle said. "He will sort out what he needs. Come, finish the good wine."

There was a void in the gathering after Jeffrey left. Still, spirits were high for the day's outcome.

P. B. and Ma Belle left the remaining food for Rosamund, who insisted she do the clean up.

"This'll fill the empty spots in your fridge for a day or so," P. B. teased, as he kissed her good-bye.

She quizzed Gebadd on more of the business with Warner. Midway through a clarification, Rosamund covered her mouth with her hand.

"Forgive me. My yawn doesn't mean I'm not enjoying your company. I feel overwhelmed, almost as much as Jeffrey. When I wake up in the morning, it will be a dream, won't it?"

Chapter Twenty-One   189

"No, I assure you what you've been through is real. You'll have no more surveillance. I do not know what Townley will do about your return to Dectel. You're only on leave," Gebadd said. "Don't worry."

Rosamund shuddered. "I don't know if I want to go back. It's been a bad dream."

"I suggest you get a good night's rest. I leave for Frankfurt in the morning. I will call en route. And, my dear, I am not upset with your Mr. Shuggs."

Rosamund opened the door for Gebadd. He leaned toward her and kissed her on the forehead. "Sleep well," he said.

She touched her head where Al had kissed. She left the kitchen until morning, "No battlefield traffic, hoorah." On her way to bed, she stopped at Caryl's room. The pieces of rock and metal on Caryl's bed gleamed in the semidarkness.

Aklud Gebadd's chauffeur asked, "Was it a good evening, sir?"

"I honestly do not know, Khalil," Gebadd said. "I have a tangled rug to unroll." He leaned back in his seat and closed his eyes as Khalil drove him to his jet.

"Is it Shuggs she cares for, or is it me that she does not care for?" Khalil had turned off the intercom. Al's question was not answered.

Pet heard. "She cares for both of you. Caring and loving are not exactly the same. There are degrees, like on a thermometer, mister." Pet had, again, followed her curiosity, wandering from the monad that was monitoring the children, Darren scaling to Jarrett's Bald on Nantahala Mountain and Caryl telling Nana what she learned from Aunt Pet about dreaming.

Nana did not tell her such things were not so. She vaguely remembered her own grandmother telling stories around the fireplace on cold winter nights in Ohio fifty years earlier.

Munje and Frank found Pet. "Stay with us; we have more energy together than when one of us wanders off," Munje said.

"The same as in life time," Frank added. "Exponential is the name," he said.

"My own lessons add, don't they?" Pet wanted to know.

"Naturally," a different monad energy pulsed. Pet knew the signal was not telepathy; she hadn't been told how the 'sending' was accomplished.

"We enjoy you so much we want you with us. We move forward faster," Mina said.

"Oh," Pet said. "I'm an asset, then. I like that."

Jeffrey unlocked his apartment door. Whistling, he went inside and dropped his jacket on the dining table. He remembered Darren wasn't here. *I don't have to set a good example.* He sprawled into a chair, turned on the television, and sat, blankly staring at an off channel. "Damn, I didn't have to blow up. Cool Jeffrey I was not." The empty screen annoyed him. He turned off the set and stared at the blackness. "I don't know if I dislike that man because he was able to do what I couldn't or because Rosamund likes him." He sat in the darkness waiting for his unease to lift. Before the black screen with no sound, his mind played back the recent weeks.

He went to his room to undress for bed. He thought, *I believed that if I did my work accurately I would be just fine. Maybe I was a naïve mountain man.* He yawned, unfastened his tie—why was he wearing one? he wondered. Dectel was no longer a factor. It had been a long day. He noticed his answering machine's light flashing.

"Honey, this is Eva Lee. Where is my boy? He didn't answer or call back. I'll be in Atlanta Saturday. We're singing at the Country Court. I'm coming by first chance I get."

Jeffrey dropped into a chair letting the tape run out, bleep, and stop. "Oh, Lord," he groaned.

CHAPTER 22

Atlanta is exciting and a paradox. To begin, the weather can vary from warm, sun-filled days to icy treachery within a few days. Greenery lines the old, curving, hilly streets and spring rains glisten on natural and man-made surfaces, giving the city and environs a magical feel. The once-gracious, old, Southern city jumped to twenty-first-century megastatus in less than a generation.

Rosamund was awakened by chirping birds at the hanging feeder on her balcony. Her coming to consciousness was gentle. She listened to the birds, enjoying their small cacophony. *It's time for Caryl to get up,* she thought, stretching up and outward. She remembered that Caryl was not there and that today was the first day of spring vacation. Rosamund no longer missed the interruptions that school and college vacations presented, but she would pretend that her hiatus from work was a spring break.

She pulled the drapery open to better view the birds and the morning sun. A chickadee and several robins pecking at things too tiny to be seen suddenly saw one another. They flew in disparate directions as if in mortal dislike. "Silly," she said, pulling herself to the edge of her bed, her long legs searching for her slippers. They act like some people I know. Running away form nothing."

Once she'd showered, real time pushed into day. A rumble began in her stomach and radiated up and down her body, ending in a half groan, half grunt. She felt a panic she had not known since Carl died. An image, familiar in dreams, of Caryl, smiling in a brightly lit, colorful room. She played with her dolls and toys. This happy vision changed to a spare, dull space with a few stark, wooden chairs and a chest with broken hinges. Caryl was nowhere to be seen. Rosamund looked down a long stairwell into an empty street.

Today, the flash of recognition was not a dream. Never before had it come when she was fully awake. She had asked herself, before, what the dream meant. Now, she was positive she knew. The possibility of losing what was most precious to her, her daughter, was a fear that tied directly to her ability to care for Caryl, to provide a home, safety, and opportunity for her. Having a job to support Caryl was inseparable from her love for her daughter.

The office was no longer a draw, so what would her days include? Her body wanted to follow its routine: rush to her car, rush through traffic, rush to her office. To rush was normal.

In the kitchen she poured juice, shook a few flakes of cereal into a bowl, and boiled water in the microwave. She drank the juice but could swallow none of the cereal. She stroked her throat. The tea went down easily. Mrs. Jones-Keyes was full from her stomach to the back of her throat.

The birds and sunlight drew her back to the balcony door. "I need to move," she said. Minutes later, she soothed her panic with the rhythm of her footsteps on the soft cinder chips of the park path.

Breathing freely, Rosamund was home again. She opened the door. A male voice was saying, "Thank you. I hope to hear from you." By the time she reached the phone, the message had ended.

Upon rewinding the tape, she remembered the voice that said, "I wanted to reach you before you left for work. This is Evan Thomas, Caryl's core teacher. Will you have dinner with me? If you are available any evening, please call." He repeated his number.

"A change of pace might be good," Rosamund said, jotting the number before she remembered it was already in her phone list.

Blocks away, Jeffrey ate a solitary breakfast. He called Lois to ask about Liam. Lois said, "I'm expecting a call from Dr. Ziegler. I'll let you know what he says. He is so happy when you call, Mr. Shuggs," she said.

"It's past time for you to call me Jeffrey," he said. "We are going through too much together to stick to formalities."

"I'll try," Lois said. "At work it has to be Mr. and Ms.; it gets to be a habit."

"Try your durndest, will you?" he cajoled. "I'll check after lunch to see what the doctor says."

Jeffrey didn't notice that he sat with the newspaper in front of him, open to page one of the sports section, without seeing a word for nearly half an hour. Did he want to see his wife, Eva Lee? He called Darren at his cousin Lottie's. Darren and his cousin Frank were setting up gem-mine trays at the farm. Vacationers to the former "gem-mining capital of the world" would begin arriving in the mountain area in a few days. The smallest visitors thought they were "gold-mining," shining bits of stone gleamed in the buckets of sand. Locals knew it was fool's gold.

"I think I'll come home and do a little washing myself," Jeffrey told Lottie. "I have time on my hands."

Lottie said, "It's too early for sand-washing right now, but come on. We've plenty of room."

Jeffrey did not wait to hear from Eva Lee. He drove to the train station and took the MARTA to the Country Court. Eva Lee and the backup singers would be rehearsing with the Ridge Boys; he knew the way they operated. At the combination restaurant and dance hall, he took a seat in the dark rear. In blue-jean skirts and pink-and-blue-fringed tops, the girls worked the new stage, finding their marks, adjusting to the size of the room. The lighting technician made final adjustments.

A voice from the control booth called, "We don't need to work it to death, folks. Back at six, OK?"

Jeffrey stopped at the edge of the stage. Except for the sound of instruments being stored, the room was quiet. He called, "Eva Lee, it's Jeffrey." He called again. A shapely, red-headed woman just offstage ran to its edge, stopped just short, and held out her hands.

"Well, I sure didn't expect to see you so soon," she said, giving him an admiring glance. "You look good, Jeffy. Let's go get a cup of coffee." Eva Lee led him to the back of the stage, "Y'all remember my husband, Jeffrey," she said to the men and women who were laying out music for the night's show and putting on jackets.

The Ridge Boys—two brothers, a cousin, and a former neighbor—shook hands with Jeffrey and said how glad they were to see him. The girl singers gave him a hug. Everybody looked tired.

Eva Lee linked her arm in Jeffrey's. They went to a fast-food eatery.

"I'm going to be in town through Tuesday," Eva Lee said. "We're all pretty worn out. I sure do want to see Darren."

Jeffrey wasn't going to tell her the whole story. "He's at Cousin Lottie's on spring vacation from school. He'll be home Friday. I'll be going up for him."

"How come we can't go up to see him while I'm here?" she asked. "Can you take off Monday?"

He wouldn't tell her about Dectel, either. "Yes, I can take off. I'm on a sort of vacation."

Eva Lee touched his hand. "I miss you, Jeffy. I'd like for you to come see our show, tonight. Will you?" She sounded like a little girl—looked like one, too.

"I think I can manage it," he said. Jeffrey wanted to get away. He had feelings he did not want, thought he had lost.

Eva Lee acted as if she wanted to say something but changed her mind. "We have a fitting for new costumes. I'd better get back. See you tonight," she said.

"Right, later," he said, wondering why he had agreed to come to the show. The shows had taken Eva Lee away from him and Darren.

Jeffrey's call to Lois brought the news that Ziegler would be at her house in the morning. Something special was going on, but Lois didn't know exactly what.

Rosamund called Evan Thomas.

"Do you like basketball?" he asked.

"I do," she said. "Are you a basketball player?"

"I played a little, but my sport is football," he said. "I have friends who play for the Hawks. One of them gave me tickets. We can eat first and go to the game."

"I'd love to go. My schedule hasn't given me much time for fun things until now," she said.

Dinner was not Coaches Six but better than adequate. Evan Thomas didn't pry and he didn't talk about himself. He looked her in the eye when she asked if he were married.

"No, I tried it once," Evan said. "It was too early for us."

Rosamund forgot Dectel, Jeffrey, and Gebadd. "I forgot how much fun a live game could be," she said. "Television doesn't make it."

Evan—he asked her to call him by his first name—wanted to know if they could go out again.

"I'd like that," she said.

Gebadd's message waited for her. He would call tomorrow, 9:00 AM her time. He was in London tonight.

Rosamund calculated, "Nine in the morning. He will have finished lunch by then. Time around the world." She sang as she prepared for bed, too late to call Caryl.

Munje sent a vibrating silver cord to the eighteen souls who were in the monad with him, Frank, and Pet. The cord gave off a steady mmm. Munje beamed. "The problem with our souls at Dectel is working out. Has Liam decided which route he will take?"

Frank spread his energy across several moon craters. "He has, but he hasn't shared it. We'll know in one or two more earth days." He waved to Pet. "Memories coming back, Sister?"

"Oh yes, for some time now." Pet wafted near to Belden, who had joined their monad. "Fun, isn't it, remembering?" Frank and Mina floated nearby. To Caryl and Darren, the vibrations in Pass On sounded like thunder a long way off. Jeffrey felt as if a weight had rolled from his shoulders, and Rosamund snuggled into her pillow.

Mina said, "Pet almost forgot to put the stones and flint into Caryl's gift doll."

"We reminded her 'in time,' the morning she went to buy allspice and cayenne pepper," Frank said. "Can't let a talisman lose its continuity; we would have to create a whole new variation if that happened.

Jeffrey liked the Ridge Boys, no matter how much he didn't want to. Their stylized country wasn't the old bluegrass, but *everything changes,* he thought. Eva Lee was good. He saw the pleasure she got from performing. He always had good feelings when he worked a mathematical solution and when he walked in the mountains. There were lots of things he enjoyed; he had loved Eva Lee's singing since they first met. He had those same feelings as she walked toward him.

"What did you think, honey?" Her eyes questioned. Her face was not as happy as she had looked on stage.

"It was good," he said. "You're better than ever. How about us leaving bright and early Monday for Ola? You might want to stay at the apartment after the Sunday show, if you want. I'll bet you're tired of hotel living." When Jeffrey was with anyone who spoke the cadence of his mountains, he fell, naturally, into the slower-paced twang and pattern.

"That's real nice of you, honey," Eva Lee said, squeezing his hand and jiggling her shoulders in a familiar way.

Friday morning, Jeffrey went to the Hardys'. When he parked his car, a black couple and he said, "Good morning," as they passed. He saw a church steeple down the curving hill from Lois and Liam's house. "There's the church where we had Aunt Pet's funeral," he said. "I didn't know this was the same neighborhood."

Lois was pleased to see him. He joked about not having to go to Dectel, and he wanted to see how she and Liam were—because they didn't have to go to work either.

Lois was packing a small carry-on. "Dr. Ziegler is taking Liam to a clinic in Fulton County. The doctors from Italy and Germany are there," she said. "The clinic has special equipment and the new doctors are going to give Liam a treatment they used in Italy on those other workers who were sick from phiofomel. They say he has a fair to good chance to regain the use of his legs."

Her eyes were red from crying, but she seemed happier than Jeffrey had seen her before. "The twins have been so good. I've got to do something special for them," she said.

"We'll do something that's fun for all the kids," Jeffrey said. "We've put them under a strain, haven't we?"

Dr. Ziegler saw to Liam being placed in an ambulance van. Jeffrey, Lois, and the twins waited in the yard until the ambulance was long out of sight.

"I know where I want to be and what I want to do," Jeffrey said.

Lois was taken aback by the force with which he spoke.

"Be where, be what?" she asked.

"I'm going to offer my work as a statistician to the medical consortium that's helping people like Liam. People who have been hurt by chemical pollution and accidents." The worry frown that often hung at the corners of Jeffrey's mouth was turned in the opposite direction. There were no furrows on his brow when he said to Lois, "I'll be on the right side of the numbers and won't have to worry about the games the 'system' plays."

"Those guys don't have lots of money," Lois said. "They won't be able to pay you like Dectel."

"I have a feeling in my bones that everything will be just fine." He laughed. "I'm beginning to sound more like some weird, psychic mumbo jumbo." He paused and screwed up his mouth for a moment. "No, I don't think so. I used to pay attention to my senses in the mountains. I'm going to follow my feelings this time."

Lois didn't know for sure if his plan was a good one, but she said, "You have the clinic's telephone number and address, don't you?"

"I do, and I'll call Ziegler as soon as they have had time to do their stuff with Liam. This is the right move for me." Jeffrey gave Lois a hug, then caught himself.

"Don't be ashamed," she said. "Mr. Shuggs is almost family, isn't he, kids?"

"Sure," Meryl said.

Mark added, "He's got a boy. He's okay with me."

Monday morning, Jeffrey cooked breakfast for Eva Lee. He kept very quiet because her last show had ended at two AM. She came to the kitchen door, red hair mussed, no makeup, looking less than twenty, the age she was when they were married.

"You're making those super hotcakes," she said, sniffing the aroma across the room.

"I haven't made them in a long time. The recipe jumped to my mind when I got to the kitchen," he said. "Bacon, hotcakes with peach preserves, and eggs with cheese, just like you used to like them."

"I like 'em, not 'used to'," she said.

Jeffrey was whistling.

The two-and-one-half hour drive to Ola, North Carolina, passed more quickly than Jeffrey remembered. Darren was like a puppy when he saw his mother—and his parents together. Jeffrey dropped her at her hotel on their return to Atlanta. He said, "I'll be glad to see you next time you're in town."

"I'll be back real soon," she said. Eva Lee went to the hotel entrance. The musicians were loading their van. She came back to the Trooper and looked up at Jeffrey with a sober, sweet smile. "Honey, I know every scratch on every guitar in the band. I'm getting tired of gigs up and down the country. If you don't mind, maybe we can talk, sometime."

"That's a possibility," Jeffrey said. "I don't know how long Darren's willing to wait, though." He nodded at the boy sleeping in back.

"I hear you," Eva Lee said, swinging the quilted duffel her mother made over her shoulder, pulling her red hair from under the straps.

Gebadd's call was not expected until morning. Rosamund sneaked a glance at her watch; it was 9:30, dark. And the evening had turned cool.

"I was thinking of you and didn't want to wait until morning," he said." His deep baritone seemed no further than downtown in Atlanta.

"It's two-thirty AM in London. You haven't been asleep yet?" she asked.

"My internal clock has been confused most of my life," he said, laughing. "Thank you for your concern. I had a meeting until midnight. I tried to sleep and keep waking. Do you mind if we talk for a little?"

Something in his voice gave Rosamund a sad feeling. *He's lonely,* she thought. *He has everything a person could want and he's lonely.* "Talk away," she said. "My clock will not run down for several hours. Are you working on NetLink?"

"We are," he replied. "The game that Warner was playing threw us behind schedule, but it is better to have the system done properly from the beginning. When I return, I will want your keen insight to assist me in determining new procedures."

"Me? I don't know what I can offer," she said.

"I have been impressed with everything you have suggested and done so far. Why should I not expect more?" Al Gebadd was emphatic. "Do you only mistrust yourself in special circumstances?" he asked. "You were very assured in Chicago."

"I have not had anyone so high up, I mean, as well placed as you ask my advice before. I'm surprised and flattered," Rosamund said.

"Like me? My dear, I am merely another of the Almighty's humble creatures."

Rosamund recalled Aunt Pet's admonition. "Why is it so hard to remember?" she asked.

"Remember? Remember what?" he asked.

"My Aunt Pet said, 'Everyone gets in their pants the same way.'"

He laughed louder. "A wonderful woman, your aunt, without doubt. I would like to have known her. I suggest you take her advice seriously."

"I promise I will stop being in awe of you—I'll dress you in blue jeans and a straw hat in my mind to remind me." Rosamund was warming to their conversation.

"Excellent," he said. "I will be back to Atlanta in two days. Will Caryl be there? I want to meet her."

"She flies in on Friday. If you are not here then, next time, for sure," she said.

In London, Gebadd smiled. In Atlanta, after the conversation ended, Rosamund realized what she had said.

In the morning, a cool, officious someone called Rosamund to come to Dectel, that the CEO, Mr. Townley, wanted an appointment with her. Rosamund told Miss Cool Caller she would be available at 2:30.

Rosamund phoned Lois.

Lois said that Liam was responding well to the new treatment. She bubbled, "The doctors think he will regain his ability to walk—maybe not run but no more wheelchair. Isn't it wonderful?"

"Absolutely," Rosamund said. "We are going to have a boss celebration. You, Liam, Jeffrey, P. B., Ma Belle, the children—all of us. I can hardly wait."

"I haven't met Mr. Gebadd. Jeffrey says he was the key in getting rid of Mr. Warner." Lois was a generous woman who included the whole world in her good wishes.

"I don't know if he will be here for our party." Rosamund remembered their talk the night before. "We will see. There's something new happening. Mr. Townley, the CEO himself, wants to see me this afternoon. I don't know why. I made a quick appointment with André. I'll go into the den of the beast looking my best," she said. "You'll get the blow-by-blow when it is over."

Townley told a sharply dressed Rosamund he wanted to end her leave of absence as of the first of the week, with a larger office, private secretary, and bonus for her good work with NetLink.

"I would like my former secretary, Lois Hardy, Mr. Townley. And will Mr. Shuggs be returning?"

Townley blushed. "I don't know if we can do all you ask. We have to maintain a semblance of protocol for the stability of the organization, you understand," he said.

"You mean, if you admit to Dectel having made an error, it will look bad to the employees?" she asked.

"Not exactly, but in the corporate arena," Townley began, "we feel that you are a very valuable employee. That's why you were hired. We will give Mrs. Hardy and Mr. Shuggs ample severance."

Rosamund felt her "Jones" rising. She confronted the man in the most impressive office she'd ever seen. "Neither of them has done one wrong thing. Mr. Shuggs uncovered the problem Mr. Warner made for Dectel. I had nothing to do with the problem or solution that was not a direct consequence of Mr. Shuggs. Mrs. Hardy's husband was injured—probably permanently-because of exposure to phiofomel. Jeffrey Shuggs brought the phiofomel expenditures and the chemical's danger to my attention." Rosamund stood and pressed her clenched knuckles on Townley's desk.

"There are some things you do not understand. You are a very young woman and . . ." Townley sputtered.

"I am not so young, Mr. Townley, that I cannot comprehend Dectel's desperation to hide a major embarrassment. I do not believe that Mr. Shuggs and Mrs. Hardy would survive the undercurrent that would surround them if they did come back—nor will I." Rosamund calmly lifted her purse from the chair behind her and walked out of the office of the chief executive officer and president of the most powerful communications industry in the nation.

On her way home, Rosamund thought, *I just burned every bridge over which I have ever passed. Now what?* She drove without turning on her radio or playing a CD.

In her building, Miss DeLong and other neighbors were nowhere to be seen. Sariah Rosamund Jones-Keyes filled her tub with water, as hot as she could take, poured jasmine oil, and climbed in to listen to her newest Luther Vandross CD.

"Why not meet me in Cincinnati? We can pick up Caryl at your parents', and she won't have to fly home alone." Al was in New York, headed to Los Angeles. "I have a proposition for you, a professional offer," he said.

"I like it," Rosamund said, "—your chance to meet Caryl. I don't want to be presumptuous, but I am, currently, one of the unemployed."

"I have been informed," Al said. "We will discuss options." He hesitated. "I am looking forward to seeing you again." He said a quick good-bye.

In Gebadd's private plane, Caryl said, "I've never known anyone from Egypt. Have you been to the pyramids?"

"A number of times," he said, taken by her alertness. "I have taken my nieces and nephews."

"Don't you have kids?" Caryl asked.

"No. I am a widow. My wife and I did not have a child," he replied.

"I'm sorry," she said. "But sometimes kids can be a pain. Right, Mums?"

"Not too bad a pain that a little medicine won't cure," Rosamund said.

Caryl slipped earphones under her chin and was soon caught up in music.

Once Al saw that Caryl was occupied, he said to Rosamund, "My people and I want you with us, running JCN-American NetLink." He put his hand over hers. "You are absolutely the right person. You know the process, as it was developed at Dectel. You understand the NetLink concept."

Rosamund felt a surge of confidence. "I'm flattered. I hope you're confident I'm the person you want because of ability and not friendship—or pity."

Gebadd stifled a laugh. "Pity? You must be kidding. Madam, you would never elicit that emotion from anyone. You have the carriage of a lioness. My people remember you from Chicago. You are it," he said.

"Do we have to move from Atlanta? I like Atlanta," Rosamund asked.

"Not unless there is a major change of plans—that's always a possibility in our world. We'll expand our Atlanta satellite, make it our U.S. NetLink base."

"I accept, with thanks," she said. "I expect you to be honest with me if there is ever a problem." Rosamund was more comfortable with Aklud Gebadd than she would have presumed to be less than a week ago.

"One little matter, if you please," he said. "I want to do right by Jeffrey."

"Jeffrey is going to work with the Complementary Medical

Consortium—CMC—which Belden and Ziegler started. He is happy with the idea of 'detective statistics'—that's his new term." Rosamund shifted the sleeping Caryl to a more comfortable position. "Our silver lining may be here right now."

"That's wonderful for him," Al said. "And I nearly forgot, your title will be chief of operations."

She repeated, "Chief of operations. Sounds neat to me. I like it."

Caryl murmured, half asleep. "'Neat' is my word."

Gebadd deposited the Jones-Keyes ladies and continued to Los Angeles.

"Mums, what are these things in this bag?" Caryl was getting dressed for the long-postponed picnic.

"I found the bag in your gift doll from Aunt Pet. By the way, have you given her a name?"

"I'll bet this is extraspecial family stuff, and Aunt Pet put it there for me to keep, always." Caryl spread the stones and flint on her dresser. She ran her hands over each piece. "I get a buzzy feeling when I touch them, even when I almost touch them, Mums."

"Nope, I haven't got a name for my African-Indian doll. When it comes, I'll know." Caryl continued to stroke the objects. "If I sleep on the stones, maybe I'll get a name," she said.

Three cars arrived at Lake Lanier. P. B. and Ma Belle drove with Jeffrey and Darren in Ma Belle's ancient sedan. Rosamund and Caryl came together. Liam, walking with a cane, came with Lois and the twins. Everyone applauded and yelled when he walked from the car to the picnic table. The long-planned picnic was a reality. The table was spread with a carmine red tablecloth—for good luck, Ma Belle said. The brazier was filled and lit. P. B. Preston held forth—seafood, barbecue, salads, and grilled Creole bread.

Darren and Mark took a few seconds to become acquainted and five minutes to become friends. Mark was happy to have another boy along. The fact that he was younger was no problem because the others were girls.

P. B. called, "Chow time." The picnickers settled down to the loaded table, bringing with them a quiet that descended like a warm cloud.

"I think twin names are neat," Caryl said between mouthfuls. "M-m-m . . . my second great-grandfather's name had an 'M' sound. His name was Munje."

Meryl said, "Caryl and Meryl have the same ending."

Darren jabbed his fork into a shrimp. "Remember the funny name in our families: Sariah?"

"I told you it is not a funny name," Caryl said. "It is unique." Caryl fixed him with a superior gaze.

"Hush," Ma Belle said. "You two fuss like you're kin."

"Mums," Caryl called to the far end of the table, "Guess what? Darren has the name 'Sariah' in his family, just like us."

"You don't say? Maybe we're related," Rosamund teased.

"Don't joke," Ma Belle said. "Could be true."

"My dad knows the story, don't you Dad? It's a hundred years old." Darren said.

"When I finish this super meal, we'll explore family trees." Jeffrey pointed to a pile of shells in a basket in front of him.

"Cousins is better than friends," Darren said, jumping from his seat.

Mark said "Maybe we're all cousins, Meryl and Caryl look alike."

Darren and Mark darted around the table, chanting, "Cousins, cousins, everybody's cousins."

Washing his hands at the nearby pump, Jeffrey pulled a pad from an ever-present valise. "You begin," he said to Rosamund.

"Let's see, our Sariah was my great-great grandmother," Rosamund said. "She had two children, Monroe, who was called Munje, and Ula. Ula was Aunt Pet's grandmother. Aunt Pet called Munje 'Uncle,' although he died long before she was born."

Ma Belle said, as Rosamund groped for connections, "We pass on family by telling stories to the young ones. Calling family folk 'uncle' and 'aunt' keeps family alive and close."

"Same with us," Jeffrey said. "I'm Jeffrey, after my great-grandfather Jeffrey. He had a nurse named Sariah. She kept him alive when his mother was too sick to take care of him. He named his daughter Sariah out of love for his nurse. Aunt Sariah was like a grandmother to me."

"Was your Sariah black?" Rosamund asked.

"Yes, she was a slave to my great-great-grandfather Frank Shuggs," Jeffrey spoke softly and looked at the ground.

"Don't feel sad, Mr. Shuggs," Caryl said. "You didn't do it."

"Caryl, I know, but it pains me anyway," Jeffrey said.

Slowly turning her gaze around the circle of friends, Rosamund said, "Hold on to your seats, folks. I'll tell you what I found in the family Civil War records Aunt Pet kept."

Something in her voice made the twins stop eating their ice cream.

"My Sariah had a son by her owner, Big Frank. He was my great-grandfather Munje," she said slowly and evenly.

"I should have known," P. B. said. "All mixed up, twixt and tween."

Jeffrey drew lines connecting the names he had written. "Rosamund Jones-Keyes, you and I are first cousins twice removed—what most people call third cousins. I'll be hogswaggled," he said, a look of great discovery filling his face.

"So that's why I hated you," Rosamund said, pushing a mock fist in his face.

"Yeah, country kin always fight." Jeffrey said. "With you and me, it's city and country feuding, North-South, too."

"Cousin Darren?" Caryl said, hiding her face in her hands. "Oh no!"

He pulled her hands down. They slapped high-fives.

P. B., Ma Belle, Liam, and Lois passed the sketch of the family tree Jeffrey had made.

"If we talk long enough, you'll find my Chinese mother in there," Liam said.

"Sure enough," said P. B. "We'll latch on up and down one branch or another, kissin' cousins, after all."

Filled to satiation, Ma Belle and P. B. lounged in deck chairs, Jeffrey lay on the grass under a tree. Liam and Lois dozed in the warmth of the lakeside.

Rosamund went to the edge of the water. Ma Belle joined her. "What's on your mind, child? Where is your friend, Mr. Gebadd?"

"He is in Hong Kong," Rosamund said. "Ma, he wants to be a special friend, but he's always somewhere else."

"What about Caryl's teacher you told me about?" Ma Belle asked. "The one that was a football player before he became a teacher?"

Rosamund picked up a stone and threw it into the lake. It skimmed above the water then dipped out of sight. "He's nice. Busy, too. Evan spends a lot of time in his business. After pro ball, he invested in a company that develops video learning for kids. He, also, has interest in a TV and radio group." Rosamund pushed back her hair. "Ma," she smiled, "I have two men in my life who like me. I like them. I'm excited by the new work. Jeffrey is happy in his new job with CMC. Liam is improving and Lois will be my assistant. You and P. B. are a delight. I don't know that the world can be better—Caryl and good friends."

"What do you think Pet would say?" Ma Belle said.

"I don't know," Rosamund said. "You know that dynamic lady. She's probably talking to me in my dreams, but so far, I don't seem to be hearing her."

"Like I say," Ma Belle hugged Rosamund, the breeze ruffling her filmy skirt, "plenty of time."

"Indeed, Sister," Pet said from the breeze that circled the friendly party. People on the lakefront glanced to the sky, thinking the little thunder roll and wind signaled rain. To reassure them, Pet, Munje, and Frank moved aside, letting the sun shine through.

"Each time of unfolding is a great satisfaction, is it not, Brother?" Munje said, wiping moisture from what would be an eye if he were in form. A robin landing on a plum branch chose to be Munje's feelings. He sang loud enough to catch attention from Caryl and Darren.

"Is it 'time' to find other relative?" Frank asked.

"We'll know at first light," Pet replied. "Wow, I'm remembering more and more."

Ma Belle and Rosamund headed back to the picnic table, the wind off the water at their backs. As they walked—the older, golden hued and exotic; the younger, darker toned and lithe—a male figure crossed the beach from the woods. Rosamund could not discern who it was. She realized that Evan and Al were similar in size and coloration. The man waved. He could be either of them.

Caryl called, "Hi, Mr. Thomas," as she kicked a soccer ball.

Darren waved, trying to steal the ball.

"This is the darndest thing," Evan said when Rosamund met him—and before she could introduce him. "I finished my work earlier than I expected and I kept thinking of water. From nowhere, I remembered you had invited me to join the picnic, so I followed my impulse—late or not. This is very uncharacteristic of me."

Rosamund said. "I know the feeling. Once in a while, following an impulse is the 'neat' thing to do."

The late sun slid under the horizon. Its warmth gave promise of more to come.

Munje wove around Evan. "I don't remember this one. Is he one of us?"

The others sang. "Of course, he is."

Rosamund introduced Evan Thomas.

Ma Belle looked him over with care. "Qui, mon ami, you fit." Her smile was one of approval.

"Fit?" Evan saw acceptance, so he smiled.

"We've been digging up family stories. We discovered that we're an unusual mix of family," Rosamund said, leading him to the brazier. She said, "Don't worry I'll fill you in later—after you've eaten."

"Under the circumstances, I think I'd rather be a friend," Evan said.

"We may be both," she said.

Caryl slipped her hand into her mother's. "Mums, I've found a name for my doll; I'm naming her Patricia."

Rosamund Jones-Keyes' and Jeffrey Shuggs' Family Lines

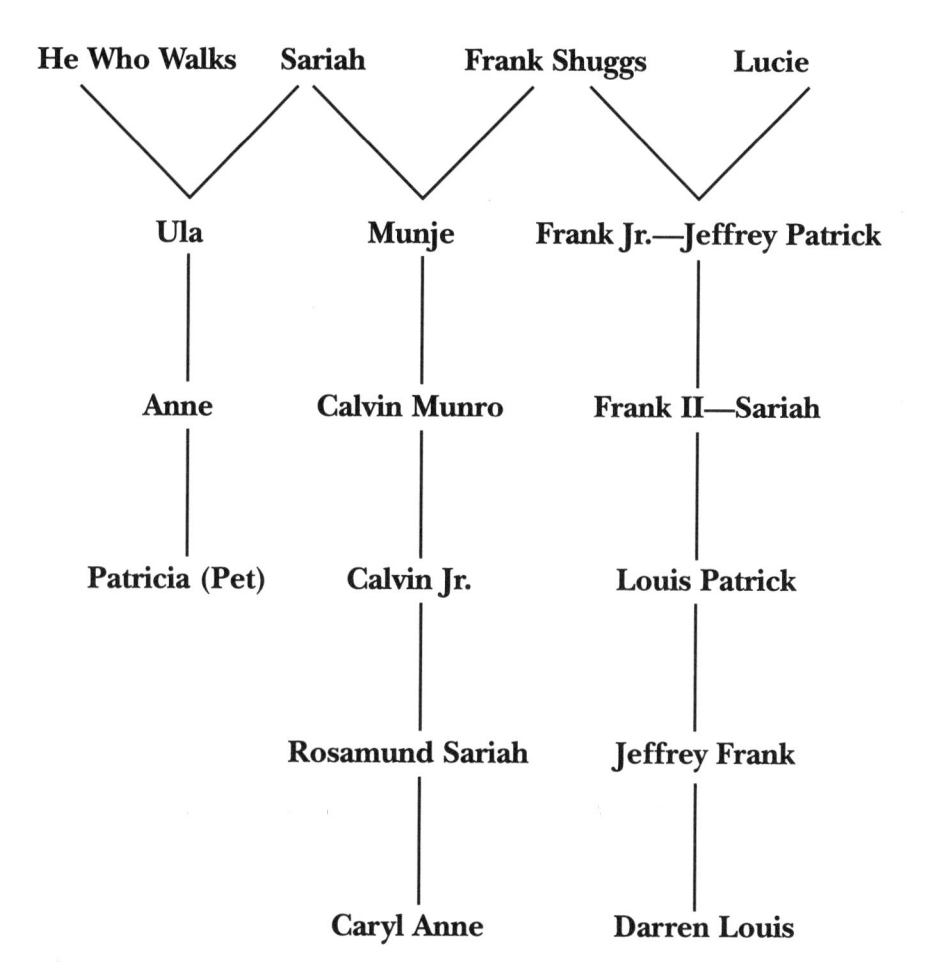

He Who Walks — Sariah — Frank Shuggs — Lucie

Ula — Munje — Frank Jr.—Jeffrey Patrick

Anne — Calvin Munro — Frank II—Sariah

Patricia (Pet) — Calvin Jr. — Louis Patrick

Rosamund Sariah — Jeffrey Frank

Caryl Anne — Darren Louis

GROWING UP NIGGER RICH
A Novel
By Gwendoline Y. Fortune

"Nigger rich" is a colloquialism encompassing class distinctions, a term used mainly by African Americans in reference to other African Americans, with an intent similar to that of other people's use of the term "nigger" to refer to any person of color. It was, and remains, an expression of fear, of anger, and of envy.

Through the complex web of this narrative, Gwendoline Y. Fortune juxtaposes "old South" and new, privilege and powerlessness, and various visions of racial identity in this refreshing, heartbreaking novel about growing up and coming home.

From the moment Gayla Tyner returns to her hometown of Carolton, South Carolina, after thirty years away "up North," she is struck by the reminders of her segregated youth. As she seeks to ease the pain of having grown up "nigger rich"—with relative privilege in some places, reviled and teased in others—she must also come to terms with her philandering husband, domineering father, and all of the relationships, secrets, and pleasures that continue to call her home.

ABOUT THE AUTHOR
Born in Houston, Texas, Gwendoline Y. Fortune grew up hearing stories of her "mixed blood" heritage: a free-born black great-grandfather, Native Americans, Scots-Irishmen, a cowboy grandfather, a Confederate great-grandfather, and relatives who were missionaries in pre-World War II China. She went to college at the age of fifteen and has been writing ever since. Selections from *Growing Up Nigger Rich* placed in the top twelve entries of the annual Pirate's Alley Faulkner Society competition and second place in the National Black Writers' Conference Awards. She lives in Saxapahaw, North Carolina.

GROWING UP NIGGER RICH
By Gwendoline Y. Fortune
256 pp. 6 x 9
ISBN: 1-56554-963-5 $22.00

All rights held by Pelican Publishing Company, Inc.

**Readers may order toll free from Pelican
at 1-800-843-1724 or 1-888-5-PELICAN.**